SIX-GUN JUSTICE

WESTERN STORIES

SIX-GUN JUSTICE PODCAST

SIX-GUN JUSTICE

Western Stories

Edited by Richard Prosch

CONTENTS

Introduction	7
1. Three Days to Pine River *Michael R. Ritt*	11
2. The Fox and the Snake *Jeffrey J. Mariotte*	41
3. Trackdown *Wayne D. Dundee*	59
4. After Black Jack Dropped *Jackson Lowry*	87
5. Dulcie's Reward *Easy Jackson*	111
6. Ghost Town Gambit *Scott Dennis Parker*	145
7. Night Horse *John D. Nesbitt*	179
8. A Requiem for Lord Byron *Richard Prosch*	207
9. Hired Guns: Mule's Gold *Steve Hockensmith*	211
10. Holly Jolly Courtship *Jacquie Rogers*	231
11. Merrick *Ben Boulden*	257
12. Shot for a Dog *Cheryl Pierson*	291
13. Headwaters *Vonn McKee*	339
Acknowledgments	355

Six-Gun Justice - Western Stories

Collection Copyright © 2021 by Six-Gun Justice Podcast

Individual stories Copyright © 2021 by the authors

All Rights Reserved. No part of this book may be reproduced in any form or by any means without the prior written consent of the Six-Gun Justice Podcast, except where permitted by law.

Cover image from Shutterstock.

Design by Lohman Hills Creative, LLC.

First Edition

These stories are works of fiction. Places and incidents are the product of the author's imagination or in the case of actual locations, are used fictitiously. Any similarity to any persons, living or dead, past, present or future is coincidental.

Visit us at: www.SixGunJustice.com

INTRODUCTION

Welcome to the very first *Six-Gun Justice Podcast Anthology*—perhaps even the first ever anthology connected to a podcast. Our *Six-Gun Justice Podcast* celebrates the blazing six-gun action of the western genre in books, movies, TV, and any other media at home on the range—and as of September 2021, has done so now for over 150+ episodes.

Richard Prosch and I have had a blast co-hosting the podcast and have learned more than we ever thought possible about so many different aspects of the Western genre—which is as alive and kicking as it has ever been. In 2020 alone, over 150 new Western novels were published in paperback, as well as an uncountable number of new Western ebook titles available from Amazon and elsewhere.

Westerns are also currently making a good showing with new feature films being released from

INTRODUCTION

major studios, and being made directly for numerous streaming services. TV is also sprouting new Western series—perhaps sparked by the popularity of *Longmire*—such as *Yellowstone*, *The Son*, *Big Sky*, the rebooted *Walker: Texas Ranger*, and more finding slots on the schedules of the traditional networks. Admittedly, many of these are contemporary Westerns, but stripped of their modern trappings, they are traditional Westerns to their core. In recent years, cable series such as *Hell On Wheels*, *Deadwood*, and *Godless* have garnered saddlebags full of awards, and retro cable stations proliferate delivering a never ending choice of episodes from the Golden Age of TV Westerns from the '50s through the early '70s. All of which means there is a big audience out there still hungry for bullet blazing Western action.

When Rich and I began the Six-Gun Justice Podcast, we also began a Patreon page for the podcast for those fans who wished to support us financially with small donations (www.patreon.com/sixgunjustice/). To reward those supporters, we solicited short stories from a variety of our Western writing trail pards as monthly give-backs. Now, we have collected those stories in one volume, the proceeds of which will go directly toward the operating costs of the podcast—monthly fees for the use of Zencastr's virtual recording studio, Internet

INTRODUCTION

podcast hosting from Buzzsprout, Descript editing services, and more.

For a niche interest, Rich and I have been gratefully surprised with how popular the Six-Gun Justice Podcast has become. Every Monday we alternate uploading new full-length episodes (which Rich and I co-host) with our shorter Speed Listen installments (which we host individually), and every Wednesday, we release a Six-Gun Justice Conversation segment, in which either Rich or I get to chat with writers and friends who love the western genre as much as we do. That's a lot of new content to create every month, but the reward has been seeing the number of downloads for each episode, installment, and segment increase every week. By the time this anthology is published, we will be nearing over 30,000 downloads since we began the podcast in January 2020.

Rich and I hope you will enjoy the Western short stories contained in this anthology and will go on to track down and read the full length Westerns from the wordslingers represented here.

And as we say at the end of every podcast—Be kind to others, be kind to yourself, and keep listening...

Paul Bishop
Somewhere out West
Summer 2021

THREE DAYS TO PINE RIVER

MICHAEL R. RITT

Marshal Logan Califf wasn't sure what was giving him greater grief at the moment. It seemed to be a tossup between the infernal Colorado heat, and the man with his hands tied to the saddle horn on the horse behind him. He stopped his mount and peered ahead down the trail that led through a grove of aspens as it snaked its way down the side of the mountain. He didn't like trails. Too many people used them. That's how they became trails in the first place. He preferred going cross country, but mountain travel didn't leave him many options.

Beads of perspiration coalesced into drops that ran down his temples and disappeared in the growth of stubble that had cropped up on his face over the past week. He removed his hat and, with a heavy sigh, ran his sleeve across his forehead.

"What's the matter, old man? Getting a little hot for you?"

Logan half-turned to face the man doing the talking. Looking down, he satisfied himself that his prisoner's hands were still tied securely. He had spent the better part of a week tracking him through these mountains after he broke out of jail in Pine River. He wasn't about to lose him again.

He turned his grulla mare and walked it up alongside the other man's bay. The two horses stood nose-to-tail while Logan lifted the canteen that he had looped over his saddle horn. Pulling out the cork, he tilted his head back and took a couple of swallows. Then he held the canteen up to the younger man's mouth. The prisoner jerked his head away. "I don't need it. I can hold out a lot longer than you can." In defiance he tried to work up enough saliva to launch in Logan's direction, but his mouth was too dry for the effort and he wound up merely making a dry spitting sound that was more bark than bite.

Logan shrugged. Replacing the cork in the canteen, he looped the strap back over the saddle horn. "It bodes well for you that you are so fond of the heat. There's a powerful lot of it where you're going."

They started down the trail again; Logan, his prisoner, and a packhorse bringing up the rear. The trail was steep and treacherous, littered with boulders and fallen trees, so Logan let the horses pick their own way down.

The San Juan Mountains rose over fourteen thousand feet, but they weren't up that high. They were well below the tree line. Logan glanced at a nearby peak and thought how much cooler it would be closer to the summit. This had been a particularly hot summer and Logan found himself calculating the number of months until the first possible snowfall. Funny, he thought; it wasn't that long ago that he was speculating on how soon summer would arrive.

The horses picked their way through some Jack pines and approached a scarred area that had been burned over the previous summer. New, green vegetation and pine seedlings were sprouting up over the blackened terrain. Moss was already growing on some of the charred stumps and timbers that littered this side of the mountain.

Logan stopped the horses and scanned the burn area as well as the ridge that jutted up about halfway across. *Too open*, thought Logan. *Looks like a good place for an ambush.* Avoiding the open area and staying just inside the trees, he turned the horses east to skirt the exposed side of the mountain.

The younger man began to laugh. "Are you worried about something, Marshal? Seems like a waste of time to take the long way 'round. 'Course, I don't mind none. You take as much time as you want. I just figured you were in a hurry to stretch my neck."

"We'll get around to that, Lou. I don't want your partner taking potshots at me. Besides, it's cooler here in the trees than it is out in the open."

"I keep telling you, I don't have any *partner*." Lou Beck spat out the word as though it was an insect that had flown into his mouth. "I don't know why you find that so hard to believe."

Logan stepped his mare over a fallen log that lay across his path. The other horses did likewise. "Let me enlighten you then. First off, when you were picked up outside of Hermosa, a week after the robbery, you didn't have any of the money on you. If you had had any of it, you would have been whooping it up in town. Witnesses inside the bank saw you run out of the back of the building after you shot the banker, Stevens, and took the money from the vault."

"I didn't mean to shoot anyone." Lou interrupted. "That fat old banker went for a gun he had hidden in the vault. I didn't have a choice."

"You had a choice. You just chose what was easy and convenient for you." Logan waited for a response from Lou, but none came. "Anyway, as I was saying, other witnesses saw you and one other person come tearing out of the ally hell-bent for leather. Your partner must have been back there holding the horses."

"Like I told the judge, I don't know who that guy was."

"So he just happened to be racing his horse through the alley behind the bank just as you robbed it and ran out the back?"

Lou stuck his chin out insolently. "That's right. That's exactly what happened."

"Well, suppose, for the sake of arguing, that's the truth–which we both know it ain't–but just for the sake of argument we'll say that it is. Where's the money?" Logan stopped the horses, turned to face Lou, and waited for his answer."

"I hid it somewhere where no one will find it."

It was the same story that Lou had given at his trial. It wasn't any more believable now than it was then. "You're still sticking to that tired, old story? No matter. There's still reason number two why I know that you had a partner."

"What reason is that?"

"Someone broke you out of my jail."

"Hell, that was easy. I just overpowered your deputy, grabbed his gun, and shot him. Then I took his keys and let myself out." Lou smiled like his great accomplishment was destined to become the stuff of legend.

"Then explain to me, genius, why his body was found in the outer room and not next to the cell. How did you get the jump on him from across the jail?"

Lou didn't have an answer. A fly kept landing on the tip of his nose. Lou, whose hands were still tied to the saddle horn, was shaking his head trying to shoo the pesky insect away. In one futile attempt to rid himself of his adversary, Lou shook his head with so much force that his hat flew off and landed on the trail beneath his horse, who shied when it hit the ground, side-stepping slightly to avoid it.

Logan sat waiting for an answer, growing more frustrated with each moment that passed. His eyes narrowed and the muscles in his jaw were drawn tight. He spoke through gritted teeth. "My deputy was a good man. He had a wife and a young son. He had his whole life ahead of him."

Lou hung his head in a rare display of contrition and spoke in hushed reverence. "I didn't know that about him. I'm sorry to hear that, I sure enough am."

"Well there's something we both agree on, Lou," Logan said as he started the horses back down the mountain. "You are about the sorriest person I know."

"What about my hat?" Lou shouted as the packhorse behind him stepped on the brim, mashing it into the dust.

"You don't deserve a hat," Logan shouted back.

The trail leveled off as they came to a small mountain meadow. Lupines and columbine quilted a patchwork of blue and red wildflowers. There was the faint, sweet peppery scent of scarlet gilia in the air. Three mule deer were grazing on the far end of the meadow a couple of hundred yards away. They looked up and spotted Logan and the horses approaching, then slipped into the trees that boarded the far end of the field.

Logan brought his horse to a stop to survey the field in front of him. Once again, his instincts were to skirt around the outside and avoid the open area. Instead, he turned to face Lou. "You know, Lou, a thought just occurred to me."

"Well congratulations on your big achievement." Lou was still sore about losing his hat. His head was drooping and his eyes were closed. He looked half asleep.

Logan just sat there, staring, without saying a word.

Finally, Lou lifted his head and looked around. Then he noticed Logan staring at him. "What?"

"It occurred to me that if you do have a partner, then it may not be me that he would be taking potshots at."

"What are you talking about?"

Logan took another look out across the meadow and then turned to face Lou. "Well, the way I see it, this partner, that you say you don't have, he is obviously the brains of the outfit. He gets you to rob the bank in broad daylight–with witnesses–while he stays concealed in the alley with the horses. He gets away with the money, but you get caught and thrown in jail. He then breaks you out of jail before you have a chance to tell anyone his identity."

"Sounds like this make-believe partner that you keep saddling me with has got my back, busting me out of jail and all. What's your point, Marshal?"

"My point is this, Lou… he only busted you out of jail so that you wouldn't be tempted to tell anyone who he is. The judge said he would commute your sentence to twenty years in prison if you gave back the money. I'm willing to bet that the only reason you're being so stubborn about it is because of your partner. He convinced you that you didn't need to worry; that he would bust you out of jail if you got caught. What did he do…offer you a larger share of the money if you keep your mouth shut?" Logan leaned forward in the saddle and patted the side of the grullas' neck as he spoke, "So the way things stack up now, he has the money and the only one who knows his identity is no longer safe behind bars. He didn't bust you out to rescue you. He busted you out so he could silence you."

Lou sat for a moment without speaking, thinking about what Logan had just said. His mouth hung partway open as he stared with blank eyes at the back of his horse's head. Finally, shaking his head, he answered, "You're reaching, Marshal. You can speculate all that you want. I keep telling you, I don't have a partner."

Despite what Lou had said, Logan caught a

glimpse of something in his eyes when he looked up. It might have been doubt, or maybe fear. It was just a hint, but it gave Logan something to work with. "All right then. If what you are saying is true, then neither one of us has anything to worry about, do we?"

"That's just what I keep telling you, Marshal."

Without another word, Logan dug his heels into the sides of the grulla. "He-yah," he shouted, as the mare jumped out into the open meadow with the other two horses in tow.

Lou grabbed hold of the saddle horn and held on for dear life. "What are you doing? Are you trying to get us killed?" he shouted, bouncing from side to side as Logan raced the horses across the field.

They were a third of the way across when the first shot rang out. It had come from the trees to the right of them and kicked up dirt just in front of Logan's horse. Intuition took over and both men ducked lower in the saddle. Logan turned the horses to his left, galloping away from the shooter who was now somewhere behind them.

A second shot soon followed that tore through the trousers of Lou's right leg, punching a hole through the meaty part of the calf. Lou cried out in pain.

Logan changed directions again, heading the horses back to his right. Two more rifle shots rang out, both missing their marks before the horses made it to the safety of the trees on the far end of the meadow.

Twenty yards or so inside the trees, Logan brought the horses to a stop. Dismounting, he pulled his rifle from the rifle boot. Keeping his mount between him and the meadow, he did a quick check to see how Lou and the horses had faired.

"Damn you to high heaven." Lou's face was contorted in pain and he winced as Logan tore open his pants leg to examine his wound. "What did you have to do that for? Were you trying to get me killed before you could hang me?"

"Quit your belly-aching. It's just a scratch." He tore a strip of cloth from the cuff of Lou's pants. Removing the bandanna from around his neck, he used it to tie the wadded up cloth in place over the wound. "That will stop the bleeding in no time."

Lou sat on his horse; shot in the leg, hands tied, hatless, hot, and hungry. He made a pretty pathetic looking spectacle.

Rifle in hand, Logan worked his way from tree to tree as he inched closer to the edge of the meadow looking for any sign of the shooter. Satisfying himself that there was no longer anyone there, he went back to where the horses and Lou were waiting in the trees.

"It's a good thing that partner of yours isn't a better shot. You could have got a lot worse than a little flesh wound." Logan replaced the rifle in the boot and mounted up.

"You just don't give up, do you?" Lou grimaced as he slipped his boot out of the stirrup to relieve some of the pressure on his wounded leg.

"If that wasn't your partner shooting at us just now, then who do you suppose that it was?"

"I reckon that it was some hunter that mistook our horses for those three mulies we saw."

Logan shook his head in disbelief. "Your ma is one of the kindest, most God-fearing women I know, and your pa was the finest lawman I ever served with. How did you ever turn out to be such a mean, stubborn jackass?"

"My pa was a self-righteous son-of-a-bitch who cared more about his work than he ever cared about his family. He wasn't happy unless he was on the trail of some horse thief or some murderer. He didn't even know that ma or I existed, so don't go telling me what a great man my pa was or what a good example he was. The fact of the matter is that he was never around long enough to be anything at all to me." Lou's face flushed with the anger that had risen in him. The bitter taste of bile momentarily took his mind off of the pain from the gunshot to his leg.

"Well, you see things one way and I see things another, I guess."

"You see things his way because you are just like him."

"You think I take any pleasure in this? You think I want to see you hung? I don't particularly relish the thought of having to tell your ma that her only boy has been hung as a murderer and a thief." Logan took a deep breath and softened his tone. "Son, I have been doing everything I can to get you to tell me who it is that you are working with. Tell me where the money is so you don't have to hang. Take Judge Nichols up on his offer. Twenty years with the possibility of parole. You can still have a life. You can turn things around."

For a moment Logan thought that he saw Lou hesitate like he wanted to say something but wasn't sure how to proceed. His eyes seemed to soften for just a second or two. Then, just as quickly Logan saw the stubbornness and lack of cooperation return. "Let's just get on with it, Marshal, and get off of this lousy mountain."

The rest of the trip down was uneventful and the two men soon found themselves in the foothills of the San Juan's. The temperature had dropped noticeably and the wind had picked up as they sat watering their horses along a small stream. Logan figured it was about three more days to Pine River where he and Lou were headed.

The sky grew darker and there was a coolness to the wind that brought a measure of relief to Logan, but threatened the prospect of rain. Logan was well aware of how quickly storms came up in the mountains and how dangerous it could be for a man caught out in the middle of one. He looked up at the gathering clouds. "We better find ourselves someplace to hole up."

They followed the little stream through the timbered foothills until they came to an open area. Here the country leveled out into a broad valley about a mile and a half wide and maybe three or four miles long.

About halfway across the valley on the northern end, Logan could make out several small buildings. There was a cabin and a barn with a little split rail corral, as well as an outhouse and a smaller building that was most likely a tool shed. Logan could make out a couple of horses loose in the corral and he saw smoke rising from the cabin's chimney.

"Looks like a hot meal and a dry place to spend the night. What do you say, Lou? Should we go down and introduce ourselves?"

Lou's leg was throbbing. He was hungry and tired and wanted nothing more than to get down off of his horse and stretch out in a nice warm, soft pile of straw and sleep for about twelve hours. "If it's a chance for better company than you've been for the past three days, then I'm all for it."

The homestead sat nestled in the north end of the valley. There was good grass and the stream they had been following flowed right through the center. Logan thought that it was a great location for raising cattle or horses, but for a pair of horses in the corral, there wasn't any livestock to be seen on the entire spread.

They walked their horses into the clearing and up to the cabin, which had a little lean-to porch jutting out from the front. A man was sitting on the porch. They could hear him singing as they approached the cabin.

"Sitting by the road-side on a summer day,
Chatting with my messmates, passing time away,"

The man was somewhere in his sixties, as near as Logan could tell. He was heavyset and had a long white beard that hung down over a barrel of a chest. He had a piece of oilcloth that he was using to wipe down a Winchester rifle that lay across his lap. Logan noticed the man's blue eyes, bright and sharp. They peered out beneath two bushy white eyebrows and didn't seem to miss a thing as he took in the two mounted strangers. He continued to sing as Logan brought the horses to a rest in front of him.

"Lying in the shadow underneath the trees,
Goodness, how delicious, eating goober peas."

"Howdy." The old man remained in his rocking chair as he spoke, but Logan noticed how his hand rested on the butt of the rifle.

"Howdy. I'm Marshal Logan Califf from Pine

River. This man," he nodded toward Lou, "is my prisoner. We're headed back to town."

The old man got to his feet. Logan noticed the initials "T.A.B." carved into the walnut stock of the Winchester as he leaned it against the wall next to the rocker.

"Pleased to make your acquaintance, Marshal. I'm Jesse Aldridge, but you can call me Jess.

Logan looked up at the gathering clouds. "Jess, it looks like we're in for some rain. I was hoping we could spend the night in your barn; maybe get a hot meal from you."

Jess gave a furtive glance at Lou. "What about your prisoner there, Marshal? Is he dangerous? I live here with my granddaughter. I wouldn't want any trouble."

As if on cue the front door opened and a young woman appeared. She looked to be in her mid-twenties with long blond hair that hung straight down to the middle of her back. She was a work of art in all the places that a man was prone to look, and she had deep blue eyes just like her grandfather. She had on a blue and white calico dress with an apron tied around her waist. Wiping her hands on a towel, she stepped out and stood next to Jess.

"Marshal, this is my granddaughter, Ann. Ann, sweetheart, this man is Marshal Califf. He is on his way to Pine River and was hoping to spend the night."

"It is a pleasure to meet you, Marshal."

"Likewise, miss."

Ann looked directly at Lou but addressed her question to Logan. "And who is this?"

"This is Lou Beck. He's my prisoner. I'm taking him back to Pine River to be hung."

"Is Mr. Beck dangerous, Marshal?" Ann repeated the question that her grandfather had asked. Logan didn't detect any fear in her question. Instead, she seemed almost thrilled by the prospect.

"Not currently, Miss Aldridge. I assure you, he will remain in restraints during our stay. He won't be any trouble to you or your grandfather. Isn't that right, Lou?"

Lou smiled down at Ann. Even hatless, and with a week's worth of stubble, he was a good looking young man. He had no doubt charmed more than one lonely, female homesteader; particularly the ones who didn't get to town much.

"Sweetheart, you have my word that I will be on my best behavior. Besides, you are about the prettiest thing I've seen in a coon's age." He gave Ann a wink that caused her to blush. "And me shot up the way that I am," Lou shifted in the saddle, wincing for dramatic effect, "I'm hardly in any condition to cause trouble."

The color drained from Ann's face. Her eyes grew wide with concern. "Marshal, is this man injured?" Lou started rubbing his leg. Ann stepped down off of the porch and moved quickly to the right side of Lou's horse to get a better look.

"Ann, honey," Jess called after her. "You be careful."

"Some hunter mistook our horses for mule deer." Logan was quick to offer. "Lou took a bullet in the leg. It went clean through though. He'll live...at least 'till I get him back to Pine River."

Ann scowled at Logan's remark. "Help me get this man inside so I can look after his wound."

Just then, a big raindrop splattered in the dust in front of Logan's horse. Then another fell and made a thud as it hit the brim of his hat, rolling off of the tip and landing on the saddle swell.

Jess stepped down off the porch. "Why don't you help Ann get your prisoner inside, Marshal? I'll get your horses settled in the barn."

Logan drew his knife and reached over to cut the rope that bound Lou to his saddle. Although the razor-like edge severed the rope freeing Lou from his anchor, his hands remained tied to each other.

Jess led the horses to the barn while Logan and Ann helped Lou into the cabin. They set him in a chair next to the fireplace. The logs crackled and popped inside and shifted position as the flames ate away at them, transforming them into glowing embers.

Ann poured some hot water from a kettle into a

small basin. Lou winced in pain as she removed the bandage and proceeded to clean the wound.

Logan glanced around the little cabin. There wasn't much in the way of furnishings, but it was warm and dry. It was divided into three rooms. There was the main room with the fireplace, a couple of chairs, and a plank table with benches on either side. A pot of stew simmered over the fire and the aroma of fresh-baked bread made Logan's mouth water. The far side of the cabin was partitioned off into two rooms for sleeping; one for Jess and one for his granddaughter.

Logan noticed that there wasn't much of a woman's touch about the place. There were no curtains on either of the two windows. There were no wildflowers stuck in vases, or no table cloth or fancy dishes or any of the other things that women seem to put such store in.

"How long have you lived here with your grandfather?" Logan asked as Ann finished placing a clean bandage on Lou's leg.

"I've been here about six months. I ain't permanent though. I'm headed to San Francisco."

"Is that where your folks are?" Logan had seated himself on the near side of the table closest to the fireplace. The chill and dampness of the storm had taken a quick hold of him, and the heat from the burning logs felt good. One at a time, he stretched out his legs and rubbed some of the stiffness out of his knees.

"Pa was killed at Antietam when I was a little girl. My ma died of consumption last year. That's why I came out here to be with grandpa. But like I said," she added quickly, "I'm headed to San Francisco."

The front door opened and Jess walked in brushing the rain off of his arms. "It's starting to come down pretty good out there. Looks like you boys made it here just in time." As if to emphasize the point, a bolt of lightning lit up the sky and thunder rolled down the valley, rumbling off of the mountains as it faded into the distance. Darkness had settled in, hurried along by the storm clouds that hung low over the cabin.

Jess sat down on the bench opposite Logan, setting the Winchester on the table in front of him. As they sat facing each other, Logan carefully slipped the loop off of the hammer of the Colt in his holster. He nodded toward the rifle. "That's a good looking firearm you have there. I can see that you take good care of it. How long have you had it?"

"This is a good shooting iron, Marshal, but it ain't mine. I was cleaning it when you rode up but it belongs to Ann."

Logan turned quickly, at the same time reaching for his gun. But it was too late. Ann stood there with a .44 caliber Colt Army revolver that she had hidden in her apron. She had it aimed right at Logan.

"Don't do it Marshal. I put a bullet in your deputy without any difficulty. I can do the same to you if I have to. Pull your gun out easy like and toss it over here."

Logan did as she said.

Jess hadn't moved an inch. The shocked look on his face was evidence enough for Logan that he had had nothing to do with any of this. "Ann! What are you doing?"

"Just stay out of this grandpa." She kept the gun aimed at Logan. "Toss your knife over here too, Marshal. SLOWLY!"

Logan slipped his knife out of the sheath and slid it across the floor.

Keeping the Colt pointed at Logan with one hand, she picked up the knife with the other and cut Lou free, tossing the knife aside when she finished.

Lou was rubbing his wrists, opening and closing his hands and flexing his fingers to get more circulation back into them. "Who's the genius now, Marshal?" He bent down and picked up Logan's gun. "For the past three days, you have been badgering me about who my partner was. I could hardly keep from laughing out loud when you rode right up to the cabin."

"I've got to hand it to you, Lou," Logan spoke calmly and with a confidence that belied the fact that there were now two guns pointed at him. "I didn't see this coming. But I understand now why you didn't want to give up your partner – even after she tried to kill you up on the mountain."

Lou shook the gun at Logan like a schoolmarm shaking her finger at an unruly pupil. "That ain't gonna work, Marshal; you trying to turn us against each other like that. Ann and I are in love. We're gonna go to San Francisco together and get hitched."

"That's right sweetheart." Ann smiled and fluttered her eyelashes at Lou. "Besides, why would I try to kill you when you ain't told me where you've hid the money?"

"Don't worry none about that, darling. I hid it in that hollow cottonwood log where we had that picnic a few months back. It's as safe as can be."

"That's good, Lou." Ann indicated the rope that had bound Lou's hands. "Take that rope and tie them up. We're leaving right away."

"You want to leave now?" Lou questioned. "It's storming out. It ain't safe to travel in weather like this."

"Do what I say," Ann shouted in reply.

Lou hesitated a moment; then, with a shrug, picked up the rope and tied Logan's hands together. When he was finished he proceeded to do the same to Jess.

Ann moved toward the door. "Let's get going, Lou." She picked up the rifle that was on the table. Turning to Logan she said, "Something tipped you off. It was this rifle, wasn't it? I was hoping that you wouldn't notice the initials."

"T.A.B.–Thomas Allen Beck. I know that rifle well. I gave it to Lou's pa about six years ago when he made Captain of the Rangers. Lou got it when his pa was killed. The only way you could have gotten it was from Lou. When I saw your grandpa cleaning it when we rode up, I figured he was the one that had been shooting at us. It never occurred to me that Lou's partner could be a woman. Guess I'll have to ledger that in the mistake column."

"If you want to live long enough to make more mistakes, Marshal, you'll just sit tight while we ride on out of here. All I want is to get that money and get out of these God-forsaken mountains and back to someplace where they've got restaurants, and shops and theatres."

Jess had a hard time understanding what was unfolding in front of him. "Ann, you can't do this; it ain't right. Just put down the gun and untie us. Let's talk this out."

"There's nothing to talk about, grandpa. I can't stay here another day. I can't stay here another hour. If I do I swear I'll lose my mind!" She opened the door and motioned for Lou. Outside the lightning flashed and the rain ran in sheets off of the edge of the porch roof. "Let's get out of here, Lou" The two of them stepped out into the darkness, closing the door behind them.

Logan stood up and wasted no time crossing the room to the fireplace where his knife still lay on the floor. Lou had picked up his revolver but had neglected the knife. Although his hands were tied securely together, Logan had no problem grasping the handle of the knife with both hands.

Jess had his eyes on the knife as well and made his way over to the fireplace. He held his hands out in front of him while Logan began to saw at the ropes. "I can't begin to tell you how sorry I am for all of this, Marshal. I just don't understand Ann carrying on this way."

Logan could see the pain and confusion in the old man's eyes and felt sorry for him. There are a lot of different kinds of pain that a man can learn to endure, but the pain of having to watch someone that you love make bad choices is one of the worse – and one that Logan was familiar with.

After freeing Jess, Logan handed the knife over to the old man who soon had Logan's hands-free.

They headed for the cabin door but stopped short when a shot rang out. Both men hit the floor and waited a few seconds to make sure that they were not the ones being shot at. Crawling forward on his stomach, Logan reached up to lift the latch and slowly inched open the door.

It was too dark out to see anything. Then a sudden flash of lightning lit up the night and Logan could see Lou lying in the mud between the cabin and the barn. He wasn't moving. The falling rain, and the thunder which rumbled overhead, made it difficult to hear the moans coming from the injured man.

Running out to where he lay, Logan bent down to examine Lou and determine what kind of shape he was in. It didn't look good. There was a bullet hole in his chest and his breathing was shallow.

"You were right, Logan." His words were strained and came between gasps for breath. "She played me for a fool. You were right all along. She's going for the money." Lou began a coughing fit that started streams of frothy blood from the corners of his mouth. It mixed with the rain and flowed down the sides of his face into the mud.

"I'm sorry, son. It looks like she's killed you. Tell me where the money is hid. Where is this picnic spot you mentioned?"

Lou's words were slow and choppy and made with great effort. Each one seemed to cost him a little piece of what life he had left. "The stream...in this val...cough, cough, in this valley...cough, cough, cough, enters the Rio...de Los Pinos. There..." Another coughing fit followed and then a moment of silence. Suddenly Lou's body shuddered, followed by a long, slow exhale. His chest stopped moving and his eyes stared, unseeing, into the falling rain and the eternal darkness of the storm.

Jess had gone straight to the barn while Logan

talked to Lou. He now emerged with Logan's horse saddled and ready to go. He looked at the body of Lou lying still in the mud, and then he looked at Logan. "She's my granddaughter, Marshal," was all he could say.

Logan took the rains from Jess and stuck his foot in the stirrup. "I have no desire to shoot a woman, Jess, but she's killed two men and I don't aim to be the third."

A moment later his grulla was making its way down the valley, following the stream that would take him to the Rio de Los Pinos. The rain continued to fall and the lightning flashed almost continually, which made Logan nervous, but it also lit up the way so that he was able to keep his horse to a steady pace.

Ann didn't have more than a ten-minute head start on him, but she was more familiar with the country than Logan was and knew exactly where she was going. Logan only had a general direction to follow, so he kept his horse close to the stream, which was growing wider and flowing faster with the rain that had fallen.

A few miles from the cabin the valley started to narrow. The way grew steeper and Logan had to hold the grulla to a walk as he made his way past boulders and the trees that were growing more numerous as the open valley gave way to more pine and aspen.

He came to a sudden drop-off and brought his

horse to a halt. Here the stream, which was now swollen to the size of a small river, emptied over the edge of a forty-foot cliff. Logan could hear the roar of the Rio de Los Pinos below and knew that he had to be near the spot where Lou had hidden the money.

A sudden flash of lightning illuminated the far bank of the stream opposite Logan. Ann sat on her horse; the Winchester aimed right at him. She pulled the trigger. The bullet ricocheted off of the saddle horn and cut a furrow across the back of Logan's hand. Diving off of the far side of his horse, Logan saw another flash of lightning and heard a deafening boom that left his ears ringing for several seconds as he lay in the wet grass.

Minutes passed as Logan lay still, waiting for another rifle shot, but none came. The storm seemed to be letting up some. The rain had slowed to a steady, drizzle, and the thunder and lightning had moved further east.

Logan lifted his head slowly and tried to look across the stream to the other side, but it was still too dark. He got to his knees and then stood up. The grulla hadn't moved, so he gathered the reins and mounted up.

About a half-mile upstream was a place where the streambed widened out. Even swollen as it was with the recent rain, the water was only belly-high on the mare, so Logan crossed over without any difficulty.

By the time that he made his way back downstream, the rain had stopped and most of the clouds had parted. A full moon was shining down with a brightness that lent a silver glow to the rain-soaked vegetation.

He approached the area carefully, but his caution was unnecessary. Ann and her horse lay motionless in the wet grass. Both of them were dead. The Winchester was on the ground a few feet from Ann. The stock had been completely blown to bits and the barrel was split open from the lightning bolt that had shattered it.

SIX DAYS LATER, Logan stepped off of the train onto the platform in Cheyenne. He had arranged for the pine box containing the body of Lou Beck to be loaded onto a buckboard he had rented from the livery.

Hannah Beck lived alone on a small ranch three miles north of town. Its real ranch days had passed some time back. Other than a few cows, a half a dozen horses or so, and some chickens scratching in the dirt, there wasn't much to keep a widow woman busy. She passed her time by working in her flower and vegetable gardens and by thinking about her son, Lou. She hadn't heard anything about him in almost two years. Every night she would sit in the rocking chair in her bedroom and read a passage from the Bible out loud and pray for her boy. Then every day she would watch the road that cut through the wind-swept plains that surrounded the ranch for any sign of his return.

She saw the wagon while it was still a long way off. Sitting on her front porch peeling apples for a pie, she watched the wagon's progress as it kicked up a wake of dust that hung in the air for several minutes before settling back down on the lonely road. When the wagon turned and headed through the gate and down the road to her ranch, she stood up and walked to the edge of the porch. Squinting, and shielding her eyes from the noon-day sun, she waited for the wagon to approach. A smile lit up her face when she recognized the driver. Stepping down off of the porch, she started across the yard.

Logan brought the wagon to a stop and set the brake. Climbing down from the seat, he walked toward Hannah, meeting her halfway. They embraced for a long moment; Hannah with her face pressed tightly against his cotton vest, smelling the dust of the road which had settled on his broadcloth suit, and feeling the rhythmic swell of his chest with each breath he took.

She let go and stepped back, taking both of Logan's hands in hers as she looked up at his face–so handsome and rugged. She wanted to take in every inch. "It's so good to see you, Logan. It's been a long time."

"It's been too long, Hannah."

There was something in his face, in the set of his jaw, and in the tone of his voice that wasn't right. There was sadness in his eyes that she hadn't seen since her husband, Tom, Logan's best friend, had been killed. Her smile faded and her eyes narrowed. "What is it, Logan? Is it Lou?"

Logan dropped his gaze and stared at the ground without speaking. What words are appropriate at a time like this? How do you break the news that no parent should ever have to hear? He put his arm around her waist and led her to the side of the wagon. Looking over the edge of the box, she saw the pine coffin inside.

Logan wrapped his arms around her and held her close while she wept. At last, pushing away, she dabbed at her eyes with the corner of her apron.

Logan reached out and grabbed her by the shoulders. "Hannah, I want you to know something." He bent slightly forward so that he could look her straight in the eyes. "With his last breath, Lou helped me catch a murderer. You can be proud of him." She didn't need to know any more of the details.

Hannah turned to look at the coffin where her only boy was laid out, then turned back to look up at Logan. Placing her hand gently on the side of his face, she felt the stubble that had grown there over the past few days. She managed a frail smile. "Thank you, Logan. Thank you for bringing my boy home to me. You're a good brother."

MICHAEL R. RITT is an award-winning author currently living in western Montana. His short stories have been published in numerous anthologies, and his first novel, *The Sons of Philo Gaines*, was released in November of 2020. You can read more about him and his writing at Michaelrritt.com.

THE FOX AND THE SNAKE

JEFFREY J. MARIOTTE

Fox Caldwell filled a tin cup at the cast-iron stove and carried it outside. The coffee was bitter and steaming, the air crisp and still. A light snow had fallen overnight, bending the grama grasses in front of the old adobe under its weight. Through the covering of white, thin as an old Army blanket and just as useful, the stump of a desert willow poked up defiantly. In the near distance, Fox could see creosote bushes and mesquites and ocotillo and soap-tree yuccas, all dusted with it. Snow capped the mountains to the east and north, and he expected it would be for some time.

He stood there drinking his coffee and enjoying the cold. Too long would make his old joints ache and every injury he'd ever suffered—knife wounds, gun wounds, a few broken bones—would start to complain. But for the time it took to polish off a cup, he'd be fine.

When he got down to the dregs, he tossed them into the snow. He was turning to go back inside when he heard the sound of automobiles coming up the road, frozen dirt and small rocks crunching under their wheels. When he'd found this place back in '92, there hadn't been a neighbor for ten miles in any direction. That had changed—like everything else, he reckoned. Now he knew of at least five houses within a mile or two. He didn't like feeling crowded, but there wasn't much he could do about it.

He hurried inside and barred the door, then checked every window to ensure that the curtains were closed. That done, he shoved a fresh ten-round magazine into his Winchester 1905 and placed it against the wall in the front room, right beside the window. He rounded up several revolvers, checked the loads, and put them near the other windows, along with a box of bullets for each. The last one, he holstered. The belt didn't fit around his waist the way it used to, but he was able to buckle it.

Then he drew back the curtain just enough to peer outside, hoping the automobiles would keep traveling up the road and bypass the little stem that led to his place.

They didn't. Instead, they turned up the stem and kept coming. Fox didn't know much about motor cars and didn't care to. Had someone asked him to identify these, he couldn't do better than "mechanical monstrosities." All he really knew about them was that they were noisy, smelly, and ugly. The three horses presently in his corral could be all of those things, too, but not usually at the same time.

One of the automobiles, a red one, came to a wheezing halt about thirty feet from his front door. The other two kept going, circling around his house. He heard one stop around the west side, out of sight from here, and the other continued on until it came to rest near the southeast corner. Each vehicle carried six people, but Fox couldn't get a good look at them. In the car he could see, he recognized only one man: Sheriff Cooter Diggs.

"Dammit," Fox said. He didn't care much for visitors in the first place. And in the second place, he didn't care at all for Diggs. Thirdly, Diggs's presence here meant only trouble.

Diggs sat next to the driver in the red automobile, staring at the house and waiting for something. Fox watched from the edge of the curtain, crouched down, one hand on the rifle. If the lawman had come to take him, he wouldn't find the task an easy one.

In the quiet aftermath of the automobile noise, he heard people fanning out around the house, boots breaking through the thin crust of snow. He was surrounded, then. Eighteen men. They were taking no chances.

Fox's gaze lit on the stump of the desert willow again, thrusting up through the snow like a defiant fist. Thirteen or fourteen years ago, jackrabbits had been scalping the bark around the base of the trunk. To protect it, he had bought some netting and tied it to a series of stakes surrounding the tree. It held the rabbits at bay, sure enough. But one summer day he'd stepped outside and been greeted by a deafening buzz. A diamondback had tried to slither in and out through the netting and become hopelessly tangled.

Had he been alone then, like he was now, he might have left it there until it starved, or killed it and cut free the corpse. But his wife and their daughter Ella had lived with him then, the latter just a tyke. She loved every creature, however wild or wicked, and he didn't want to take a chance on her getting too close to the thing. When he went back in for his gun, Ella came to the door to look and broke down crying. "Don't kill it, Papa!" she said. "Let it loose!"

He debated whether to argue with her or simply overrule her, but in the end, he took a sharp knife outside and crouched down, just out of the snake's reach. He started at the tail end, cutting through just enough of the netting to free the rattler. It buzzed and thrashed and tried to bite, but he stayed back from its fangs and spoke gently to it. "Easy now, friend," he said. "I'm trying to set you free. You just got to be a little patient with me, 'cause I ain't doing this in no kind of hurry."

After a few minutes, the snake seemed to realize that Fox meant to help, or at least it wasn't going to be able to get to him. It settled down, stopped shaking its rattles, rested its head on the ground and just watched as he sliced through the netting, closer and closer to the biting end.

The hardest part was freeing the head. That was when he might be bit. But if he simply cut around the part that the snake's head was tangled in, the thing would probably get caught on every branch, twig, and thorn out there—and in the high desert, there were plenty. He hadn't gone to all this bother just to have the rattler starve to death in another day or three. "All right, snake," he said. "Be calm, here, because I'm fixing to come real close to those fangs, and I want you to keep 'em sheathed."

The snake didn't answer; it just kept those cold, lidless eyes on him as he cut closer and closer. Finally, Fox sliced through the last bit. Instantly understanding that it was free, the diamondback slithered away, moving faster than Fox had ever seen a snake travel. From the doorway, Ella cheered.

Ella's mother was long gone now, buried behind the house eight years back. Ella was gone, too—not dead, so far as Fox knew, but not here, either.

No, Fox was alone in the house, and had been for a very long time. For the moment, though, he had plenty of company. Sheriff Diggs was walking toward the house, a scatter-gun in his hands. The brass star on his vest gleamed in the slanting sunlight. His handlebar mustache was silver, his hat black and pulled low to shade his eyes.

"You in there!" the sheriff called. "Come on out, peaceful-like!"

Answer, or not? Ultimately, Fox couldn't resist. "You got anything to say to me, say it from there!" he shouted.

Diggs stopped where he was and shifted the gun so he was holding it at his waist, more or less pointed toward the window. All the other men Fox could see were armed, as well, and several had their rifle stocks up against their shoulders, aiming at different windows and the front door. If he showed himself, he'd be cut down.

"I know it's you in there, Fox Caldwell," Diggs said. "You was in Bisbee a couple days back, layin' in some supplies. You was seen, and follered back here. You been out of the trade for some years, but that don't matter to the law."

He'd been followed? Fox remembered noticing somebody on his back trail a couple of times, riding back from the store. But the route he'd taken was well-traveled these days; for someone else to be using it was not unusual.

"Leave an old man be, Sheriff," he said.

"I ain't no youngster myself, Caldwell. But there's

things you got to answer for," the sheriff continued. "Reckon you know what matters most to me."

Fox saw no advantage in denying any of it. "You know when I shot your boy, it was in self-defense, Cooter. He was gunning for me."

"You bein' an outlaw who honest men oughta be gunnin' for," Diggs countered.

"Cade weren't no honest man, Diggs. He was riding with Alvord and them, same as me, until we got crosswise with each other."

"Sometimes boys take the wrong path," Diggs said. "Most times, they come to their senses and find the right one. Only you never gave my son that chance. Cade looked up to you—you were the oldest in the bunch, the one who'd known the Dalton brothers and Bill Doolin and Cattle Annie and them. Time you came here, you already had a name and a reputation. The Territorial Fox, the one no lawman could touch. Never spent more than a few nights in any jail, always slipped out somehow before bein' sentenced. You were like a legend to him. Then the minute he started to figger things out for his own self, you gunned him down like a dog. You'll get a fair trial, Caldwell, I promise you that. I hope you hang, but that's up to the circuit judge."

Fox didn't think it wise to tell the lawman that he'd never do a dog that way. Instead, he said, "I've been out of it since the day Jeff Milton killed young

Jack Dunlop, back in Fairbank. I didn't want to wind up the same way."

"Just because you stole enough to take it easy for the rest of your days don't mean you didn't steal it in the first place," Diggs argued. "Southern Pacific still has a reward out for you, and these boys as came out with me today mean to split it. I ain't takin' a share. My reason for bein' here is personal. Plus also, I'm a lawman and you're hiding out in my county."

Fox couldn't argue with the sheriff's reasoning. He was still living off the proceeds from several train robberies he'd pulled with Burt Alvord and Billy Stiles and their outfit. He was wanted by the law, and he'd known it. But he'd thought himself safe out here, on his little piece of land far from town. Twelve years, it had been, since he'd left banditry behind. Why couldn't the law see that? Surely the county sheriff had better things to do.

"I hope you don't think I'm going easy," Fox warned.

"Some of the boys thought you might," Diggs said. "Me, I'm hopin' they were wrong."

The lawman shifted the gun to his shoulder and aimed at the window. Fox's tailbone hit the plank floor and he scrambled, putting some thick adobe wall between himself and Diggs. The gun roared and window glass flew throughout the room, some of it embedding itself in a wooden table pushed up against the far wall.

As if that had been a signal, the other men surrounding the house started shooting, too. The thunder of their guns outdid all but the heaviest of the hundreds of monsoon storms Fox had seen. All through the house, glass shattered. Rounds punched into walls, shredded curtains, smashed dishes, and more.

In the sudden stillness after the first volley, Fox hefted the Winchester and fired three shots blindly through the big window. A cry of pain sounded, right before return fire drowned everything else out.

Fox scooted under the window and raced into the kitchen, crushing glass shards beneath his boots. Snatching up the six-shooter he'd left by the sink, he emptied it through that window, then dropped it and dashed into the bedroom. He did the same there, and again from the bedroom that had been Ella's. Each time, the men outside concentrated their fire on where he had been, not where he was. His swollen knuckles ached from pulling triggers, and by morning all of his joints would be complaining about what he'd put them through. Acrid smoke bit at his nostrils, and he sneezed twice.

But he was out of windows now, and three of his pistols were empty. The cracks of the guns from outside dwindled while he reloaded, and as they did, he heard a woman's voice, sobbing and screaming. It sounded like she said, "You said you'd let me see him! You promised! Diggs, you bastard!"

"It ain't safe, Ella." That was Diggs's voice. "You saw that your own self. He was firin' blind, tryin' to kill whoever he could."

Ella? Could he have heard that right? Sometimes these days, his ears played tricks on him. His eyes, too, especially at dusk or in bright sunlight, like today's, with light bouncing off the scattered snow.

"You started shooting first, Diggs! Not him, you! After you promised me!"

That, Fox was sure he'd heard. "The lady's right, Cooter!" he called. "You did shoot first!"

"You're damn right I did!" Diggs replied. "You're a murderin' son of a bitch, Caldwell. And the boys get their reward money, dead or alive. Don't matter none to me or to Southern Pacific."

"Papa," Fox heard, and the word took him back years. "I'm no lady! It's me, Ella! Diggs said I might be able to talk you out!"

"Ella? It's really you?"

"Of course it is! Who else would it be?"

It could be a trick. He wouldn't know his own daughter's voice, after so long. That might be anyone out there. "You remember that snake, got caught in the netting around that desert willow?"

She hesitated. A trick, then. He finished loading the guns, and carefully moved from room to room, staying below the windows, putting them all back into place. He started to raise one, to start shooting again while the men were distracted by her.

"Of course I do," she said.

Fox released the trigger. "What kind was it? Was it that king snake, lived under the porch?"

"It was a rattler," she said. "Made the most ferocious noise until you started cutting him loose. I'd never been so happy to see a snake wriggle off through the brush."

It *was* her. Nobody else would have known that. "Diggs," he called. "Let her come in. Just her, no tricks. I won't hurt her!"

"I don't trust you, Caldwell. You're still a cold-blooded bastard. You'd kill anyone to get away."

"Not her! Not my daughter."

"Oh, please, Sheriff," Ella pleaded. "Let me go in. I can talk him into coming out peacefully, I know it."

Some of the other men spoke up—the ones who didn't wear badges and were just here for the money. If there was a chance that Fox would come out with no more trouble, they wanted to take it. He could tell from the whimpering and chatter that he'd wounded at least a few of them, and maybe done worse than that.

He hadn't meant to kill anyone. What he'd told the lawman was true—he was done with that life, done with banks and trains and killing. But they'd forced his hand, and he would have to live with the consequences.

Finally, Diggs agreed. "She's coming in!" he

shouted. "You can open the door for her, we won't try anything."

Fox risked a quick peek out the shattered front window. The men he could see, including Diggs, had lowered their weapons. He went to the door and pulled the bar, and when he heard her outside, he swung it open, staying out of sight behind the wall, just in case. Ella stepped inside, and he shut it again, replacing the bar.

As she entered, she wrinkled her nose at the stink of the smoke hanging in the room. She must have been nineteen now. Maybe twenty; he disremembered exactly. Her hair was long, light brown like her mother's. Tall and slender, like him, but pretty. Luckily, she took after her mother that way. "Ella, is it really you?"

"Of course it's me, Papa. Can't you tell?"

She spoke with an educated tone, so unlike either of her parents. His voice caught in his throat. "I mean," he managed, "you still look like you, but you're so grown up. When you went to live with your mother's people, you were just a little girl."

She came into his arms then, and he held her tight, feeling her heartbeat against his chest. He thought there might have been tears in her eyes. "I didn't want to go, but Mama insisted. You know that."

"I know. When your mama got an idea in her head, she wouldn't let go of it for nothing. She was always that way, and I always let her have her way. Especially when it was her deathbed wish. But you know, you could've come back any time."

Ella broke off the embrace and stepped away. "I was in *Kansas*, Papa. It wasn't so easy. When I did come back, things had changed so much I didn't know if I'd be able to find the place. Then Sheriff Diggs recognized me. He said if I'd bring him out here, he'd make sure you weren't harmed. I didn't trust him, so I told him I couldn't remember how to get here. When you were spotted and someone figured out where you were, he said I could come along. But he promised to let me talk to you first, before any shooting started. I thought I could convince you to come out and stand trial."

"And spend the rest of my life in prison?"

"At least I could visit you. At least you'd be alive!"

"One word for it, anyway," Fox said.

"Is it true, what those men said about you on the way over?"

"Depends on what they said."

"That you're a thief, a murderer. That you never put in an honest day's work in your life."

Fox shrugged. "Could be a mite exaggerated, but I reckon it's mostly so."

"They'll kill you if they have to. Some of them talked about it all the way here."

"Riding in those infernal motor cars? Those

things are a sign of the last days, I think. It's all downhill now."

"Papa, they're all the rage in the cities. In civilized places."

He scoffed. "Like Kansas City?"

"Among others."

"Well," he said, "I reckon you're still my daughter, even though you got some strange ideas in your head."

From outside, Diggs shouted. "Ella, come on out, now! That's enough!"

"He said five minutes," Ella said. "He has a pocket-watch in his vest."

"Five minutes? It's been eight years since I've seen you, or thereabouts. We got so much to talk about."

"I'll visit, no matter where they send you. We'll get to know each other all over again."

"Ella!" Diggs cried.

"She's coming!" Fox called back. "Hold onto your britches!"

"Please, Papa. Come out with me. They won't shoot if you're with me."

He considered, briefly, then shook his head. "I can't risk that," he said. "If just one of them got a twitchy trigger finger, you could be hurt. You go on out, Ella. Get in one of those automobiles and make somebody drive you away from here, where you'll be safe."

"Then you'll give yourself up? Do you promise?"

"I'll come out," Fox said.

She put her hands on his shoulders, rose up on her toes, and kissed his cheek. "I can't wait to spend time with you, Papa. It's been much too long!"

"It has been," Fox said. "Now go on out. Tell Diggs what I said. Until you're safely away, I don't budge an inch."

She gave him a smile that made his heart ache and stepped through the door. Fox held his breath, half expecting gunfire to break out. But it didn't. He heard the murmur of voices as she explained to Diggs, then a few minutes later, the sound of one of the automobiles driving away. He chanced a glimpse through the window and saw Ella sitting in the front seat, next to the driver, as it went down the road and disappeared behind a low hill.

"She's gone, Caldwell!" Diggs called. "Come on out, now!"

"Give her a few minutes," Fox answered.

"Why? You said when she was safe, you'd come out. She's safe now."

"I need to gather my thoughts," Fox said.

"You've had years to do that."

"It ain't so easy as you might think, Cooter. Just be still, now."

Diggs started to say something, but he cut himself off before he got a word out. There was no conversation among the men outside. They were waiting, expectant. Fox moved to another window and took a quick look. Guns were pointed toward the house. Maybe Diggs had told them not to fire, but they were prepared to do so if Fox started shooting again.

Fox thought about the lawman's offer. Some nights in jail, until the circuit judge showed up. A fair trial. He would be convicted, of course—even he couldn't claim he hadn't done the things he had. He had robbed people, killed a few. Held up trains. Stolen people's savings from banks.

It wasn't much to be proud of. His years in solitude had convinced him of that. He paid for everything he took, now. He didn't threaten people, didn't even argue with them. But just the same, there was blood on his hands and on the money he paid those people with.

He would lose at the trial, and he'd either be sentenced to hang or go to prison. He was old, past seventy. If he went behind bars, he wouldn't come out unless it was in a pine box.

The net had been strung around his house, sixteen men strong. The cage would surely follow.

But one of those men outside had lied to his daughter. Put her in harm's way. For that, Cooter Diggs had to pay.

Fox drew the pistol at his hip, checked the cylinder out of habit. He threw open the door and stepped out into the cool stillness and the snow and the sunlight, already firing.

Because whatever else he was—husband, father, outlaw, killer, and more—Fox Caldwell was no snake.

JEFFREY J. MARIOTTE is the author of dozens of novels and short stories and hundreds of comics and graphic novels, most of which take place in the historical or contemporary West. Work in the Western genre includes the Peacemaker- and Spur Award-finalist novella "Byrd's Luck," weird-Western novel *Thunder Moon Rising*, comic-book series *Desperadoes* and *Graveslinger* (with Shannon Eric Denton), and short fiction in anthologies such as *Lost Trails*, *Ghost Towns*, *Westward Weird*, and *Straight Outta Deadwood*. From the bedroom of the Arizona home he shares with his wife and writing partner Marsheila Rockwell and their family, he can see the Superstition Mountains. Visit him at www.facebook.com/JeffreyJMariotte to stay updated on new goings-on.

TRACKDOWN

WAYNE D. DUNDEE

The man in black made his way down the back slope of the giant boulder in a barely controlled slide. Near the bottom, where the slope broke off sharply, he pushed away and dropped lightly the rest of the way to the ground.

A second man waited there, crouched patiently on his haunches, rolling a handful of smooth pebbles in his right palm. Some feet away, two saddled horses stood ground-reined in the lengthening shade thrown by a strand of scraggly juniper.

The climber took a minute to catch his breath, at the same time removing his broad-brimmed hat and using it to swat the fresh streaks of boulder dust from his clothes. When he was finished, he swept back his shock of gray-flecked dark hair with his free hand and replaced the hat.

The second man straightened up, tossing aside his pebbles. "Well," he said, "are they over there?"

The black-clad man nodded. "They are for a fact. Just like we figured."

"All of 'em?"

"All seven, by my count. Regrouped from the different directions they scattered. Act like they don't have a care in the world now. Camped right in the middle of a clearing, cooking coffee over a fire. Don't even have a lookout posted."

"Seven. Makes the odds just like we figured, too." The second man sighed. "Not like I haven't bet my hide on worse, though, I reckon."

"Yeah, ain't that the truth. The rotten apples always seem to come in bunches, don't they?"

Standing against the backdrop of sun-blasted rock, discussing the matter at hand in calm, quiet voices, the two men presented a number of visual contrasts. The climber was tall and gaunt, the slenderness of his long legs and arms suggesting the kind of gawkiness common to that physical type, perhaps even a certain degree of frailty. Suggesting such things, that was, to any who failed to observe the self-assured grace with which he carried himself or who had not witnessed his deceptive strength.

The second man was equally tall, much thicker through the chest and shoulders and neck, his forearms, exposed by the rolled cuffs of his shirt sleeves, sun-bronzed and corded with muscle. His strength was obvious, the deceptive part in his case being the speed and agility with which that big frame was capable of moving. Where the gaunt man was decked out entirely in black from head to toe, the big man wore faded denims and a buckskin vest beneath a flat-crowned Stetson bleached colorless by the sun except for its sweat stains and many miles' accumulation of trail dust. The abused Stetson rode atop a square, weathered, ruggedly handsome face as opposed to the gaunt man's narrow, pale, saturnine features brooding beneath the sweep of his broad, black brim.

More telling than their differences, however, were the similarities to be noted about the pair: the steeliness in their eyes, the casually confident way they moved under the weight of the guns riding low on their hips, the always-close proximity of their varied other weapons. In truth, both were bounty hunters of considerable reputation. Their partnership was only a few days old, but each had worn the brand of manhunter for several years.

The gaunt man was called Doc Turpin. If he had a first name he never used it, and no one could remember having ever heard it. Furthermore, since he evidently wanted it that way, no sensible person —considering his reputation for having a lightning draw and temper to match—was in a hurry to ask. Turpin plied his trade for the most part in Texas, making his current appearance in the borderlands of the Arizona Territory something of a rarity.

For Bodie Kendrick, the big man in the buckskin vest, it was just the opposite. The territories of Arizona and New Mexico were mainly where he did his hunting, with only infrequent forays into the lone star state.

"As far as this bunch," Kendrick said now, replying to Turpin's observation, "I guess you'd have to say they've managed to scrape together just about the rottenest collection of apples to be found anywhere."

"That's a pure fact," Turpin allowed. "This poor old world sure as hell never needed the likes of the Klegg gang and the Harrup Brothers to throw in together. The way they hit that bank in New Gleanus makes it clear enough what they add up to: they're going to flat try and outdo each other when it comes to spilling blood along with whatever jobs they pull."

Mention of New Gleanus and the slaughter that had taken place there only three days earlier made Kendrick grimace with recollection of the scene. He'd ridden into the dusty territory town barely an hour after the robbers had struck—struck with a cold-blooded viciousness that marked them as something more akin to rabid beasts than to even the fringe element of civilized mankind. Of course Kendrick had known for some time that there was little civilized about the Harrup brothers, Clem and Darrel; or the wild-eyed cousin, Huck Mather, who rode with them. And while Kendrick had heard a few stories about Otis Klegg and his marauding band over in West Texas, he'd had no first hand feel for how bloodthirsty they, too, could be.

Until New Gleanus.

The joining of the two outlaw groups had come as a surprise and something of a shock. The common link apparently was a man known as Paris, who now rode with Klegg's bunch but had once outlawed with the Harrups. The exact details of the joining were still obscure. All Kendrick knew for sure was that he'd been dogging the Harrups for nearly a week when all of a sudden, in the middle of some barrens to the north of New Gleanus, their tracks had increased fourfold.

By all reports, the New Gleanus bank money, its total abnormally swollen to meet the payroll of the railroad crew approaching with gleaming new track from the east, had been handed over obediently under gunpoint. It was then that it became clear the robbers had an appetite for more than just booty. Fattened by their take, having met no serious resistance, in a position to ride away fast and clean before an alarm could be sounded or responded to, the Harrup-Klegg kill-crazies had opted instead to blast their way out of town for no reason other than to dish out a measure of death and destruction. In the storm of gunsmoke and sizzling lead that ensued, windows were smashed, wagons and livestock stampeded, fences flattened, yards trampled, fires sparked by broken lamps, a score of innocent citizens—including women and children—wounded or injured, and half a dozen others killed.

The spilled blood had still been fresh and red on the boardwalks and in the dust of the street when Kendrick rode in. The moans and lamentations of the survivors still quavered in the rapidly warming morning air. It made Kendrick think of crossing a landscape in the wake of a battle, the way he'd done more than once as a fuzz-chinned young soldier during the War Between the States, his baptism to man's capacity for violence toward his own kind.

It was while strolling the bloodied streets of the stunned town, eavesdropping on near-hysterical accounts of what had happened, softly asking an occasional question, that Kendrick first made eye contact with the man in black whom he promptly recognized as Doc Turpin. Even partially stripped of his trademark garb as he pitched in to try and help the frantic town doctor deliver aid to the wounded, Turpin was unmistakable. And the faint narrowing of the man's eyes when he met Kendrick's gaze told plainly enough that the recognition cut both ways.

Later, after a posse of outraged, well-intentioned, but woefully inadequate clerks, shop keepers, and laborers—hurriedly sworn in as deputies by a town marshal who was himself twenty years too old and forty pounds too soft for the task at hand—rode out on the trail of the animals who had shattered their community, Kendrick and Turpin once again locked gazes in the back-bar mirror of a saloon, all but deserted and eerily quiet in that troubled hour. They were its only two customers. The bartender, a balding, grotesquely fat man, was busy picking the remaining shards of broken glass from around the framework of what had once been the establishment's gaudily painted front window, sweating profusely and muttering obscenities under his breath at having to perform the chore in the middle of the morning's heat. He seemed to have little inclination for serving his patrons or for grieving the town's wasted lives, only for bemoaning his own plight and the loss of the precious glass.

It had been Turpin who finally broke the silence between the two manhunters. Tossing back a shot of rye, he slowly turned and, in measured strides, walked the stretch of bar front that separated him and Kendrick until he paused at a new distance of three paces. At all times he carried his lean body with a subtle poise under never-still eyes, balanced, ready, hand dangling close to the brightly polished hogleg at his hip. Just as Kendrick, even in a supposedly relaxed position, elbows resting on the bar, out of habit held his torso with a certain rigidity, waist cocked slightly so that neither the big fighting Bowie on his left nor the Colt on his right were in any way blocked from quick access.

Having made his approach, Turpin said evenly, "By the height and the span of those shoulders and the rest, I make you for Bodie Kendrick out of New Mexico Territory."

Kendrick had nodded. "Guilty as charged," he allowed. "And by the all-black outfit and the way you carry yourself coiled like a diamondback inside that gunbelt with the pearl-handled Smith and Wesson, you'd be the famous bounty hunter, Doc Turpin, from over Texas-way."

"I don't know about the 'famous' part ... but I'm Turpin."

"I've heard of you, you've heard of me. Maybe we're both famous."

"In our line of work, being too well known isn't necessarily a good thing."

Kendrick had reached to snag a fresh whiskey tumbler from behind the bar, filled it from the bottle in front of him, held it out to Doc. After they'd bent elbows together, Kendrick said, "Speakin' of our line of work—what was done out there on the street a little while ago bears the stamp of the kind of men our business is all about. I don't reckon it's coincidence, Doc, the both of us showing up here just now."

Turpin had sighed with an air of weariness,

perhaps a touch of sadness. "No...I don't reckon it is."

They'd stood there together for a spell, sipping whiskey, talking, comparing notes.

Turpin told of following Otis Klegg and his bunch out of Texas after they'd botched an attempt to rob a payroll wagon, leaving behind two of their own mortally wounded and getting away with only a fraction of the money they'd been after, yet still managing to kill three guards and the driver of the wagon during the confrontation. The episode had resulted in the price on the heads of the Klegg gang being raised to a level that renewed Turpin's interest and held it even to the point of going out of state after them. Somewhat sheepishly he admitted to losing their sign for the better part of a day in a rugged stretch of unfamiliar territory and then, after picking it up again, recognizing that a rendezvous had taken place with three new riders whose identity he had no way of knowing at the time. He also spotted sign of Kendrick, doing his own tracking, and the whole thing made him that much more curious and cautious in his pursuit. Like Kendrick, Doc had arrived in New Gleanus too late to do anything about the bloody robbery.

For his part, Kendrick told of dogging the Harrups down from the north but not being able to close the gap on them before they unexpectedly threw in with four additional men and proceeded to hit the bank and the unsuspecting town with their combined savagery. Upon learning the identity of who the Harrups had joined with, Kendrick recalled the fact of Klegg's man Paris having once ridden with the Harrups and from there it seemed logical to figure him for the one who'd acted as the go-between in somehow bringing the two forces together. At any rate, both bounty hunters now agreed the New Gleanus posse that had assembled and gone after the robbers had about as much chance against them as a flock of sage hens thrown in front of a buffalo stampede.

Neither of the two men probably could say exactly how the idea of them teaming up came about. On the one hand it might be considered a fairly natural evolution out of the way preceding events had unfolded, on the other it was a prospect practically unthinkable to two independent sorts. Nevertheless, abetted in no small way by previously formed respect for each other's reputations, by the time they'd wrapped up their saloon palaver they'd also wrapped up plans to unite their individual hunts and ride out together after the seven wanted men.

With the sun beginning its descent in the afternoon sky, re-provisioned, horses grained and watered and rested, Kendrick and Turpin had put the unfortunate town of New Gleanus behind them. Their way was at first clearly marked by the chewed ground that had been ridden over by both fleeing robbers and pursuing posse. On the second day, tracking started to get more difficult; the terrain changing, growing rockier, more barren and sun-blasted. The outlaws had waited for this rugged flooring to pull the tactic of splitting up, each rider branching off in a different direction, and the posse had been foolish enough to split their force as well. The one chance they'd had going for them was sheer weight of number and by dividing what had originally been a small army into seven separate handfuls of anxious amateurs they dramatically increased the odds against their success, possibly even their survival.

Kendrick and Turpin stayed with the distinctive track of a horse with a slightly crooked shoe on its right front foot, a mark Turpin knew well, having followed it all the way from Texas. "Belongs to Otis Klegg's own black gelding," he'd explained. "We lock on this, I'm willing to guarantee the others will fall back in with it. I don't know much about your Harrup boys, but I know old Otis is bull enough to make that kind of demand, that the rest converge on him when the time is right."

"I'll buy that line of reasoning," Kendrick had agreed. "The Harrups are a little young, a little green at what they're doing still. Klegg's been around longer, got a bigger reputation. Clem and Darrel and for sure their crazy cousin Huck would be impressed by that. They'd let him do most of the bossing... for now, anyway."

So they'd locked on the track of the horse with the crooked shoe, following it deeper into the rugged sprawl of badlands.

On the morning of the third day, just before full sunup, they'd heard a series of gunshots in the distance. After covering a cautious mile and a half, they'd come upon the four posse deputies who'd been unlucky enough to draw Klegg's trail and found them shot to pieces. Two dead, one badly wounded, one creased less seriously but still not without blood loss and pain. The crafty old bastard had doubled back on them and when he saw how few they were he'd cut them down from ambush.

The bounty hunters had dressed the wounds of the living as best they could before directing them back the way they'd come, throwing in a warning for the two still alive to do everything in their power to call their posse together again into full force before others were picked off in the same manner. Temporary graves were dug for the pair of dead deputies and marked well in order to be easily found by those who would return to take the bodies home for a proper burial.

Kendrick and Turpin had then taken up the hunt once more, faces set in even grimmer expressions, resolve burning hotter in their guts to take down the animals running somewhere out ahead of them—

and for more reasons than could be measured in dollars and cents.

By afternoon, exactly as Turpin had predicted, tracks of the other robbers who'd branched off the previous day began re-converging on those of Otis Klegg. And now, with evening drawing near on this far edge of the badlands, all seven had returned to the fold and were snugly gathered in the camp in the clearing on the other side of the massive boulder. The way they saw it they had good reason to be smug, believing the posse that had been chasing them to be disorganized and riddled (there almost certainly having been other ambushes sprung in the same manner as Klegg's) and likely turned tail for home. The thing they had no way of knowing yet was that a separate kind of posse, a two-man version that was the last thing they would want to encounter anywhere or anytime, had finally closed the gap on them and was getting ready to drop the bolt across the door.

"So," Kendrick drawled, "now that we got these desperadoes right where we want 'em, any particular plan come to mind for how best we go about roundin' 'em up and takin' 'em back?"

"My way's always been to go at a situation like this head-on," Turpin replied. "When you've got a rat cornered in a grain bin, then you go in after it. That's all. I was never much for skulking around the edges looking for the right opening, or trying to lay down some fancy trap or ambush. For one thing, I don't favor giving vermin like these the notion they're important enough or dangerous enough to rate any special consideration."

Kendrick chuckled softly.

"Something funny in what I said?" Turpin wanted to know.

"Not really. Happens I ain't much of a skulker, either. Reckon that means we're gonna keep gettin' along fine…long as we don't end up with our fool heads blowed off together."

Turpin gave a fatalistic shrug. "I don't figure the good Lord woke me up this morning and pushed me through the day for no better purpose than to let my candle get snuffed out by the likes of that bunch over there."

"You a religious man, Doc?" Kendrick asked, genuinely curious.

"Not in the way you probably mean. Not in a church-going, Bible-thumping kind of way. Fact is, the life I lead…hunting men down, having to kill some of them…I expect a lot of preachers and regular church-goers would frown real serious on most things about me. But I still believe in God Almighty, and Right and Wrong and Good and Evil. At least the way I see 'em. Don't you?"

"I know about Bad and Evil, I've seen plenty of those. I keep tellin' myself there's Right and Good out there somewhere, too, balancin' things. Easy to lose track of that part, the line of work we follow." Kendrick let his eyes sweep the sky and the raggedly majestic landscape, this region where the badlands were breaking up, giving way stubbornly to grasses and trees and more gently rolling hills. "Far as God Almighty, if He hangs strictly around churches and the like then I don't reckon I rub up against him too often. But it's pretty hard to ride this country day and night under a wide open sky that takes turns being angry and beautiful and mean and breathtaking...and not grow to figure there's somewhere something bigger at work than us piddly little human beings."

Turpin let his gaze follow Kendrick's, squinting, giving some thought. After a minute or so, he said, "The thing that's at work in that sky right now is the sun. It'll be setting down on the horizon soon. We could maybe put that to our advantage." He made a circling motion with his arm. "We'll swing around that way, come at 'em from out of the west. I saw a narrow, open flat feeding into the wider clearing where they're camped. We time it right, come across that flat with the sinking sun at our backs, it could give us a small edge."

Kendrick tipped his head in an agreeable nod. "Seven to two ain't much of an edge at all—I'll take small over not much."

They swung into their saddles and rode west into some grassy, tree-studded lowlands, then looped around and headed back toward the outlaw camp. The fiery red-gold ball that was the sun beat hot against their backs, throwing their shadows long out ahead of them.

In the hours and days they'd ridden together they had discussed the men they were getting ready to go up against, assessing their strengths and weaknesses, advising one another what to expect from those each had little or no familiarity with. It was generally accepted that Otis Klegg was the meanest and strongest and had the most influence, even over the Harrups; but if bullets started flying, Klegg was too bulky and slow to be the most immediate worry.

The man called Paris, known to Kendrick and Turpin both, was probably the fastest gun in the bunch, closely followed by Darrel and Clem Harrup. Huck Mather was a brooding young giant, as strong and mean as a gored bull, but slow mentally as well as physically. The remaining two Klegg men—a whiskey-nose named Bedney and a Mex known as Chulla—were scraggly hanger-ons of little consequence but nevertheless willing and able to take life at any opportunity.

The bounty hunters rode up into the narrow flat Doc had described. Ahead, where it flared into a wider clearing, they could see men gathered around a campfire, unsaddled horses grazing close by. The timing was perfect, making their approach straight out of the blinding blast of the sun.

As they slowed their own horses, Kendrick said, "We should dismount, lead our animals in on foot. That'll look less threatening, probably allow us to get in closer."

Turpin took the suggestion, dropping lightly from his saddle. "Don't you figure they're going to recognize us anyway?" he said.

"Expect so," Kendrick agreed. "But we'll still look less intimidating for a while. And if it comes to throwin' lead—which it likely will—reckon we're better off standin' on the ground than sittin' the backs of a couple hoppin' horses."

"Done my share both ways," Turpin said stubbornly.

Kendrick took time to rearrange his weapons, pulling his Winchester out of its scabbard and slipping it behind the saddle cantle where it was wedged loosely in place by his bedroll. The Greener double-barreled shotgun that usually rode in that position (although lashed securely with leather thongs) he temporarily dropped into the Winchester's scabbard.

"I take it you don't figure to get the job done by your short gun?" Turpin said with a trace of impatience.

Kendrick shook his head. "Comes to yankin' out shootin' irons, I can't match the speed of Paris or Darrel Harrup. So I'll try to make it up with the added accuracy and punch of my rifle."

"Well, however you plan to do your part, let's be

getting to it. We're losing the sun. " As he said this, Doc was checking the load in the Colt Lightning .38 he'd pulled from his saddle bag. Satisfied the gun was ready if needed, he then slipped it under his belt to the left of the shiny buckle, butt forward and angled toward his right hand.

They took their horses' reins and began walking toward the camp. As an afterthought, Turpin muttered, "Any sonofabitch shoots my horse, I'll kill him certain."

The men in the camp had seen them by now. Some who'd been squatting or sitting on the ground rose to stand. Cold eyes followed every step of the intruders' approach. Otis Klegg stood in the middle of the group, fists planted on hips, the grimy long duster he wore fanned open by the posture, making his bulk look twice as wide as any of the others. Darrel and Clem Harrup stood off to Otis's right, their contrastingly lean bodies looking bowstring tight with anticipation. Their cousin Huck was a ways back from them, over by the horses; he had a bridle in his hands and appeared to have been repairing or adjusting it in some way. Paris was to Klegg's left, his stance deceptively relaxed, his eyes crackling with alertness. Chulla was busily stirring a pot of something over the fire and seemed content to let the others worry about whoever was coming. That left Bedney, off by himself over to one far edge of the clearing, paused in the act of breaking up tree branches for firewood.

When they'd closed to about a dozen yards from the camp, Kendrick and Turpin stopped walking and tugged their horses to a halt.

"Hello, the camp," Turpin called easily.

"Right back at you," Otis Klegg responded, squinting hard into the fingers of sunlight spraying around the figures of the newcomers.

"We saw your smoke, smelled your cooking fire."

"That's a lie."

Muscles fluttered along Doc's sharp jaw line. "Say again?"

"You heard me. That there's a drywood fire, ain't giving off no smoke. And what's in the pot ain't been cooking long enough to send no smell."

"I'm not in the habit of being called a liar."

"Shouldn't take on such a nasty habit, then."

Kendrick spoke up, "Maybe my partner was mistaken. Maybe what we smelled clear across the way was just the stink of an overripe, murderin' tub of guts wrapped up in a ratty old duster coat."

Klegg grinned broadly, showing brownish stumps of teeth and then showing the sun didn't have him all that blinded by saying to Turpin, "Partner's got kind of a mouth on him, don't he, Doc?"

"Only problem with that'd be if he couldn't back up what comes out of it."

"You figure he can?"

"Wouldn't be partnered with him if I didn't."

Darrel Harrup took a step closer to Klegg. "His name's Kendrick—Bodie Kendrick. He's from up our way. I recognize him same as you did Turpin. Makes them two vulture bastards cut outta the same cloth."

"Looks like you got your own self a partner who ain't afraid to speak his mind," Turpin told Klegg.

Klegg shrugged. "Like you said…only problem with that'd be if he can't back it up."

"So let's quit gnawin' around the edges," Kendrick said. "You know who we are, we know who you are. Reckon we can all figure out what this visit shakes down to."

"You aim to take us in—that what you're saying?"

"For a fact."

"Sort of insulting, the odds you're giving us." Klegg paused and showed his ugly grin again. Then he placed the edge of his hand above his eyes and did a mocking pantomime of sweeping his gaze carefully around. "Or have you maybe got some members of that fee-rocious New Gleanus posse lurking somewhere out there to back you up?" He and his men emitted a round of snorting laughs at this idea of a big joke.

"You try to make an argument of this," Turpin said evenly, "you'll be doing your laughing in Hell. Me and Kendrick mean business, and we haven't done our training behind store counters or hay bales like those poor posse boys you cut apart. This is it,

Klegg. Throw your guns down or make a go for 'em. One way or another, we're taking you with us."

Klegg's ugly grin turned into an even uglier sneer. "Why, you bold bastard! Who do you think you're talking to? I demand more respect than that."

"I got more respect for a diseased coyote," Kendrick muttered.

"The only thing you'll get from us," Turpin said, voice still calm and steady, "is a way to the gallows or a bellyful of lead. You choose."

Klegg jerked his arm down, sweeping his great coat open even wider, and clawed for the long-barreled Remington revolver jammed in his belt. "Damn you to hell—I choose this!"

The scene exploded into a flurry of deadly-intentioned activity. Men scrambling, dodging this way and that, feet trampling, arms flailing, fingers clutching at holsters and diving under coat flaps and vests to grab for weapons.

Two figures remained comparatively motionless: Doc Turpin and Klegg's gunny, Paris. Only their hands moved. Like twin lightning bolts. Their drawn guns roared simultaneously—the first shots to be exchanged—and Paris reeled and fell as a result with a bullet hole punched straight through his heart.

Kendrick pivoted on his heel, turning hard and sharp to the right, reaching, snatching the Winchester from where he'd placed it behind the saddle cantle. He let the turn take him full around in a continuous fluid motion, dropping into a slight crouch at its completion, the rifle braced against his hip, and from that pose began levering a rapid-fire rain of lead into the outlaw camp.

Darrel Harrup lived up to his own fast-draw reputation, Colt flashing to his fist with startling speed. He cocked and fired only a fraction of a second behind the reports of Turpin and Paris. But Darrel was confused by Kendrick's spinning move; he threw two shots wide, anticipating Kendrick's motion would pull him off to one side. By the time he started to correct his aim, Kendrick's Winchester was spitting its own brand of death. Harrup took hits to the groin and stomach, the slugs doubling him and knocking him skidding to the ground. Beside him, his younger brother Clem, sprayed by Darrel's blood, slightly slower on the draw and also confused by the whirling tactic of Kendrick, got off a single ineffective shot before he, too, was ripped by the bounty hunter's rifle fire.

Having downed Paris, Doc Turpin began to move. In long, unhurried strides he advanced directly on the camp, holding his torso twisted to the left, offering an even narrower target in profile than his spare frame presented straight-on. He walked with his right arm extended full in front of him, Smith and Wesson barking in his grip. Cock and fire, cock and fire…he squeezed the trigger with each down step of his right heel.

Otis Klegg got the big Remington pulled free of his belt but never had a chance to raise it before one of Doc's slugs smashed his Adam's apple. He dropped abruptly to one knee, teetering that way for a long moment, blood bubbling down the front of him, eyes wide as if disbelieving he'd been hit. Two more bullets tore into his chest, an inch apart, and his massive frame slowly toppled backward and down, like a tree. The Remington stayed gripped in his dead fingers, unfired.

At the outbreak of action, Huck Mather had dropped the horse bridle he'd been fiddling with and turned to grab for the Henry repeating rifle that leaned against a nearby mossy hump. He came around with it in time to see his two cousins hit the ground. Choking back a sob, blurting instead a roar of emotional pain and rage, he came rushing forward, leaping over the fallen bodies of Darrel and Clem and making straight for Kendrick in a plodding run, firing the Henry wildly. In spite of the recklessness of the charge, one of his shots managed to tear a long gouge in Kendrick's side just above the beltline.

Chulla, the Mex who'd seen fit to worry only about the stew pot until the shooting started, fell instantly into a world of problems when he finally decided to pay attention and join the fight. In trying to stand up, he somehow got his feet tangled together and ended up sprawling on his hands and knees directly in the fire. Screeching with pain and panic, he jerked away and sprawled again, tumbling this time like a smoldering log, both of his shirt sleeves and one pant leg bursting into flames. As Otis Klegg went crashing down in death, Chulla was only a few feet away, howling and flailing at the fire that threatened to spread and consume him. In his condition he presented no immediate danger to anybody other than himself, but his outcries were annoying enough to draw a pair of bullets from Doc. So energetic was Chulla's flopping about, however, that both shots missed, kicking up dirt around their intended target.

The remaining Klegg man, Bedney, had positioned himself to be a more serious threat. When the fight broke out, he had dropped the armload of fire wood he'd gathered, turned and ran as fast as he could to gain the cover of a durable oak tree on the edge of the clearing. From there, he drew his Colt and took careful aim on Doc Turpin.

Meanwhile, Huck Mather was continuing his charge at Kendrick. The bounty hunter had sent round after round of Winchester slugs thudding into the young giant and while each staggered him and slowed him, none of them stopped him. He kept coming. When his Henry rifle was empty, he flung it aside and came on with both hands reaching claw-like. His face was shiny with sweat and tears, chest and stomach streaked with blood. Kendrick's

Winchester was emptied, too, but he hung onto the heavy piece and when Mather got close enough he knocked aside the clawing hands with its stock then brought the butt up and across in a slashing chop to the jaw. Mather's neck popped like a dried corn stalk and he finally went down.

Bedney's first shot took Doc's hat off and creased his scalp, spilling an instant trickle of blood down over his face. At the same time, the hammer of Turpin's Smith and Wesson began clicking on spent cartridges. Bedney fired twice more. Coolly, with the bullets singing to either side of him, Doc shifted the spent gun to his left hand and with his right drew the backup Colt Lightning from his belt. When Bedney leaned out to fire again, a .38 slug shattered tree bark a hair's breadth from his face. Turpin kept walking, adjusting his course specifically for the tree now. Every time Bedney tried to poke his head out, another bullet crashed into the trunk where he showed himself.

While Doc was keeping his man pinned down, Kendrick walked over to Chulla, who'd managed to smother the flames that had caught his clothing and was now rolling back and forth on the ground, mewling in pain, panting to regain his breath between coughs brought on by the tendrils of smoke that still engulfed him. Kendrick paused long enough to kick him nonchalantly in the head, knocking him unconscious and putting him out of his misery. That done, he drew his Colt and turned to Turpin, saying, "Lend a hand there, Doc?"

"Join in if you like," Turpin answered. "Workin' on flushing out a yellow dog."

But before Kendrick got off even a shot, Bedney called from behind the tree, "Wait a minute! Hold it! Hold your fire. I ain't no match for the two of you, not no how. Ain't there some way we can end this without me getting blasted to pieces? I'll throw my guns out...I'll do anything you say."

"Talk is cheap," Turpin said, "but it takes money to buy whiskey. Let's see the color of your money—let's see those guns come out."

Bedney hesitated. "How do I know you won't shoot me anyway?"

Kendrick said, "If we're of a mind to shoot you, then shot is what you'll get, regardless. Comin' out unarmed with hands high is your best chance. Believe it."

After several clock ticks, Bedney's Colt sailed out and landed on the ground seven or eight feet from the tree. A handful of seconds later, a big bore derringer landed next to it.

"That's it. That cleans me out."

"Haul yourself out from behind that trunk then, where we can see you," Turpin said. "Hands high, like you were told."

Bedney emerged, visibly shaken. His hands, thrust at arms' length over his head, were trembling badly. By contrast, neither of the guns trained on him wavered one whit.

Bedney's bug-eyed stare swept over his fallen comrades. "My God, look at 'em ... all my pards... every one cut down." His eyes found Kendrick and Turpin, danced nervously back and forth between them. "You two are a couple of holy terrors, you know that?"

Turpin blinked away some of the blood dripping down off his left brow and said, "Not a damn thing holy about us, old man...we're just doing a job."

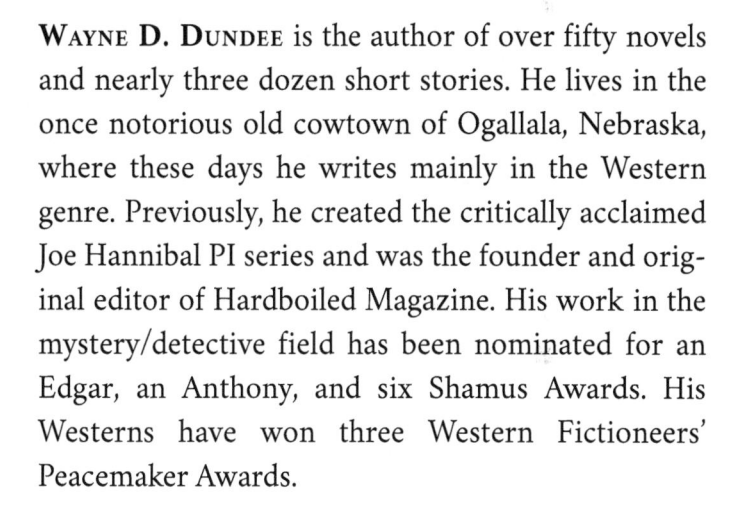

WAYNE D. DUNDEE is the author of over fifty novels and nearly three dozen short stories. He lives in the once notorious old cowtown of Ogallala, Nebraska, where these days he writes mainly in the Western genre. Previously, he created the critically acclaimed Joe Hannibal PI series and was the founder and original editor of Hardboiled Magazine. His work in the mystery/detective field has been nominated for an Edgar, an Anthony, and six Shamus Awards. His Westerns have won three Western Fictioneers' Peacemaker Awards.

AFTER BLACK JACK DROPPED

JACKSON LOWRY

"That's about the damnedest, stupidest thing I ever heard," the judge said, staring at the defendant.

"I protest," cried Thomas "Black Jack" Ketchum's lawyer. "You're malignin' an honest man."

"Nuthin' honest about him," the judge said, then spat accurately into a cuspidor at the side of his desk. "You." The judge pointed at Frank Harrington. "Tell me again about what Ketchum did." The judge glared at both the defendant and his lawyer to silence them.

"Yer honor, I worked as conductor on the train. We been robbed twice before and this time I was ready for anything. When Ketchum—"

"A point, Judge," called the defense attorney. "You are trying the wrong man. This here's George Stevens and—"

"Don't give me any guff," the judge growled. "That's Tom Ketchum, not some first timer who didn't know his ass from a hole in the ground. Now shut up and let Mr. Harrington finish. We all got better things to do. I want to get home for dinner 'fore it gets too late."

The lawyer subsided and the conductor continued his recitation of the train robbery.

"He jumped onto the train just this side of Folsom, then forced the engineer and fireman to stop." Harrington grinned savagely and smoothed his mustache. "Where we stopped was real tight, sheer rock faces on either side of the tracks. He couldn't get back and uncouple the mail and express car like he planned."

"What did you do?" the judge asked.

"I heard him walkin' on the roof of the passenger car on his way back, so I grabbed my shotgun and got to the express car 'bout the time he did. He saw me, and damn but he was quick. He got off the first shot. I let loose with my scattergun and missed. I fired the second barrel and got the varmint that time."

"Damned well blew my arm off!" Ketchum cried. He held up a bandaged stump before his lawyer could stop him.

"Didn't blow it off. Not entirely," Harrington said. "But it was danglin'. Heard tell they caught him when he run off."

"Never did," Ketchum said. "I was too weak. Flagged down the next train and surrendered. Sheriff Pinard took custody of me at Folsom, kept me on the train to the Trinidad hospital where they lopped off my arm." Ketchum glared at the conductor. "You done me in, you son of a bitch." He waved his stump around some more but the judge used his gavel to silence him.

"I'm sorry I didn't blow off yer head!" the conductor shouted. "You wounded *me*! That shot you got off hit me in the left arm!"

"Silence!" bellowed the judge. He straightened papers in front of him on the desk and continued. "Think that 'bout wraps it up. Not much left to say other than, guilty!"

"Your honor!" The defense attorney jumped to his feet. "I protest!"

"Protest this," the judge went on. "On this day of September 11, 1899, I do order Mr. Thomas Edward Ketchum to be hanged by the neck 'til he's dead. Sheriff Garcia, take the guilty party to the jail. Clayton, New Mexico's 'bout to have its first hanging." The judge brought his gavel down with a ringing bang. The few men in the courtroom let out a shout of glee that drowned out Ketchum and his lawyer's protests.

"I'll get an appeal, Tom," the lawyer said. "They can't hang you for robbin' a train. You didn't kill anyone."

"Not this time," Ketchum said. "Did before, over in Arizona. But not this time. Nuthin' went right with the robbery. I was a damn fool to try it all by my lonesome, but bad luck's been my mistress since my brother Sam was killed by that posse. I shoulda been with him. Together, we coulda got away."

"Keep your voice down, Tom. Don't go givin' the deputies anything they can testify to in court."

"How long?"

"Until they hang you?" The lawyer shook his head. "Months. With luck we can keep 'em jumpin' like fleas on a hot griddle 'til they come to their senses and let you go. Or at least reduce your sentence to a few years in the Santa Fe Penitentiary."

"Don't want to go there," Ketchum said firmly. "That's where they took Elzy."

"You mean McGinnis?"

"Elzy Lay. Don't matter what name he got convicted under. He's still locked up like an animal. And fer life. The son of a bitch shoulda looked after Sam better."

"You won't be dead."

"What's it matter? You ever seen a one-armed gunfighter?" Ketchum waved his stump around. "I can't use my six-shooter fer shit with my left hand. I can't escape and I botched killin' myself twice. Why don't they just let me do myself in?"

"It's only August. I'll get onto gettin' you out of this lockup. They got you confused with another Black Jack. You were never called that, and they confused the pair of you. That'll be good for an appeal." The lawyer stood and paused at the cell door. He turned and looked back at Ketchum. "You got money, don't you? Your last heist was more than $40,000, gold and silver."

"All spent. That bother you?" Ketchum looked at his former lawyer with desolate eyes and knew it did.

It was bright and sunny in April, but George Otis, MD, was an old man and felt his advanced years constantly from arthritic joints. No matter what he wore, he could never wear enough of a coat to stay comfortable. Still, Union County was warmer than back in Washington, DC this time of year. For all the cherry blossoms and hints of humid summer to come, the city was not this warm. Otis shuffled along, peering at signs through rheumy eyes until he found the sheriff's office.

He paused, rubbed his hands on his thighs and removed the last of the nervous sweat there. Otis always felt this way when he neared another addition to his fine collection. One day his long years of study would pay off, and Professor Virchow would be vindicated.

And Doctor George Alexander Otis would be hailed as one of the greatest forensic scientists in American history.

He was almost bowled over when the lawman came rushing from the office.

"Sorry, mister. Didn't see you." The sheriff peered at Otis, evaluating him and immediately discounting him as a threat.

Otis didn't mind. That was the way it always was on the frontier. Dangerous, deadly, though not as fierce in 1901 as it had been even 28 years earlier when he had received some of his finest specimens. So much work had been done since then, so much.

"Eh, that's quite all right," Otis said. "You are the sheriff? Sheriff Salome Garcia?"

The stout lawman's bushy eyebrows arched.

"Do I know you?"

"Uh, no, Sheriff, you do not, but I know of you. May we talk?"

"I was on my way to the saloon. A fight's gonna break out any time now."

"I am sure it will wait a few more minutes. I am with the Army."

"You?"

"Not those fine soldiers who ride forth to do

battle, no, not them. I am a licensed doctor of medicine and work for the Army Medical Museum."

"Never heard tell of such a thing," Garcia said. He glanced toward the still quiet saloon, obviously hankering more for a drink than to break up a nonexistent fight in the middle of the day.

"It is not well known, true, true," Otis said, rubbing his hands together to keep them warm against the spring breeze whipping down Clayton's main street, "but nonetheless important. We are affiliated with the Smithsonian Institution. I am sure you have heard of that organization."

"Reckon I might have," Sheriff Garcia said. "What's that got to do with anything in Clayton?"

"Your prisoner. The one about to be executed."

"You mean Ketchum? We'll get around to stretchin' his neck sooner or later. Been havin' a run of bad luck with this and that. Truth be told, we've postponed the hangin' three times already."

"I had not heard that," Otis said, frowning. The wrinkles on his high forehead vanished among those naturally there. "Will the execution be forthcoming?"

"You mean will we do it soon? I've heard rumors that some of his old gang might try to break him out. If they try, well, all I got's one deputy. That means the judge'll have to either approve another deputy or two or let me get a citizens' committee organized."

"Come along, sir, and let me tell you of my work

and how you might aid it and the future of law enforcement."

"Something to do with Tom Ketchum? He's a killer, that's for certain sure, but what's your interest?"

The old man took the sheriff's elbow and steered him in the direction of the saloon, where he had wanted to go anyway. It didn't take much to guide him inside the almost deserted gin mill.

"Looks as if your fight has taken care of itself," Otis said. "Let me buy you a drink while I tell you of my research."

"Go on," the sheriff said, pulling up a chair near the door so he could look out into the street. He might be taking a break but that didn't mean he could ignore his job entirely.

The barkeep brought a quarter bottle of rye whiskey and placed it on the table. Otis poured, his hands a trifle shaky.

"To crime," he said.

"To catchin' the damn robbers," Sheriff Garcia corrected, downing his shot.

"That's what I do. Or rather it is what I help fine, upstanding lawmen like you do, Sheriff," Otis said. His eyes glowed with an inner light. "I run the U.S. Army Surgeon General's Indian Crania Study." Otis saw the sheriff's blank look and hurried on with his explanation, taking time only to pour the lawman another drink. "We have endeavored to collect more than forty-five hundred skulls."

"Indian skulls? Why?" The sheriff looked perplexed. Otis was used to this reaction. It was more common than revulsion, though he encountered that, also, especially in the upper circles of polite Washington society.

"I am a phrenologist. I examine the bumps on the head in an effort to predict behavior. If the red skinned savages' nature can be determined, we can predict the behavior of those on the reservations."

"You mean predict which're likely to go raidin'?"

"Yes!"

"Suppose that'd be a good thing," Sheriff Garcia said, "but I don't see how that means a danged thing to me."

"Your prisoner. Thomas 'Black Jack' Ketchum is one of the worst, is he not?"

"Can't say he's *that* bad. A killer, yeah, but not as bad as some I've heard tell of."

"I want to examine his skull. Think of how this would reduce robbing and killing! If I can predict a man's behavior from the phrenological patterns, you would know the men who would commit crimes before they did so!"

"Don't take bumps on a head to figger which one'll turn bad," the sheriff said. "Right here in Union County, now, we got three or four I'm watchin' real close. They're just itchin' to rob something. I can tell."

"What if your feelings were vindicated by scientific proof? You could prevent murders and robberies."

"Folks'd like that, not gettin' themselves murdered or robbed," Garcia allowed.

"Exactly. All I would like is the chance to examine Tom Ketchum's head after the execution."

"You could do it 'forehand," the sheriff said. "He's just settin' in his cell feelin' sorry for himself. He might like the attention of somebody other 'n the priest or a deputy."

"You misunderstand. I want to take his head with me. Back to Washington where I have a laboratory with measurement equipment."

"That's not gonna happen," Garcia said. "Look, I'm a bit antsy about this execution as it is. I never hung nobody before. And the chin music around town is that Ben Owen might be thinkin' on gettin' Ketchum free."

"A gang member? Could I examine his head, too, when you catch him?"

"Look, Doc, I want this done with, and you can't have the head. We ain't like them cannibals in Africa."

"I am empowered to offer a suitable fee in exchange for the cranium."

"You'd pay for it? Nope, no way. The judge's

order says I'm to hang him and bury him. That's all. I just want this over with as quick as possible."

Garcia half stood, hand going to his six-shooter when the doors slammed open. He relaxed when he saw his deputy in the doorway.

"Sheriff, surely am glad I found you. Paco Fuentes just said he spotted a suspicious fellow nosin' around. A real tall stranger and Ketchum signaled to him out the window of his cell."

"The gallows 'bout built?"

"As ready as it'll ever be, Sheriff," the deputy said. "We need to test the drop. Otherwise, we're all saddled up and ready to ride."

"Send Billy Gilligan to the judge and get a firm date—as quick as possible—to hang Ketchum." The sheriff pushed back from the table and tried to compose himself. He looked down at Doctor Otis and said, "I got official business to tend to. You can stay in town, if you like. Even talk to Doctor Slack, but Tom's gettin' buried right after the hangin'."

"Slack is your town doctor?"

"Undertaker, sawbones, anything else that turns up. Truth is, he's better with horses than humans, but that don't stop him none." With that Sheriff Garcia left George Otis sipping another shot of whiskey and making his plans.

"What do you figger he weighs?" Sheriff Garcia poured sand into a burlap bag balanced on the grain scales.

"He's a big one. Maybe two hunnerd?" The deputy pushed back his floppy brimmed hat and scratched his head.

"Sounds 'bout right," Garcia said, adding more sand until the scales registered two hundred pounds. "Help me get this to the gallows."

The two lawmen hefted the bag of sand and staggered along to the gallows built next to the jailhouse where Ketchum could see the structure and repent for his crimes. They got it to the trapdoor. Garcia fastened a rope to the bag, then stepped back.

"Let's see if it works all proper," the sheriff said. He took the loop of rope off the trigger for the trap and let it open. The structure shuddered as the bag fell four feet and then swung about underneath.

"That's not much of a drop, ain't it, Sheriff?"

"Want this to go smooth and don't want to have nuthin' go wrong," Garcia said, sucking on his lower lip. "I ought to put some soap on the noose so it'll slip over his head easy once I got the hood on him. And maybe yer right 'bout that. We kin lengthen the drop a foot or two. Just enough so's his feet don't hit the ground under the gallows." They worked for another hour until after sundown making certain the gallows was ready for the next day.

"It's all legal and proper, Tom." The sheriff told the condemned. "The judge has given the go-ahead for a 1:00 P.M. hangin'."

"Just as soon have you do it now, Sheriff," Tom Ketchum said. "The waitin' is worse than the doin'."

"I got to agree," Sheriff Garcia said. "My nerves are killin' me."

Ketchum laughed harshly. "And it's gonna be your noose that kills me. But that don't make us even."

Garcia looked at his prisoner uneasily, nodded once and left to check the gallows for the tenth time. He stepped into the bright sun and pulled the brim of his Stetson down to shade his eyes. Looking around he saw most of the businesses in town were closed and the crowd was already gathering around the gallows although the hanging wasn't for another couple hours.

"Git yer tickets fer the best seats. Git 'em while I got 'em!"

Garcia pushed his way through the crowd and found his deputy taking money and passing out slips of paper with numbers scribbled on them.

"What 'n hell's goin' on?"

"I thought to make a few bucks, Sheriff," his deputy said. "Why not sell front row seats to the hangin'? This is the biggest thing that's happened in Clayton since . . . since forever."

"What're those?" Garcia pointed to a box of sticks. He pulled one out. A crude doll with a string around its neck was hung from the end.

"Me and Mr. Kincannon are sellin' souvenirs."

Garcia saw the owner of the mercantile going through the crowd with a handful of the gruesome toys, selling them for a dime apiece.

"Hope you get plenty for your enterprisin' nature," Garcia said, shuddering a little. He looked up the steps to where the wind caused the noose to swing fitfully. It wouldn't be much longer before that noose was filled and a dead man swung at the end. Garcia took a deep breath and remembered all that Tom Ketchum had done. The judge had pronounced the verdict, and it was up to the county to carry out the sentence. And Salome Garcia would because it was his duty. It didn't hurt much that he got a ten-dollar bonus for the extra work.

"It's one o'clock, Tom. Let's go," said Sheriff Garcia.

"About time." Ketchum swallowed hard, then straightened his shoulders and marched out. Garcia followed a pace back, hand on the butt of his six-gun but Ketchum made no effort to escape. Just outside the jailhouse door stood the deputy with a scattergun. He looked as nervous as Garcia felt. The only one not the least excited or nervous was the condemned. Ketchum walked with a slow, even stride, paused at the base of the gallows, then mounted.

The crowd cheered and jeered as Ketchum allowed the sheriff to fasten a rope around his upper arms and tie his feet together.

"Because you were found guilty of 'felonious assault upon a railway train,' it is my sorry duty to hang you, Thomas Edward Ketchum. You got any last words?" Garcia shuffled his feet nervously as he ran his fingers over the noose he had soaped to make it easier to slip over the condemned's head when he had the black hood on.

Tom Ketchum looked out over the silent crowd, saw the toys and the way the deputy and a couple merchants passed through the crowd selling concessions. He heaved a tired sigh and said, "Hurry up, boys, get this over."

Garcia placed the black hood over Ketchum's head, then pinned it to the front of the man's shirt before sliding the noose down and snugging it tight. He didn't want the hood coming off and Ketchum's death expression giving the crowd more than they had bargained for. The sheriff looked out over the throng. Some waved their dangling effigies of Ketchum and others were rapt. Most attentive of the lot was George Otis, seated in the front row. Garcia wondered if he had bought the seat or wheedled it out of the deputy.

The sheriff stepped back, hefted his hatchet and, without fanfare, swung it to sever the rope holding the trapdoor closed. In his nervousness, he twisted the blade slightly and the edge skittered along the rope. Garcia drew back and chopped again. This time he cut the rope.

The trapdoor snapped open. And then came another snap. A more sickening one followed by a gasp from the crowd.

"His head!" someone cried. "It done popped off!"

The sheriff blinked. A photographer worked his magic to capture the scene.

"Get on back. Don't crowd now. Let me see what's wrong."

Salome Garcia hurried down the steps and went around under the gallows where Doctor Slack was already working on the body—the headless body all trussed up and laying on the ground.

"Sweet Mother of God," Garcia muttered. Ketchum's head had come off and lay in its black hood some distance from the body.

"You shouldn't have put soap on the noose," Slack said. "Made the rope like wire. Sliced right through. And the drop? It was way too much. Old Tom here, he don't weigh but one-eighty-five, if that."

"We figured for two hundred pounds," Garcia said weakly.

"Don't much matter to Tom now. Help me get him into the back of my wagon."

"Will you say something to the crowd?" Garcia thought they should be told that the beheading was accidental but didn't have the words. He was still too stunned by the sudden decapitation.

"Reckon I can. What do you want me to say?"

"That it wasn't supposed to happen like this."

Doctor Slack shrugged his bony shoulders and snorted like a hog, then made his way around the gallows and stepped out into the afternoon sun.

"Ladies and gents, the sheriff wants me to relate what went wrong with the execution."

Garcia closed his eyes and tried to push away the faintness welling up inside. He had never heard of a hanged man losing his head like this. When the vertigo passed, the undertaker finished with, "So let's all give the good sheriff a round of applause for the show this afternoon."

Garcia found himself taking a bow and almost enjoying the accolade given him by the townspeople. This passed when the gravity of the situation hit him.

"Get on back to work, all of you," he said. "The doc and me, we got work to do." The crowd slowly dissipated. When everyone was out of earshot, he said to Slack, "Is there anything you can do, Doc? I mean, it's not right to bury a man like that."

"I can sew his head back on, if that's what you want."

"It is."

"Be an extra dollar."

"Done," Garcia said, willing to pony up the money from his own pocket just to have it done.

"There's only one problem," Slack said as he rounded the gallows.

"What's that, Doc?"

"There ain't no head to sew back on."

Sheriff Garcia pushed the undertaker aside. Sure enough, the body lay where it had fallen but the head wrapped in the black executioner's hood was gone.

Garcia and his deputy looked across the embalming table at Doctor Slack, who worked to get the blood drained from Ketchum's remains—or what remained of them.

"This is the damnedest thing I ever heard tell of," the deputy said. "Who'd want to steal a man's head?"

"I know who," Garcia said, a tight knot in his belly. "That old geezer from Washington. George Otis."

"Why'd he want it?" The deputy scratched his

balding head and looked puzzled. Garcia stared at Slack.

"He talk to you, Doc? The old man from back East?"

"Nope, didn't say a word to me, but I know who you mean. That withered, bent-over fella I seen going into the saloon with you earlier on?"

"That's the one. He stole the head. I'm sure of it."

"Did he, Sheriff?"

"What do you mean?" Garcia stared at his deputy. "You know somethin' I don't?"

"I was just thinkin'…"

"Always a danger with someone like you," Slack muttered, but the deputy plowed on.

"If this Otis did take the head, is it stealin'? It's not like property that belonged to somebody. Rob Mr. Kincannon, say, and you stole somethin' that belonged to him. But the head didn't belong to nobody."

"It belonged to Tom," pointed out Garcia.

"I don't think he's going to file a report, Sheriff," Slack said. He dropped a long silver needle into a tray and took tubing from under the table, preparing to pump in embalming fluid. He stopped and looked puzzled. "If I try puttin' this formaldehyde in, it's going to leak out his neck."

"Hold off a spell, Doc," Garcia said. "I've got a thief to bring to justice."

He left the undertaker's parlor and looked up and

down the main street. He hadn't expected Otis to be standing there, holding Ketchum's head like Herod with John the Baptist's, but he had hoped. Stride turning into a fast walk just short of outright running, Garcia went to the town livery stables.

"Bart!" the sheriff called. "You in here, Bart?"

The owner's head poked up from a rear stall. He came out with a pitchfork in his hand. He tossed it aside and wiped sweat from his face.

"Gettin' mighty hot in here. Good thing you came along, Sal, so I have an excuse to take a break. What kin I do you for?"

"The man from Washington. George Otis."

"The doctor fella? He said he was a doctor, at any rate, but he didn't look like one. Didn't even have a black bag with him when he came."

"Where is he?"

"He left, maybe twenty minutes back. Same way he came to town. In a buggy." Bart scowled and wiped more sweat. "Funny thing, now that I think on it."

"What's that?"

"He didn't have a black bag when he came but did when he left. I woulda seen it."

"Which way was he headed? Toward Santa Fe?"

"More likely to Folsom. Saw him with a railroad schedule."

Sheriff Garcia wasted no time saddling his horse and getting on the trial toward Raton Pass and

Folsom, the spot where Black Jack Ketchum had held up three trains in as many years. He rode steadily and within ten minutes spotted the dust cloud kicked up by Otis' buggy. In twenty he was standing beside the old man.

"I'll buy it, Sheriff. I'll pay good money," George Otis pleaded. "Twenty dollars. I'll give you a twenty dollar gold piece!"

"It's not mine to sell or yours to take."

"It's not doing Ketchum any good now. Bury it and science will lose! I'll give you forty! It's all I have."

Garcia reached past the old man and pulled out the black hood. Stains on the bottom showed where Tom Ketchum's blood had spewed forth, but the heavy cloth was otherwise untainted. Garcia could understand how the livery owner mistook it for a doctor's bag.

With some distaste, he pried loose the corners of the hood and peered in. He had seen some terrible things in his day, but never had he seen a man's head come off like this. The skin had stretched and then the slickened rope had cut right through like a knife through sun-warmed butter. Part of Ketchum's spine protruded whitely. Garcia closed the hood up and stepped away from the scientist.

"I ought to run you in, but I won't. I can't figure what to charge you with. You weren't grave robbing. We got a law about that, but Tom wasn't buried yet.

And there's no law against robbing a corpse of money, much less its parts, if you didn't cause the demise."

"This will be the keystone of my collection. It will reveal the terrible criminal nature. Please, Sheriff."

"Don't let me set eyes on you again, Doctor Otis. I'd hate for you to end up like this." Garcia held up the head.

Otis slumped as if he melted in the sun. Then he turned and climbed painfully into his buggy and drove away slowly. Garcia watched him for a minute, then mounted and rode back to Clayton, Ketchum's head precariously balanced on the saddle in front of him. If he hurried, Doc Slack could sew the head back on and they could finish the funeral before sundown.

Sheriff Salome Garcia wasn't a superstitious man, but he didn't want to take any chance of Tom Ketchum's ghost haunting him because there wasn't a head to go along with the corpse in its grave.

JACKSON LOWRY IS the pen name (among many) of Robert E. Vardeman, the author of almost 200 westerns, many in series such as Jake Logan, Trailsman, West of the Big River, and Blaze! He has garnered award nominations for novels *Drifter*, *Sonora Noose*, *China Jack* and was honored with the Western

Fictioneers Life Achievement Award in 2017. Current titles written for the Ralph Compton series include *Tin Star, Never Bet Against the Bullet, The Lost Banshee Mine, Shot to Hell* and *Flames of Silver*. His website is www. jacksonlowry.cenotaphroad.com/

DULCIE'S REWARD

EASY JACKSON

It took Grandpa three weeks to die. Emzy had warned him to replace the new latigo on his leggings with old rawhide, but he'd been in a hurry to round up the few cattle he owned and hadn't listened. When a spreadin' nanner spooked the high-strung mustang Grandpa was riding, he was thrown, the new latigo catching on the saddle horn. The horse dragged him hundreds of yards before Emzy could grab the reins and pull it to a halt.

I cried and cried, and when Grandma grieved herself to death two weeks later, I cried some more. Death had taken my mother early, my father during the Second Battle of Sabine Pass, along with my betrothed, Tom.

So, I reckon I was crying for all of them. I stopped blubbering long enough to stoop down, pick up a clod of dirt and throw it in on Grandma's coffin.

Lula Mae, with her short chubby arms, reached around my shoulders and hugged me. "There, there, honey," she said in a loud voice, her blowsy dark hair enveloping my blonde locks and threatening to overwhelm not only my hair, but the rest of me. Lula Mae liked to put on a good show at funerals.

The preacher put everything he could into the emotional finale. It pleases him when womenfolk shed tears at funerals—he believes his words have roused up the Holy Ghost. Maybe so, but I would have cried for my family even if it had only been me and old Emzy.

We proceeded back to the cabin where I managed to dry my eyes. While people feasted on the food they brought, I contemplated the pickle I was in. We had no money. Grandpa and Emzy had managed to round up three hundred head of cattle to take to the new market in Abilene. They were supposed to catch up and tie in with Wilbur Nettles and his herd, but by the time Grandpa had his accident, Wilbur had already left and wasn't going to turn back, along with most of the rest of the able-bodied men, excepting Lula Mae's husband, Catfish, and Ponton Degan.

Everyone said Catfish was so lazy that Lula Mae had to force him to get up and go outside; otherwise, he'd just wet himself sitting in the chair. And

Ponton, tall, rotund, with bulging eyes and fleshy lips, spent the war years working for the government in Austin. He had enough money to pay drovers to take his cattle because he wasn't about to get on a horse if he could help it. That's what buggies were made for.

I sat in a chair, staring at a cold fireplace and pondering my predicament, pausing only long enough to say goodbye as people left one by one. My thoughts tumbled around—sell the land that had been in my family since 1824? And then what? Take the money, buy a place in town and run a boarding house? And what about Emzy? He had lived here over forty years—Willow Branch was as much of a home to him as it was to me.

I became aware the only people left in the house were Lula Mae and Grandma Eggers bustling around. Plus Emzy, who seemed to be hovering in the background, twisting a tattered and stained hat in his hand.

Ponton Degan came in holding his favorite fawn-colored flat topped English hat with its big black ribbon around the band. It looked like something just out of a mail-order box. He turned to the two other women.

"Miss Lula, would you and Grandma excuse us? I'd like to talk to Miss Dulcie alone, please." He looked across the room. "Scat, Emzy."

They scattered, Lula Mae giving Grandma

Eggers a knowing look as she left the room. I wondered what that was all about.

Ponton came closer. I made a slight movement back.

"I apologize for being so precipitous, speaking to you at your grandma's funeral and all, but I'll come to the point, Miss Dulcie. I know you have been left in a bad way because of the war and will need someone to take care of you. I would be honored if you would take my hand in marriage and become my wife."

It took several seconds for his words to sink in. When they did, I swallowed hard to keep from gagging. My training took over, and I answered him with as much politeness as possible.

"I'm so honored, Ponton, but it is much too soon after the loss of my family for me to consider anything of that nature."

Ponton nodded with dignity and understanding. "I just wanted to get my oar in."

"Yes, yes, thank you," I muttered. I turned back to the fireplace, wishing he would leave. He did, saying his goodbyes. He had no sooner left the room than Grandma Eggers reentered.

"Dulcie, don't you be fiddling around. You say yes to Ponton before somebody else grabs him. You can't run this place by yourself. Emzy is too old to be much help to you."

The only way I could get her to stop yapping

SIX-GUN JUSTICE

about Ponton was to walk to the door. She joined Grandpa Eggers outside, while Lula Mae joined Catfish as they readied to leave. I paused in the doorway, watching Ponton's buggy recede down the tree-lined road. Emzy appeared behind me and began to talk low.

"Miss Dulcie, I heered what Mr. Ponton said. I justs wants to warn you that when Mr. Tom was alive, he told me Mr. Ponton once tried to…. kiss him."

I turned my head to Emzy. "Kiss him?"

"Yes, ma'am, Miss Dulcie. Mr. Tom said Mr. Ponton one of those men what likes other men, not womenfolk."

"Good heavens." I didn't know there was such a thing.

"Course, you can marries him if you wants to, but he gonna want to be loving up on some man when your back is turned. He just want you for the show."

"Thank you for telling me, Emzy," I said. I took a deep breath and went out into the yard to say goodbye to the last of the funeral goers.

Catfish gave me a big grin. "Now you just holler if you need anything, Miss Dulcie."

I nodded my thanks, absentmindedly surprised to see the change that came over Lula Mae's face. Instead of hugging me, she looked about ready to smack me.

I thought no more of it. I had other things on my

mind. That night before turning in, I stood on the porch while Emzy sat whittling on a stick.

"Emzy, we've got to get those cattle to market, or we aren't going to have enough money to pay taxes or anything else."

"Yes, ma'am, but how we going to do that? I cans still ride, but I can't handle no three hundred head of ornery longhorns by myself."

"We'll just have to find someone, that's all."

I waited a day before heading out to Lula Mae and Catfish's place. Rusty farm implements were scattered everywhere; one side of the porch looked like it was about to fall down. I was keenly aware that with just me and Emzy to work the place, Willow Branch would soon look the same way.

I slid down from Lover Boy; the brown gelding Tom had given me. He had named him when he saw how attached the foal was to me. Tom was always full of fun. I regretted that Pa and Tom had insisted we wait to be married until the war was over. It looked like I was going to be joining the army of old maids the war had created.

Lula Mae came to the door, frowning when she saw me. As Lover Boy drank from their trough, she walked toward us but did not invite me inside.

"I came to see if I could hire Catfish to take my cattle to market."

"No, you can't," Lula Mae said. She narrowed her eyes. "And don't be coming around here anymore.

Take that sapling waist and high bosom of yours that makes you think you are so high and mighty and get on out of here."

I was so flabbergasted; I didn't know what to say. It hurt to the core to be told I thought myself above my raising. It began to dawn on me what was behind her words.

"Lula Mae, I got no designs on Catfish whatsoever."

"Don't matter. I don't want him getting no designs on you. He ain't much, but he's all I got. Take my advice, Dulcie, marry Ponton, because if you don't, you're going to find yourself being shunned by every married woman in these here hills."

I turned, stumbling a little as I led Lover Boy away from the trough. I got on, and with only so much as a click to Lover Boy, left without another word. It took me a while to calm down and settle my breathing. The sting of Lula Mae's comments hurt. But that's the way people were. All over you being nice in public, but cutting loose in private to tell you what they really thought.

Over the next few days, Lula Mae's words proved true as I met with a couple of more cold shoulders from wives who didn't want me asking their husbands about doing anything. The ones with gumption were already gone anyway.

I wondered if I should I go farther afield looking for help. The roads were unsafe for men to travel alone, much less women. Fear filled me, and I walked around the house almost unable to think, to breath.

I was cleaning the kitchen after dinner when the worst happened. Emzy had said he was going to look after the stock, but he had probably found a snug place in the barn for a nap. I gave the scratched and dented table one last swipe when someone grabbed me from behind. He put one rough hand over my mouth while another squeezed my breast. I didn't stop to think of who he was—I bit his hand and started fighting back.

He hadn't expected such a tussle. I scratched, kicked, and bit any piece of flesh I could get a hold of. He flung me across the room, and I landed against the wall with a thud. An old muzzle loader was leaning against the wall. I grabbed it and fired off a shot.

It grazed his cheek, stunning him. Before he could react, I flipped the rifle around, ignoring the hot barrel and whacked him with the butt. I was still beating on him when he made for the door. He stumbled outside and ran to his horse, jumping on and riding away, blood flowing from his cheek.

I sank to the floor and began to weep. I thought about who he was, and it took me a minute to remember—a sorry piece of trash from another community. It didn't matter how no good he was—there was no use in crying foul. People like Lula Mae would only rub it in my face that I needed to marry Ponton.

Everybody wants somebody to take care of them, but I didn't want that someone to be Ponton. That night on the porch, I talked to Emzy.

"I'm leaving for San Antonio in the morning. Somebody, somewhere, has got to be willing to help take our cattle to market."

"I can't let you go off like that by yourself, Miss Dulcie," Emzy said.

I looked down at the hair that was beginning to grizzle. Like most black people, it was impossible to judge Emzy's age, until one day they suddenly looked a hundred and fifty. Tall, rangy, in his time, he had been the best cowboy in five counties. Grandpa had explained to Emzy at the war's end that he was a free man; he could go as he pleased. If he wanted to stay, he could, but Grandpa couldn't afford to give him much wages. Emzy had thought about it and replied that if he had been a young man, he would have welcomed the opportunity to be on his own, but now, he was too attached to Willow Branch to leave.

"You have to stay here and look after the stock, Emzy. I'll be fine." Emzy was always singing about angels watching over him or coming to get him, so I added, "I'll be surrounded by a whole passel of angels looking after me." God had already shown me I could get attacked in my own home same as I could out looking for help on the road to San Antone. The angels could watch out for me just as easily there as they could at Willow Branch.

Mindful of Lula Mae's prediction, I left the hills behind me before stopping at any ranches along the way. The early spring days were slipping too quickly into summer, reminding me that cattle needed to be on the trail now to take advantage of good grass.

Every place I stopped told the same story— widows trying to raise large broods of children, the only men left home were too old or missing limbs, crippled by the war. The poverty I saw everywhere almost overwhelmed me. People were kind, however, to any stranger who could bring a breath of newness to their stale lives, even a young female they believed touched in the head for wandering around the countryside by herself. That I was transient and not situated in one place long enough to lure any male down the road of sin meant that I did not face the same prejudices I had at home. I was here today, gone tomorrow; therefore, more of a blessing than a threat.

I slept on pallets on the floor, ate meager portions of cornbread, and entertained my hosts with news about far flung friends and relatives. Emzy had managed to hide Lover Boy and the few other mules and horses we owned from troops bent on conscripting everything for the army, but others had not been so fortunate. That did not stop them from admiring and petting Lover Boy. Sixteen hands high, with a deep wide chest and powerful hindquarters, he got fed better than I did. Since the only way I could get on such a tall horse was to throw myself up in the air with one leg over, I had to ride astride, and just watching me get in the saddle gave people cause for amusement.

But none of this helped me in my quest. On the road, I rarely met anyone. I tried to pick a decent ranch or farm house way before dark to spend the night. There were times I followed a path only to have it take me to a house that made Lula Mae and Catfish's place look like a palatial castle. Twice I had to turn away and hope I hadn't been seen.

As I neared San Antonio, I began to worry. People in the country welcomed strangers stopping for the night because they brought news and relief from tedium and boredom. But town people weren't like that. And I had no money for food or shelter.

Lover Boy and I had just turned a curve in the road when a stagecoach overtook us. I hadn't expected the driver to halt, but he did.

"Everybody, get out and stretch your legs," he said, hopping down. He looked at me as I pulled up on the reins.

"Where you heading, Miss?"

"San Antonio. Looking for trailhands to take some cattle up to that new town in Kansas."

A small man, he was joined by the taller shotgun messenger. They paused to spit tobacco.

"You might find somebody, but he most likely won't be no count if he's still hanging around San Antone."

I shrugged. He wasn't telling me anything I didn't already know, but I had to try.

Two passengers alighted from the stagecoach and tried to find their legs. They saw me and removed their hats.

"Howdy," I said, looking them over. One was a little redheaded drummer. The other was older and looked too fat and soft to be much use on a horse. Both were dressed in suits, and the one on old baby hands was sharply pressed, his waistcoat made of quilted silk. His hat matched Ponton's, and he held onto a new valise.

"You best ride alongside us, Miss," the stagecoach whip said.

"I say, can't she ride in here with us?" the man in the expensive suit said.

"Not without a ticket." He climbed up in the driver's box, spitting again as he waited on the passengers to get in.

The quilted waistcoat swelled as the man in the expensive suit leered at me. "I'll be happy to pay for her to ride."

"Thank you kindly," I said in a hurry. "But I prefer to ride my horse."

"Suit yourself," he said heaving into the stagecoach, grabbing on to the door frame with one hand while holding the valise with the other. The little drummer followed as meek as a mouse in church.

To keep from eating their dust, I rode to the side. The whip and shotgun messenger spoke only to the horses pulling the stage, keeping them at a steady pace. Bored, the little drummer hung his head out the side but said little. The chubby man did the same, but talked almost nonstop. He informed me he was a prominent banker, on his way to San Antonio with important business. He had acquired large tracts of land he hoped to sell to "the greenhorn Yankees in San Antonio."

That thought depressed me. If I didn't do something, Willow Branch would land in Yankee hands, too. Tiring of his boasting, I reined Lover Boy around to the other side of the stagecoach and rode up to the messenger.

"Do you know of a ranch hereabouts where I could stop for the night?"

The messenger and the whip exchanged glances. "Not that I would recommend. We're going to be stopping here directly at the next station. You can stay there."

I shook my head. "I don't have any money and can't be beholding to nobody either."

The messenger gave me a long look. "They's

always needing help at the next station. You can earn your keep by washing dishes."

I nodded. The rest of the trip passed uneventfully, except when we made the sharp turn into the driveway of a log cabin station, the stagecoach lurched to one side. When it righted itself, the banker spoke in sharp tones.

"Get your hands off my valise," he told the drummer.

The station fare wasn't much to brag about. The banker insisted on keeping his valise next to his chair, making me wonder if he had robbed the bank or something. As soon as supper was over, I began in on a mountain of dirty dishes that was almost as tall as my head.

To my surprise, the little drummer put an apron on, grabbed a towel and starting drying. The banker sat on the porch, regaling the owners of the station with stories of his standing in the community that I'm sure didn't impress them, but they had to be polite to the passengers of the stage line.

"What's he got in that valise anyway?" I asked.

The little redheaded man turned his head in the direction of the porch and then went back to drying.

"I heard he was in cahoots with the local sheriff and district attorney. He'd get widows to borrow a little money against their property, saying that when their sons came back from war, they could pay it back at their leisure. When they returned, he swore up and down the women had sold him the property. Since most of them couldn't read, they didn't know what they were signing."

I nodded in understanding. Tom, who had aspirations of one day studying for law, had warned me before he left never to let anybody even look at the deed to Willow Branch. One slick man came by talking big about how he had always wanted to see one of those old Spanish land grants, and grandma, proud of it, wanted to show it to him, but I wouldn't let her. He finally gave up and left.

The banker must have been a really smooth talker and had every government official in town in his pocket. It wouldn't stand up in court anywhere else, but I remember Tom saying possession was nine-tenths of the law. And the banker was in possession of the deeds.

"What a crook," I said, and the drummer agreed with me.

The bed they gave me to sleep on was a rickety cot, and I had to cook breakfast the next morning, but I didn't mind. Neither did the passengers or stagecoach employees since it tasted better than what we had endured for supper. Plus, the stagecoach whip made sure Lover Boy got oats.

Despite being somewhat nauseated by the unwanted attentions of the banker, I rode beside the stagecoach. Our next stop would be San Antonio, and I grew jumpy just thinking about it. Lover Boy picked up on my emotions, and he became nervous and distracted by even the flapping noises of birds flying from tree branches as we approached.

We were coming up to a blind bend when an armed and masked man stepped out from behind a large rock and pointed a shotgun in our direction. The whip pulled the team to a stop.

"Throw down your guns and keep those hands up," he ordered.

I looked him over. He wore old clothes and his boots and hat had not been in good shape for a long time. The gun belt he wore, however, looked new, and the shotgun still had an oily sheen to it. The blue neckerchief covering the lower part of his face was faded silk—at one time, an expensive luxury.

Meanwhile, the rifle and pistols were thrown down, and still holding the shotgun on them, the robber picked up the weapons and tossed them far aside. He did not act disconcerted by my presence, and I wondered if he had been following us, watching for some time.

Keeping one eye on the whip and messenger, he strode to the stagecoach and flung open the door.

"Out!"

The banker and drummer came out, holding their hands up. Remaining on guard against the men in the driver box, the bandit felt inside the coats of the passengers. He pulled a small derringer out of the banker's inside pocket and threw it aside. He took a fat wallet out of the other pocket. The banker made a movement, but a shotgun shoved into his belly stilled him.

"Empty your pants pockets."

The drummer was an experienced traveler and only carried a small amount of money in his pockets. He dutifully emptied them, throwing what little he had on the ground.

The banker looked as if he wanted to faunch, but he didn't want the shotgun shoved at him again, so he complied.

The bandit picked up the banker's money but left the drummer's lying on the ground. He backed up and addressed the whip and messenger.

"Throw down those trunks."

The messenger reached for the smallest one, and this time the drummer lost his meekness.

"Please! Please, be careful. Those contain my salesman samples."

The bandit motioned for the drummer to take the case. He brought it down and opened it gingerly, showing the bandit rows of bottles.

"I'm an apothecary salesman."

The robber motioned for him to set the suitcase aside. He looked up at the messenger. The messenger picked up the other trunk and threw it on the ground. The robber addressed the drummer.

"Open it and throw everything out."

As I sat on Lover Boy watching, it came to me

that the bandit was looking for something specific. I could sense his disappointment when the drummer revealed nothing inside the trunk but the banker's extensive wardrobe.

The bandit gave every appearance of being disgusted. His glance went back to his captives, scanning them for signs of trouble. His eyes stopped and rested on me. Without moving my head, I let my eyes purposely go to the valise lying half hidden inside the stagecoach.

He followed my gaze and shoving the passengers aside, reached in and grabbed the valise.

"Unhand that!" the banker said, making a grab for the valise.

He was rewarded with the butt end of the shotgun against the side of his head. He reeled back. Opening the valise with one hand, the robber's eyes momentarily paused on the contents. He shut it and looked up at me. He walked closer, admiration for Lover Boy showing in eyes that were clear blue with dark lashes.

"That's a mighty fine horse, sister."

"Don't even think about it."

He laughed. Lover Boy, already a bundle of nerves, reared. The bandit grabbed for the reins. When his head came up, his mask fell down, and I saw a fairly young man's face with regular features except for a deep ugly scar under his left eye. He instantly pulled the mask up and helped calm Lover

Boy. His back had momentarily turned when he grabbed the reins, so the others did not get a look at his face. It happened so fast; he could not be certain how much of a glimpse I had gotten.

Holding the shotgun and carrying the valise, he backed away until he could slide behind the rock he had come from. We heard the sound of hoofbeats as he rode away.

"Are you going to let him get away with that?" the banker yelled. "Why didn't you try to stop him?"

While he fumed and threatened to sue the stagecoach line, the whip and messenger calmly got down from the coach. The drummer began picking up his money. The banker bent down, picked up a bill and started for his pocket with it. The whip stopped him with one harsh sentence.

"That ain't your'uns."

The banker let it flutter to the ground with obvious reluctance.

"I'll have your jobs for this," he said.

"Yeah," the whip said, and went to fetch his pistols.

In San Antonio, the messenger shared a little feed for Lover Boy and told me where I could stake him near grass and water where he wouldn't be bothered. The drummer offered to buy my supper, but I thanked him and told him I wasn't hungry. The banker informed me in the most pompous way possible that the sheriff would want to talk to me. I ignored him and led Lover Boy away.

Later, walking the streets of San Antonio, I wasn't sure where to go. I wondered if I should find a church and throw myself on the mercy of a pastor. I decided to try to take care of business first. I could always throw myself at someone's mercy later.

I passed by men, but they were rough looking, and I did not like the insolent stares they were giving me. Many others were German merchants, or at least that's what they looked like to me. And they would have no interest in going on a dangerous cattle drive into strange territory.

I was about to give up and go look for a church when I came upon yet another saloon. I stood to one side and looked over the swinging doors. There was a crude painting of a half-dressed lady on one wall and a mirrored bar on the other. Cattle and deer horns cluttered the walls. The floor was covered in tobacco-stained sawdust that looked as if it hadn't been swept clean since the beginning of the war. It smelled of urine. My eyes scanned the men inside, searching for a likely one to approach. At the far end of the bar stood a cowboy with a dark hat, old boots, and faded blue silk kerchief around his neck. He turned, showing the left side of his face with its vivid scar under one eye.

"Ma'am?"

I jumped about six inches and turned. A tall,

older man stood behind me. A tin star pinned on his vest said "Sheriff."

"Yes, sir?"

"I heard you were with the stagecoach that got robbed."

I nodded, and he went on.

"The banker said you might have caught a glimpse of the robber, that his mask appeared to have come down when he was looking in your direction."

I shook my head. I wasn't about to get involved in any of the banker's shenanigans. Instead, I changed the subject.

"I'm looking for someone to hire to take my cattle to market," I said, turning back to the saloon. "What about that cowboy standing at the end of the bar? The one with the scar? You reckon he's got any cow sense?"

The sheriff looked over the door. "That's Temple Holden. Before the war he trailed quite a few head up into Missouri. He's dependable, but not a man I'd ever want to get crossways with. The war did not sweeten him."

The sheriff turned and gave me a keen look. "Before she died, his ma supposedly got took by that banker who was on the stage today, her and a lot other folks in his part of the country. You sure it wasn't Temple that robbed him?"

Before I could answer, he spoke again. "I better

tell you; the banker has offered a two-hundred-dollar reward for information leading to the arrest of the thief."

Two hundred dollars would pay the taxes and a lot more. I calculated what three hundred head of cattle might bring in Abilene. I thought about the banker and wondered how many ways he would try to get out of paying it.

I shook my head. "I would have recognized those clothes."

The sheriff looked almost relieved. "Where're you staying?"

"I don't know. I don't have any money."

He frowned in irritation. "You can sleep on my deputy's cot. But just for tonight."

"Thank you kindly."

He sighed. "Supper at sundown. Don't be hanging around town come dark."

"I won't. I'll talk to this Holden fellow when he comes out, and then I'll walk straight to your office."

"See that you do," he said, making his voice sound gruff. "I got enough trouble in this town without you causing more."

He left and I looked back at Temple Holden. He had seen me talking to the sheriff, seen that the sheriff had left. All I had to do was wait.

He didn't leave me standing too long. It was half an hour before sundown when he came out, carrying a package wrapped in brown paper.

He gave me a hard stare. I plunged into conversation.

"Mr. Holden, I'm looking for a man to take three hundred longhorns to Abilene, Kansas. I'll go in halves with you, and I've got one good trailhand to help you."

He gazed at me a full minute before speaking.

"And if I say no?"

I swallowed hard. "My memory will suddenly improve with the sheriff."

Men staggered out the door. He took me by the elbow and propelled me along the sidewalk, the set of his jaw and the flare of his nostrils telling me just how angry he was at being caught.

"You better change those clothes. I recognized you by them before I even saw the scar."

He stopped, pulling me off the sidewalk onto the edge of an alley.

"Start from the beginning."

I knew what he meant, and I told him about Grandpa dying just after roundup, Grandma's passing and what a good cowhand Emzy was.

"I've got to get those longhorns to market, and there ain't a soul around left to take them. That's why I come to San Antonio. You just made it easy for me."

Witnessing the frost in his eyes made me realize why the sheriff was relieved he did not have to arrest

Temple Holden. My knees got a little shaky, but I held my ground.

A change came over him. He relaxed, and the eyes that had been full of cold steel now sparkled in amusement.

"Well, little sister, you have just given me the perfect excuse to pay my debts and leave the countryside for a while. When do you want me to start on this here cattle drive? I guess you'll be wanting to stay around town and shop for a day or two."

"Can't shop. Don't have a cent to my name. The sheriff said I could spend the night on his deputy's cot. Besides, those cattle should have been on the trail three weeks ago."

"Those cattle should have been on the trail six weeks ago."

He paused in thought, pushing his hat back and rubbing his forehead with a few rough fingers, the nails on two of them black.

"Where's your horse?"

I told him.

"Meet me there at dawn." He pulled me back onto the sidewalk.

"There's the sheriff's office over yonder. Go straight there and don't stop to talk to anybody."

He disappeared into the throng of people milling the sidewalks of San Antonio. I couldn't figure out why he trusted me not to blab to the sheriff. Maybe it was a test. I took a deep breath and crossed the road, heading for the sheriff's office.

The grub at the jail wasn't too bad. The banker came in, raising Cain and blaming me for not noticing more. Every time the thick and rather slow-witted deputy spoke, the sheriff yelled at him to shut up, while the banker just kept a gabbing. When he finally left and things calmed down, I tried to rest on the deputy's cot while he slept on two chairs pushed together in the next room. Thoughts of Lover Boy being stolen worried me so much, as soon as I knew by his snoring that the deputy was in a deep sleep, I rose and left as quietly as I could. Once on the darkened street, I felt a moment of panic, troubled that I might not be able to find the place I'd left my horse.

Slipping from one darkened doorway to the next, I made my way, worrying all the while that Temple Holden might have taken Lover Boy and left town. When I did arrive, I could make out Lover Boy's big form and that of another horse and a mule.

Just as I exhaled in relief, someone grabbed me and placed a cold knife next to my throat. I caught a whiff of leather mixed with fresh soap, like someone who had just come from the barber. After that first second, I was struck with so much fear, I didn't notice much else.

"Oh, it's you," a voice spoke low, and Temple Holden let go of me. "What are you doing here?"

After I caught my breath, I explained about Lover Boy.

"Shh!"

My tongue froze in midsentence. There came the sound of footsteps stealing toward us.

"Lay down on the ground," Temple whispered, pushing me downward. I got down on my belly. I was just making out a shape when a pistol fired, flame spewing from its barrel, lighting up the night. The bullet sang over my head. Temple fired back and jumped aside. I turned to look at Lover Boy, who was kicking up a fuss. The mule began braying. The other horse stood still and quiet. He had probably been through the war with Temple.

I could hear footsteps, but there was no more gunfire. Sounds of scuffling came, getting closer. I could see two figures fighting and the flash of a knife. The blade of the knife disappeared, and one of the men slumped down. The one left standing was immediately attacked by another man, and another struggle ensued. I did not know what to do. I was about to crawl toward Lover Boy when the thrashing men fell on top of me. I let out a yelp, spooking one of them. He paused long enough to give the other man time to drive a knife home.

A hand reached out and jerked me to my feet.

"Let's get out of here."

Temple propelled me toward the horses. I calmed Lover Boy while he untied the rope. I jumped in the saddle so fast, the horse tried to bolt. Pulling on the reins, I soothed him while Temple untied his horse and the mule. I followed them out of the lot, his horse stepping nimbly over dead bodies while Lover Boy tried to avoid them. The mule trod on one, and I heard a soft groan.

We were heading out of town when a voice boomed behind us.

"Stop right there, Holden."

We turned to face the tall form of the sheriff holding his rifle on us. He twisted his head and called over his shoulder.

"You men can come on."

Lanterns were lit and lights bobbed before us. We were soon surrounded by the sheriff's deputy, the banker, and to my surprise, the little drummer.

"See sheriff?" the banker said, pointing at us. "They were in cahoots all along. Search them!"

"No, no, sheriff," the drummer said. "I'd swear she had nothing to do with the robbery."

Everyone began to talk at once, except Temple and me. Lover Boy began snorting and pawing the ground. He didn't like guns being held on him.

The sheriff's voice boomed above the rest. "I got no proof that Temple Holden and this girl had anything to do with that robbery. You talked me into this fiasco, but I can't arrest them without proof."

"Miss Dulcie is only seventeen and never been married," the drummer's voice faded to a halt.

There was a momentary pause before the banker burst into excited speech.

"Arrest him then for corrupting a young maiden! He's trafficking in white slavery, I tell you!"

In the dark, the sheriff seemed to be mulling this over.

"Is that true, Miss Dulcie? That you are only seventeen and unmarried?"

I nodded. That's the reason Tom and Pa wouldn't let us get married. I was only thirteen when he left.

"It was that shapely bosom that fooled you," the deputy said.

"Shut up!" the sheriff thundered at the deputy. He turned back to Temple. "Leading an innocent girl into a life of vice is a serious offense."

My mind raced. Not only was Temple in trouble, if the sheriff found out about the dead bodies we left behind, he could keep us in San Antonio for weeks, not to mention having to face a judge and jury. I could see my chances of selling cattle in Abilene slipping away.

"Sheriff, you've got it all wrong," I said. "Mr. Holden and I are on our way to get hitched before leaving to sell cattle. He ain't got nobody, and I don't either, so we are putting our team together."

"You will be unevenly yoked for certain," the sheriff said. He turned to the banker and drummer. "Go back to your hotel. I'll handle this."

The banker tried to keep yelling, but the sheriff

cut him off. With great reluctance, he and the drummer walked away, their lanterns bobbing up and down, fading as the darkness swallowed them.

The sheriff pointed his rifle at us.

"You two, get down and start walking."

We did as we were told. As we headed toward the center of town with the sheriff and his rifle behind us, I was too scared to even look in Temple Holden's direction. He had not said a word, but I knew he must be furious. I remembered something else Tom had told me about the law, and I began to feel sick. A woman couldn't testify against her husband. There went my clout with Temple. I turned and looked back at the sheriff. Even in the dark, I knew by his firm footsteps he was not going to relent and let us go before reaching the church we were headed for.

We rousted the preacher out of bed, and although his wife protested, he insisted on taking us to the sanctuary next door for the ceremony. As we stood at the altar waiting for him to start, I hissed at Temple out of the corner of my mouth.

"Don't you try nothing, buster. This here marriage is in name only until you get those longhorns sold, and then we are getting an annulment." Tom had told me the difference between an annulment and a divorce, too, and I intended to see that those grounds were not compromised.

"You reckon?"

His savagery and sarcasm made me draw back, but not enough to make me shut my mouth.

"Just so we're clear. And don't forget you made a deal to take those cattle to Abilene."

"We're clear," he said through gritted teeth. "I just hope I don't murder you before this is all over with."

The preacher got in place and cleared his throat. In a loud voice, Temple spoke.

"Make sure you put in the part about 'obey.' She's a feisty little heifer."

He glared at me. I gave him a dirty look. Behind us, the sheriff stifled a chuckle. The preacher proceeded normally. Evidently, he was used to having brides and grooms being brought before him with a gun at their backs.

Once the deed was done, Temple paid the preacher, and the sheriff walked out with us.

"Both of you, do me a favor and get out of town."

He didn't have to ask us twice. I rarely rode Lover Boy in the dark, but he didn't mind night traveling. Temple didn't mind either, and we made good time getting back to Willow Branch.

Emzy was surprised to see Temple and even more surprised when I told him we had married. I explained about the annulment.

"Yes, Miss Dulcie," Emzy said, nodding his head.

The dismissive way he said it caused me to give him a sharp look. He paid no attention and began leading our horses to the barn. Temple turned to me.

"You didn't tell me your cowhand was a hundred and one years old."

"Hush! You'll hurt his feelings."

But Emzy had heard. He turned around. "Don't you worry, Miss Dulcie. He'll find out I knows so much about them ornery longhorns; he be thinking he's still sucking on his mammy's teat when it comes to them."

Emzy's words didn't bother Temple. Instead, he looked Willow Branch over with a critical eye I didn't much care for. Maybe the fences were in bad repair around the house, and the roof of the cabin did sag in the middle. I loved it anyway.

He followed Emzy into the barn to have a look at the other horses and examine the tack. Emzy and I hung back, watching him look over the old halters and creaking saddles. Temple took one last look around the barn.

"Is the house like this?"

I exchanged glances with Emzy. "Pretty much."

Temple pushed his hat back and sighed. "I can't leave you here by yourself. I've got an uncle who owns a good hotel. I can drop you off there when we go through Bastrop. He'll let you stay, but you'll have to help out to earn your keep."

I didn't much like the thought of leaving Willow Branch. Emzy could see my mulish feelings bubbling to the surface.

"He's right, Miss Dulcie. You be a lot better off up

there than down here by yourself. Mr. Ponton probably start coming around again, trying to run things. Willow Branch ain't gonna go nowheres."

I caved in. "All right."

"My uncle's hotel has the reputation of serving the best food of any stagecoach stop in Texas, so don't embarrass both of us."

"I can cook!" I turned to Emzy, "Emzy, tell him I can cook."

"He be finding that out for hisself pretty soon I reckon."

I took the hint and flounced from the barn. My steps slowed as I looked around Willow Branch. The shady, dappled trees, the grass growing like a green carpet—they made a lump rise in my throat. I swallowed, determined to accomplish what needed to be done.

Two days later, I was sitting on a wagon seat, holding the reins of an old mule. Temple wanted to stop by his hometown and give people their deeds back. He thought his younger brother would want to go along, and I could leave the mule skinning to him the rest of the way to Bastrop.

We were just about to head out, when to my surprise, Lula Mae and Catfish drove up in their wagon.

"Oh Dulcie, I heard you got hitched and just had to meet your new husband," Lula Mae said with a squeal, like we were kissing kin or something.

I introduced them to Temple. Catfish got out of the wagon to look over the herd, just as if he knew what he was doing. Lula Mae batted her eyelashes at Temple and simpered flirtatiously. I looked at Temple and realized what a dashing figure he cut, even in old clothes.

Temple excused himself and rode over to Catfish. Lula Mae looked at me with envy.

"Oh Dulcie, he's so handsome."

"Lula Mae, you call Catfish over to that wagon to take you home. And if I ever see you batting those eyelashes at my husband again, you hussy, I'm going to pull every one of them out one by one."

Her mouth dropped open. Her flabby throat bobbled up and down like a turkey's wattle.

I refused to remove my gaze from her face, and she hollered out to Catfish. "Catfish, it's time to leave and let these people get on their way."

Catfish did as he was told after Lula hollered at him a few more times. When they left, Temple rode up to the wagon. He twisted in the saddle and looked over the herd of longhorns.

"You're taking a gamble. You may wish you had taken the banker up on his reward money."

"Oh, I think I may have already gotten my reward, or at least part of it."

Temple gave me a puzzled look and laughed. "Get in front of the herd. Giddy-up, mule," he said, popping it with his hat. The wagon lurched forward. Temple waved his hat to Emzy.

"We're moving them out. Abilene, here we come." He raised his eyebrows and added, "Lord help us."

EASY JACKSON IS a pseudonym for author Vicky J. Rose, who also writes under the name of V. J. Rose. Born in a small Texas town with a wild and woolly past, Rose grew up listening to enthralling stories of killings, lynchings, and vigilantes—excitement she tries to add to her writing so the reader, too, can experience the thrill of the Old West. In addition to short stories, Jackson's novels are available online, in Walmart, and fine bookstores everywhere. She has written and is working on producing *Lost Pines*, A Christmas Western set for filming in 2021.

GHOST TOWN GAMBIT

SCOTT DENNIS PARKER

The sky above gambler John Denton was the same color as the bruise on his face: dark, purple, and angry.

The tall man, dressed in a gray suit, red ribbon tie, with a dapper black hat pulled down low on his brow, scanned the ridge up ahead and culled his memory. The ridge up ahead, just above the arroyo, looked like the one he remembered. If it was, he knew salvation lay on the other side.

"Let's go, Queenie," Denton told Queen of Spades, his gray horse named for the distinctive black fur on the face and nose that, more or less, resembled the spade symbol from a deck of cards. The question now was simple: would he make it to the ghost town before the storm deluged the countryside or would he be washed away in a flash flood?

Queenie moved.

Denton watched the sky. This was tornado weather. The wind kicked up into his face. Dust found its way into his eyes. He held up his hands, but the dust still came. He dug his heels into Queen's ribs and urged her to go faster.

She complied. Now she openly galloped.

Denton held on with all his might, charging into the wind.

As man and horse crested the ridge, the rains started. Not the kind that gears up to a full downpour. One moment no rain filled the sky; the next, it was like standing under a waterfall.

Denton cursed. He wore one of his best suits. He hoped it wouldn't shrink.

Down below, the remains of Oakley stood against the torrent. Twenty years abandoned, Oakley used to be the only town between Fort Davis and Fort Stockton. The arrival of the railroads had diminished Oakley's importance. Soon, all the people just left.

Denton had been there as a boy, and thanked his childhood memory for being correct. Already soaked to the skin, he let Queenie find her own way and speed down the other side of the ridge.

Ten minutes later, Denton rode down what used to be Main Street. The town had gone to hell in the years since he and his father passed through to Fort Stockton. Even in the darkness that had overtaken the land, Denton noted which buildings had damaged roofs. He bypassed them, settling on, of all things, the saloon. It was a two-story building. Even if the upper floor had holes in the roof, the ground floor would still remain dry.

Denton dismounted and, without a second thought, guided Queenie through the front door. The batwings had long since broken. The horse balked at first, somehow knowing a saloon wasn't the right kind of housing for her. With more urging on by Denton, Queenie finally entered the building.

"Well, ain't that just bad luck?" Denton asked Queenie.

The beast blinked water out of her eyes.

Denton set about taking the saddle off Queenie, rubbing her down with a dirty blanket he found behind the bar, and feeding her by hand from a small bag of grain he always carried with him in case their camps didn't have any foraging available. Only after Queenie was attended to did Denton see to himself.

He stripped to the skin and laid out all his clothes across the remains of a few chairs. He pulled on more clothes from the oiled saddlebag. The old cast-iron stove in the corner was still intact enough to accept a fire Denton built in its bellows. The heat warmed him. He ate some jerky, took some swigs from his canteen, and rewarded himself with two nips from his whiskey flask.

"They ain't caught me yet," Denton told the horse. "I bet they're still out there in the rain." He laughed and positioned himself near the front, facing it. He pulled his Colt from his holster. He lay down on the floor, using his saddle as a pillow, and fell asleep, gun in hand.

THE SUN SPEARED into Denton's eyes and he woke with a start. For a few seconds, he forgot where he was. He stood, gun up, aiming it around the saloon, looking for the sound that woke him.

He found nothing other than Queen of Spades. The roan softly pawed at the floorboard. Grass grew among the cracks. Her lips sought the sweetness.

"You scared me, girl." Denton looked outside. The early morning sun shone brightly down on old Main Street. He cursed himself for sleeping so long. He wondered if he was still comfortably ahead.

Hurriedly, he put back on his favorite suit, the one he had laid out to dry the previous night. No shrinkage. Maybe it was a good omen, although Denton prefer to make his own luck. He saddled Queenie, ate another bit of jerky, and gave her a handful of grain. He led her out onto the muddy street, taking care not to dirty his boots. Denton mounted, pulled the reins, and set off at a slow trot.

He made a point to keep his eyes peeled on the east ridge, the one he had passed the previous day. True, he faced west and was doing his best to put distance between himself and the men looking for him, but it never hurt to manage one's rear.

John Denton smiled. He was free and clear.

Riding to the top of the western ridge, he angled Queenie around mesquite trees and a wall of rock where he saw all the layers of geology. He didn't hear the gunshot, but he felt the pieces of rock flake off from the bullet's impact.

"Son of a bitch!" Denton slid off Queenie and scrambled behind a small rock outcropping. He drew his pistol. His horse, trained to keep her cool amid excitement, only moved a few paces from him.

Another gunshot. This time, he heard it. The slug found a home in the limestone. It knocked rubble down beside him.

Whoever was shooting at him was getting closer to the mark. It couldn't be the men chasing him. They came from the east. It made no sense to come all around the town and ambush him from the west.

Denton got his feet under him. He whistled for Queenie. Snapped his fingers. The horse obeyed and approached him. In a swift move, Denton reached up, snagged his Winchester rifle, and ducked back behind the rock. A bullet pinged off the outcropping. Denton barely made it in time.

From down below came a man's voice. "We know you're up there! Come on out and bring the rest of your gang with you!"

"Gang?" Denton muttered to himself. He cupped his hand to his mouth. "You're wrong. I'm…"

Three rifle cracks sounded in quick succession. Hot lead found new homes in the limestone.

Denton ducked lower.

As trained as Queenie was, even she got restless. Not being a stupid animal, she hung close by the ridge.

"Why in tarnation do they think I'm with a gang?" Denton asked.

Another voice, much closer, and behind Queenie, said, "Because we're here."

Denton whirled, bringing his Winchester up with both hands.

A man crouched behind another rock. The sun glinted off the pistol in his hand. His face hadn't seen a razor in days. His body and its stench needed a good cleaning. His red shirt showed wrinkles on top of wrinkles. The bandana around his neck used to be green. The brown hat atop his head was missing chunks and bits along the brim. It drooped low over his face.

"Who are you?" Denton demanded.

"Name's Butch. I'm part of the gang that there posse from Fort Davis is lookin' fer. I was sent out to scout their location. A better question is who are you?"

Denton didn't lower his rifle. "John Denton. I'm just passing through. Stayed the night in Oakley."

"Funny. So did we. Wonder why we didn't hear you."

"I was in the saloon. You?"

"Livery and the hotel."

Denton thought about the town's layout. He had passed the livery on the way to the saloon.

Butch said, "I need to go back, talk to Musgrave."

"Who's Musgrave?"

"The leader of my gang the posse's after." He indicated the Winchester. "I think it might be a good idea if you were to come along."

Denton considered his options. He wasn't sure the trigger-happy posse looking for the Musgrave gang would give him a chance to explain. And the men pursuing him would happily welcome him. In handcuffs.

Lowering the rifle, Denton nodded. "Lead the way."

LORAN MUSGRAVE WASN'T much to look at. Short, stocky, with muscles that barely stayed inside the seams of a shirt that appeared a size or two too small, the leader of the gang jolted to his feet when Butch brought Denton into the hotel.

Denton kept his hands away from his Colt. He had stashed the Winchester back in the leather scabbard on Queenie's saddle.

"Who the hell is this?" Musgrave's hand shot to the butt of his pistol hung low on his thigh.

Two other men looked up from the meager meal they were eating. Both drew iron and aimed it at Denton.

Butch extended his hands. "Loran, hold up. This here's John Denton. Turns out he was here in town last night, too. He stayed in the saloon."

Musgrave cocked his head and studied Denton. "You look mighty doodied up to have spent the night in a ghost town."

Denton bowed at the neck. "My clothes got soaked in the deluge last night. I laid them out to dry. Slept in my skivvies." Grinning, he presented his clothes in a flourish. "This morning, it was like they had been professionally cleaned by a Chinese laundry."

One of the two men who stood off to the side said, "Where was your horse?" He was the tallest of the bunch, three or four inches over six feet as best Denton could tell.

"With me." He chuckled. "You wouldn't believe how much prodding I had to do to get her inside."

"You feed her?" the same man asked.

"Yup. Always carry spare oats for my girl."

Musgrave took back the floor. "Why you here?"

And there it was. Denton's choice. How much did he reveal to this gang of outlaws? He wondered if there was a way out of the vise in which he now found himself.

Quick thoughts swirled in his mind. He started with a question. "Butch here tells me y'all robbed a bank up in Fort Davis. That true?"

Musgrave gave Butch a withering look. "Yeah, that's right."

"We even kilt a man in the process," the fourth gang member said. If Musgrave was stocky, this fourth man was downright fat. Denton wondered how he even kept up with his skinnier brethren.

Denton appeared impressed. "I guess there was no other way?"

"What?" said the fat man.

"The man y'all killed. There was no other way around his killing?"

"Kill or be killed," the fat man bragged.

"How much y'all take?" Denton asked.

"Listen here," Musgrave interrupted. "I already asked you a question. Why are you here?"

Denton inhaled, considering the words to use. "Let's just say there's a group of men looking for me, too."

The fat man appeared impressed. "What'd you do?"

Denton looked at him, and at each man standing in the room. He wondered how much to say to them, how much to divulge of the real reason why he was here. "Let's just say there's a good reason for a posse to be chasing me." He held up a finger. "But that's not the real reason why I want to talk to y'all today."

Musgrave narrowed his eyes. "What do you mean 'talk'?"

"We have a problem out there," Denton nodded outside toward the east, "and I have a way for us to get out of here. Want to hear it?"

Butch actually raised his hand. "I do."

Musgrave shot him an angry look.

Butch lowered his hand.

Musgrave, reasserting his leadership, edged nearer to Denton. His hand never left the butt of his gun. "Go ahead."

Denton shook his head. He held out his hand, palm up. "It'll cost you." He looked at each man one at a time. He settled on Musgrave's face. "How much y'all take?"

"I ain't saying."

Denton withdrew his hand. "Then I'm not telling. I'll take my chances with the posse out there, yours or mine. I can evade the law, maybe even better than you can. Want to put it to a test?"

He waited a few beats. No one spoke.

"I've got a plan that will get us all out of here."

The tall man idly scratched his chin, his fingernails rasping on the stubble.

Butch suddenly found something in his teeth worth worrying about.

The fat man sweated.

Musgrave just stood there. Finally, he said, "Six thousand."

Denton did quick math in his head. Six thousand divided by four outlaws meant there was about fifteen hundred apiece. He pondered how much each man would be willing to hand over to Denton in exchange for safe passage. Inwardly, he shrugged. Might as well aim high.

"Tell you what, each one of you men give me five hundred and I'll guarantee you get out of this ghost town alive." He smiled, waiting for them to haggle.

It didn't take long. "Why in hell would we give you some of our money?" Musgrave blurted. "You got a posse after you. We got one after us. Way I see it, we're all trapped, and you are smack dab in the middle of it." He grinned, showing teeth that hadn't seen a toothbrush in weeks. "How you expect to get out of that?"

Denton smiled. "Oh, I'll get out of here alive. I got no doubt about that. The only question is, will y'all?" He kept his palms up. "I'm going to step outside, roll a cigarette, and have a nice long smoke while y'all discuss y'all's options. When you're ready to do business, come and get me. Otherwise, given about thirty minutes or so, I'm gonna ride out here and I might not ever see y'all again. Alive, at least."

John Denton kept his face to the four outlaws as he backed out through the hotel door. He sidled up to Queenie and patted her head. "Let's see how long this takes."

Turned out to be only about five minutes. Butch proved to be the emissary. He walked out into the bright sunshine, eyes squinting. "The boss wants to see you."

Denton leaned off the post and followed the owlhoot inside. He had heard some of the arguing so he had a pretty good idea of the specifics.

Inside, Musgrave, the tall man, and the fat man sat around a table. The leader indicated the two empty chairs opposite. "Take a seat."

Denton did and waited.

"Me and the boys've talked. We're willing to part with four hunnerd each."

"Sixteen, huh?" Denton hid his true feelings. He had thrown out the two grand price tag never thinking he'd come close. Sixteen hundred was more than enough to get him out of this jam.

He extended his hand across the table.

Musgrave took it.

"Done," Denton said. He brought his hand back to his lap.

"Now," said the fat man, "let's hear this fancy plan."

"Shut up, Hezekiah," Musgrave said. "I know'd

you didn't wanna do this, but having more money than you ever had before and bein' alive to spend it is better'n bein' dead or in jail."

Denton said, "It's true, Hezekiah. Spending money, especially money that isn't yours, is one of the great joys in life."

"How you know that?" the fat man said.

"Because it's the way I've made my living for the past ten years."

For the first time, Musgrave put on a genuine grin. "I'm all ears." He indicated the tall man. "That's Mort Ackerman. You know Butch and me. What's your big plan?"

Denton held out his hand. He rubbed his thumb and forefinger together. "Payment is due prior to services rendered."

The smile on Musgrave's mouth vanished.

Denton's remained in place.

"Gentlemen." Denton indicated his right hand, which remained under the table, "This is a business arrangement, plain and simple. Now I thought you might be trying to put one over on me so I have my gun drawn. It's aimed at one of y'all."

He waited while the outlaws all started. Denton wagged a finger. "No sudden movements."

"You double-crosser!" Hezekiah yelled.

"I haven't double-crossed anyone," Denton replied. "I'm merely ensuring our business arrangement. You pay, I talk, and we all get out of this town alive."

Musgrave leaned on the table. "You're one against four. You shoot me, my boys'll kill you where you sit."

"And y'all don't get out of this town alive." Denton stared at the leader. "Besides, my gun isn't aimed at you."

The eyes of the other three men widened.

Denton's eyes remained fixed on Musgrave. "Payment first. Then freedom."

A muscle in the leader's cheek twitched. A bead of sweat rolled over his unshaven face.

"Loran, come on!" Hezekiah said. "You gonna let this chiseler tell us what to do? This is our money. We can get outta—"

The gunshot boomed in the old hotel lobby. The bullet slammed into Hezekiah's body. He fell backward in his chair. The old wood couldn't support his weight. It cracked, then broke. The fat man landed on his back in a heap. Blood poured out of his lower gut.

His screams pierced the silence.

"Don't move," Denton said, his hand still under the table. Gun smoke curled around the table's edge. "Any of y'all."

The three bank robbers remained frozen in place. "The deal's still on. My price is the same. Y'all just earned dividends. Don't think too hard on this. I might be liable to cull another one."

Hezekiah grabbed his belly. "Oh, sweet mother of God, this hurts. Loran, do something!"

Loren Musgrave glanced at Denton who nodded.

Musgrave pulled his pistol and shot Hezekiah in the head.

The screaming stopped.

Denton smiled. "Y'all just earned an extra five hundred dollars each. But don't be thinking of killing another member of the gang. The plan that'll get y'all out of this town is based on there being a small band of men. Now, with all of the objections out of the way, who wants to hear the plan?"

"That's it?" Ackerman, the tall man, said.

"Yes, indeed." Denton pulled out papers and tobacco and rolled another cigarette.

"We're supposed to just ride out there and meet up with the posse chasing you?"

Denton held up a finger. "And convince them y'all are chasin' the Musgrave gang."

"We are the Musgrave gang!" Musgrave exploded. "I didn't bust my hump to earn a nickname only to hide from it."

Shrugging, Denton said, "Suit yourself. You can

be alive and skedaddle outta here or die with your name." He inhaled and blew a smoke ring.

Ackerman and Butch waited for Musgrave to say something.

After about a minute, the leader sighed. "What do we have to do?"

"Excellent!" Denton tossed the cigarette to the floor and stubbed it out with a boot. "First off, y'all have to look more like a posse."

For fifteen minutes, John Denton fussed about each man. He extolled them to tuck in shirts, dab out as many stains as possible, and generally look presentable. "Remember, posses are made up of normal men pulled from their daily lives to ride out against an outlaw. Even after hard riding, they still have an appearance about them. You need to look like that."

The living members of the Musgrave gang allowed Denton to work them over. When he was done, they looked at themselves. They still wore their same clothes, but with a spruced-up look and combed hair, they came off respectable.

"This is all it takes?" Butch asked.

"You'd be surprised what a little cleaning up will do," Denton replied. "Now, who has a watch?"

Ackerman pulled a watch without a chain from his pocket.

Denton extended his hand and the tall man plopped his watch into Denton's palm. The gambler compared his watch with Ackerman's and adjusted them both accordingly. He handed it back to the outlaw. "Here you go. Both watches match."

Ackerman pocketed the watch. "Why's that important?"

"Timing is crucial if this is going to work."

"What exactly we aimin' to do?" Butch asked.

"Y'all're gonna hunt down the Musgrave Gang."

Denton moved to one of the windows and tore down an old white curtain. He ripped it in half and handed Musgrave one piece. "Find a stick so you can make a white flag."

"We surrendering?" the leader asked.

"Nope. You're getting in the perimeter of my posse." Denton tied his half of the curtain on a broken stool leg. "Once there, all you have to do is become one of them. And shoot whatever comes your way. I'll signal you when everyone's in place."

"What'll your signal be?" Ackerman asked.

"A gunshot."

With that, Denton readied himself to depart. He stowed all his new cash in various pockets. He expected trouble when he fulfilled his part of the bargain. Finished, he turned to Musgrave and extended his hand.

The outlaw shook it. "I hope you know what you're doing."

"I'm getting us out of here. Remember: give me fifteen minutes, then y'all head east. I'll give y'all thirty minutes to get yourselves set. So that's forty-five minutes from now." He snapped his fingers.

Ackerman looked at his pocket watch and started the countdown.

Denton tipped his hat to the Musgrave Gang. "Gentlemen, it's been a pleasure." He turned his back to the men and shuffled out to Queenie. Putting a boot in the stirrup, he mounted the horse. He set her on a canter out to the east. He carried the makeshift truce flag across Queenie's back. No sense getting his hand all tired.

As Denton neared the ridge, he hefted his flag. He took a deep breath. He had displayed complete confidence back in the ghost town hotel. Now, he was about to find out if his gambit had worked.

He raised the flag above the outcropping and waved it. "Hello down there." He waited. He kept waving the flag. He repeated his call.

"Who are you?" came a man's voice.

"Traveler." Denton peeked around the ridge. He kept both hands in view, the one that held the flag, the other open-palmed to the posse. "Coming through."

"You a member of the Musgrave Gang?" The voice was deep and gravelly.

"That who attacked me?" Denton put a little desperation is his voice. "I'm on my horse. Can I pass?" As good as his eyes were, Denton couldn't pinpoint the man's position.

"Dismount and walk. Don't forget I've got my rifle trained on you."

Denton dismounted. He kept hold of the flag. "Coming." He tugged on Queenie's bridle.

The gambler and his horse traipsed around the outcropping and down a small slope. Small mesquite trees dotted an otherwise grassy landscape. Above him, low hills rose from the earth. In all directions, Denton saw nothing.

But he heard the cock of a gun. He stopped. He kept his hands visible.

"What's your name?" the same gravelly-voiced man said. "State your business."

Denton cleared his throat. "Name's Cullen. Was passing through the area. Got caught in the storm last night. Took shelter in the old ghost town down yonder. This band of outlaws swooped in. They captured me. I shot one of 'em and got away."

A grunt from the man.

Denton now identified the rock behind which the man stood. It was two old boulders, side by side, a small V in the middle.

"How come I didn't hear you galloping out?"

"Because you already shot at me once. You think I want to have you do it again?"

Another grunt.

Denton continued. "When I shot one of 'em—a fat man the others called Hezekiah—I was able to escape with my horse. That mean anything to you?"

The rifleman said, "Yup. I think you need to talk with the sheriff."

"Why? I ain't done nothin' wrong."

"No, but you seen the Musgrave Gang. Maybe you can help us."

Denton pondered the question. "All right. Lead the way."

THE POSSE LED by Sheriff Tom Phillips turned out to be a rangy, scraggly band of five men. They all dressed haphazardly, with mismatched clothes that were sweat-stained and dirty. Their hats looked misshapen and dented. None of them had seen a razor in days. The sheriff himself sported a thick brown beard that made Denton sweat just looking at it.

So much for my theory about posses being well-dressed men.

Phillips looked up at Denton when the gambler walked Queenie into a small clearing. The rifleman walked behind, Winchester held at waist level, pointed forward.

"Who's this?" The sheriff stood and put his hand on his iron. The tin star flashed in the sun.

"Name's Cullen," Denton said. "As I told your deputy, I was passing through the area last night, got caught in the storm. Took refuge in the old saloon before this Musgrave Gang came in. I heard y'all're lookin' for them. I've knocked 'em down a man." He assumed a large grin.

The sheriff didn't move. "That the gunshot we heard?"

"Yes, sir."

The rifleman who stood behind Denton said, "This here fancy man said he shot Hezekiah."

The sheriff's eyes were the only thing that moved. They swept from his deputy to Denton. "How'd you know his name?"

"Because when I shot him in the gut, his pals yelled out his name." Denton put some force in his voice. "That's all I heard before I mounted up and skedaddled."

Finally, the sheriff moved. He walked over to Queenie and indicated the truce flag. "You have time to make this before or after you fled?"

"Before," Denton said with certainty. "After your deputy did his job the first time and laid a few slugs over my head, I turned back to town to figure out what to do next. I found this old curtain in the hotel and a broken stool. I made this here flag right before the gang found me. They musta been spooked by the gunfire."

The sheriff spat on the ground. He sniffed. "Where were they last you saw 'em?"

"The hotel. It's about the fifth building inside of town. South side. They were holed up in the old lobby, eating around a table." Denton paused. "You thinking of going after 'em?"

"That's our job. Bring 'em back to Fort Stockton to be tried by a judge. Or die out here." He spat again. "I'd prefer the latter. Which is why I'm draftin' you into our posse." Finally, a grin.

Denton was shocked. This wasn't part of the plan. He hadn't anticipated this. He hoped his face didn't betray his shock. "What? I'm not fit for a posse. There ain't nothing I can do."

The sheriff inclined his head to Denton's Colt. "If you're good enough to take out Hezekiah with that, you'll be fine."

"The man was a fat pig. It's like shooting the slow buffalo on a hunt. You take out the easy one."

"Be that as it may, Cullen, you're comin' with us."

Denton sighed. "I didn't want to have to do this, but you leave me no choice."

The sheriff and his men tensed.

"My name's not Cullen. It's Denton. And I'm wanted." He held up his hands.

One of the sheriff's men said, "Yer pullin' our leg."

Denton shook his head. "John Denton, wanted in New Orleans for theft, swindling, and ungentlemanly conduct with a woman." He chuckled. "That last from a father who didn't like the fact his daughter spent the night with me of her own free will." He grinned, thinking of the fake memory. "It was quite a night." He wagged his eyebrows to complete the sell.

The sheriff looked skeptical. "You lied about yore name. You lyin' now?"

"No, sir. But I'd like the opportunity to buy my freedom." He indicated his suit pocket. "My wallet's in here. Six hundred dollars. I'd be willing to part with that if you boys'll let me ride away in peace."

The amateur deputies gasped at the amount.

Sheriff Phillips just squinted. "You tryin' to bribe an officer of the law?"

"I am."

"Think it'll work?"

"Tell me after you're holdin' six hundred dollars." He moved his arm to open his suit coat. "Right inside pocket."

The sheriff spat. Tobacco juice streamed through the air. Some landed in his whiskers. He glanced at his deputies. Without a word, he stepped forward and stuck his hand into Denton's pocket.

The gambler kept a smile on his face, only following the sheriff's actions with his eyes.

Taking the fine leather wallet in his hands, the

sheriff opened it. Inside, bills of multiple denominations spilled out.

More gasps from the other men.

Phillips took in the sight. He reached in and took the cash. All of it.

"Um, could you spare a dollar or two?" Denton asked. "Travel expenses and such."

In response, the sheriff slapped the wallet on Denton's chest. "Guess you don't know how this bribin' thing works. I take what I want and you live." Putting a thumb to his tongue, the sheriff counted the money. "Six hunnnerd dollars." He whistled. "I ain't never held that much money before."

He turned to his men. The four of them stood in anticipation. He dished out a hundred per man. He kept the extra for himself. He shoved the small wad in his pocket. "Mr. Denton, looks like you bought your freedom. Out of curiosity, what's the bounty on you?"

"Only five hundred. You just made a profit."

The sheriff gave him a quizzical look. "I might be inclined to handcuff you to a nearby tree and come fetch you after we take Musgrave and his rascals. Get an extra five."

Denton kept his gaze even and nonplussed. "But how would you explain the other money? I might be compelled to let my lawyer know about that. It might call into question your integrity. That wouldn't be good for you."

Out of the blue, the sheriff laughed. "You're a smooth talker, Denton. Let's hope we don't meet again. If we do, I'm liable to shoot you." He jerked a thumb. "Git on outta here before I change my mind."

Denton tipped his hat to the corrupt lawman and his band. "Gentlemen, I wish you safe hunting." He held up a finger. "I might suggest y'all get on down there and arrest or kill the gang. It looked like they were about to skedaddle."

"That so?" the sheriff asked. "How you figure?"

"Call it a gambler's hunch. I was right about y'all. Chances are I'm right about that, too."

Denton stood by while the posse readied themselves. Surreptitiously, he checked his watch. It had been thirty-five minutes since he had left the ghost town. Ten minutes until he was to give the signal.

The sheriff and his posse mounted up. "I feel a might bad for thankin' you about the tip, seein' as how I took yer money, but thank you."

Denton mounted. He turned Queenie away from the small group. "Don't mention it, sheriff. I always bet on red."

The sheriff frowned. "What's that supposed to mean?"

"It's my favorite color." Denton indicated his red tie. "See?"

The sheriff narrowed his eyes. "Sure." Belief didn't seem to come naturally to the lawman.

"Good luck." Denton whistled and Queenie trotted away from the posse.

She didn't get far before Denton halted her. He looked back up the small rise trying to catch a glimpse of the posse. He saw nothing. He got off the horse and pulled out the Winchester from the leather scabbard. Opening one of his saddlebags, Denton filled a pocket with rifle bullets. He expected to need only one, but it was best to be prepared.

He checked his watch. Two minutes.

Not needing to tie Queenie's reins, Denton crept back up the rise. The campsite was empty. Crouching low, he peered over a boulder. His view tapered down to the ghost town.

Sheriff Phillips and his men were cautiously approaching the outskirts.

A check of the watch. One more minute.

Denton steadied the rifle on the outcropping and aimed it down at the group. He only needed to fire a single shot to sound the alarm. If Musgrave did his job, then this was it. He could turn and leave. If the gang leader didn't do his job, then Denton might have two posses after him.

Might as well kill two birds with one shot.

He took aim at the small band. He asked himself a question: *Do I take out the head of the proverbial serpent or just a limb?*

Holding his breath, John Denton pulled the trigger.

Butch Irvine never truly believed Loran Musgrave could talk his way into the good graces of an honest-to-goodness posse. The outlaw's hand twitched as his leader made the case for their false identity. Perhaps it was the easy nature of Hector Gruber, the sheriff of this posse chasing John Denton, or simply blind luck, but the three members of the Musgrave Gang found themselves among five lawmen all hunting the rogue gambler.

Now, Butch, Musgrave, and Ackerman joined Gruber and his crew in creeping along the main street. Denton had told them one thing: shoot anyone who comes from the east. When asked who would be coming from that direction, the gambler said simply, "The Musgrave Gang."

Butch, Ackerman, and two lawmen stepped lightly along one side of Main Street. Musgrave, Sheriff Gruber, and the other lawmen matched their slow pace across the street. Running west to east, the sun shone down the middle of the street. Nothing was hidden from view.

A horse blew air between its lips. All the men stealthily walking along Main Street cocked their guns. A couple of the lawmen had rifles. Everyone carried side arms.

Up the street, four riders appeared. They all

carried rifles, all pointing up in the air. Still, no signal from Denton.

From up the ridge, a gun cracked the morning air. One of the riders yelled and fell from his horse. The remaining three horsemen made to turn, but got caught in a hail of lead as all seven men, including the Musgrave Gang, fired at them. Man and horse took the onslaught of flying slugs. The men fell from their saddles. Wounded horses galloped from the scene of the massacre. In a matter of seconds, it was all over.

The gentle stillness returned to the ghost town. Acrid gun smoke fumigated the air. Butch realized he was breathing heavy and concentrated on slowing down. He hadn't been the one to kill the man during the bank robbery. He had fired all his bullets at the approaching riders. He didn't know if any hit them. He decided all of his bullets sailed high.

Sheriff Gruber holstered his piece and propped his hat atop his head. "Shit." He clapped a hand on Musgrave's shoulder. "You were right."

The living souls walked to where the dead ones laid in the street. Fresh blood caked in the dirt. None of the riders took breaths.

At a nod from Musgrave, all the members of the gang reloaded their guns. "There may be more," the leader said to Sheriff Gruber.

The lawman nodded. "That's why we shoot with

rifles first. Leaves our pistols ready for another round."

One of the riders lay in a heap on the ground, his torso slumped over his legs. The angle was such that the contents of his pockets had spilled out. Paper money wafted in the gentle breeze.

A deputy crouched and picked up a bill. "It's a twenty.:" He frowned. "And a hundred dollar bill." He gave it to Gruber. The sheriff took it and examined it. The deputy scooped up the remaining money and handed it over.

"Gather up the rest," Sheriff Gruber ordered. "We'll take it back and find out which bank this came from and return it. Then let's rustle up the horses. We'll take these owlhoots back to town and see about a reward."

His deputies fanned out to each of the new corpses. For some reason, Butch found this part of the plan most excruciating. The waiting.

A deputy swore.

"What is it, Todd?"

Todd waved Gruber over to one of the bodies.

Butch, Musgrave, and Ackerman exchanged glances. Slowly, Musgrave moved his hand to his revolver. His men did the same.

"Look." With the barrel of his rifle, Todd folded over the vest of the first man to fall. Pinned to it was a shiny silver star.

"What the hell?" Gruber cried. "Was this a sheriff? He have money in his pocket?"

Todd held up a wad of money. Two hundred dollar bills. "Yes, sir."

Gruber snatched up the wad. He compared it with the other money already recovered. "Why would a sheriff be carrying around stolen money? Actually, y'all were the ones who said the Musgrave gang was in this town." Slowly, he turned to Musgrave.

Sheriff Gruber started.

All the members of the Musgrave Gang had their guns drawn and trained on Gruber and his lawmen.

"I'd like that money back, Sheriff," Musgrave said over grinning teeth. "We earned it."

Gruber let the money slip from his fingers. His steely-eyed stare narrowed. "Y'all are outnumbered. We're pretty fast on the draw. You might get one of us, but we'll get you back. You willing to take that chance?"

Out of the corner of his eyes, Butch watched Musgrave. Butch had selected the deputy named Todd as his target. Even if Butch gave himself the happy fantasy that he'd missed all six shots at the other posse, there was no way around killing this time. Kill or be killed.

Might as well get it over with.

Butch fired his gun. Todd spun around on impact.

A second later, Gruber drew. The surprise of the gunshot gave Musgrave a pause. The slug from Gruber's gun slammed into Musgrave at pretty much the same time as the gang leader pulled his trigger. Both he and the sheriff were hit.

By that time, however, Butch had recovered enough to bring his gun around to another deputy. That lawman was slow. Butch nailed him in the chest.

Ackerman and the two remaining deputies had enough time to take cover. They were firing at each other from behind buildings. Butch realized he had an angle on the lawmen. He swiveled his arm and took aim at the men. He sent two rounds into the pair. One man fell. The other turned to shoot at Butch. Ackerman made sure it was the last thing the deputy did.

Breathing heavily, his gun hand shaking, Butch looked all around the street. He saw figures where none existed. He fired a few more rounds until Ackerman calmed him.

"Butch! We're done." Ackerman held his hands out, palms facing his friend. "We're done," he repeated in a softer voice.

"Mort, we done kilt a sheriff and his deputies. We're gonna hang."

Ackerman shook his head. "Nope. We gonna take all this money and get ourselves lost." He pointed to the bills scattered along the street. "Let's just pick'em up and get outta here."

Butch didn't move. He stood stock still. He had killed two men in the last five minutes. There was no way he could deny that. Something turned in his stomach. With a violent retching, Butch bent over and vomited in the street. He ended when dry heaves forced up only bile. He wiped his mouth and stood up. His stomach muscles ached.

Ackerman gave his a pitiful look.

"What? I got sick. I ain't never kilt a man before. Now, I done two."

Shaking his head, Ackerman said, "You knew what you was gettin' into when you hooked up with Musgrave. Now you done it. There might be more. You up for it?"

Butch thought. He actually furrowed his brow. He was looking down at the ground when Ackerman shot him in the gut. Butch Irvine fell to the ground, face looking at a clear blue sky.

A shadow darkened over him. Ackerman stared down at him. "Sorry about that. I aim to get outta here in one piece. I kinda figured you'd just slow me down." He kicked the pistol out of Butch's hand. "Don't feel bad. You just weren't cut out for a life like this." He crouched over his fallen former friend. Ackerman stuck his hand into Butch's pocket.

The next thing Butch knew, something smacked into Ackerman's face. A shower of blood cascaded onto Butch's face. A portion of Ackerman's jaw blew off. The man wasn't quite dead when he toppled onto Butch's body, but he wasn't long for the world.

New footsteps approached while a Winchester rifle chambered another round. Butch tried to turn and see who it was. His angle was off and Ackerman's body prevented any further movement. That was fine by Butch. The ache in his gut had slowly spread to his legs.

Come to think of it, I can't even feel my legs.

Butch coughed. He felt warm blood run down his cheek.

The footsteps got closer. Another figure blocked the sun. From somewhere in his dying mind, Butch wasn't surprised to see John Denton.

The gambler smiled down at Butch Irvine. He whistled low. "Gut shot's a bad way to go. Need me to ease your pain?"

Butch gave it a moment. "A question." He coughed. His breathing gurgled. "This what you planned on all along?"

Denton pursed his lips. "Afraid so. I always bet on red."

Butch frowned. "Red?"

"Red. Blood. Depending on the circumstances, men will always seek out their own best interests, even if that means killing. It's man's nature to be cruel. I just use it to my advantage. Most of the time, it pays off." He gestured to the dead men littering the old ghost town's Main Street. "It did today. And I made a profit." With that, he brought the rifle to bear.

The last thing Butch Irvine saw was the blood red tie worn by the gambler.

JOHN DENTON WHISTLED a tune as he walked around to all the bodies and collected the stolen money. He even picked up the tin star from Sheriff Phillips's vest. "This may come in handy."

He whistled for Queenie. The horse cantered down the center of Main Street. She picked her way among the bodies. Reaching Denton, she stopped.

John Denton mounted his horse and pulled her reins. He pinned the star on his lapel. It shone in the sun. "Okay, girl. Let's go spend some of this money."

THE SATURDAY COLUMNIST at Do Some Damage for over a decade, **Scott Dennis Parker** draws on his history degrees to write mysteries and westerns, many set in his hometown of Houston, Texas. Browse his books and read his long-running blog at scottdennisparker.com.

NIGHT HORSE

༄༅

JOHN D. NESBITT

Finley Cole kept a night horse in the barn for all the time that I worked for him. He didn't keep the horse saddled, as some men did, but he had it in a stall so he wouldn't have to go out and catch one if something came up in the night. He had three or four horses that he rotated, depending on how much work they were getting otherwise, so that he wouldn't have the same one penned up every night. One of my jobs was to clean the stall each day and to have it ready for that evening's horse.

On one afternoon in late August, a stranger dropped by when I was cleaning the pen. He tied his horse outside and stood in the doorway. I didn't like looking at him with the bright light in back of him, so I told him to come in.

He was a normal-looking fellow in his mid-thirties, a little above average height, not decked out in gaudy clothes but not wearing rags, either. He was dressed like a range rider, with a dust-colored hat, a greyish-tan work shirt, a brown cloth vest, denim trousers, and boots with spurs.

"What can I help you with?" I asked.

"Does this place belong to Finn Cole?"

"It does."

"How long has he had it?"

"I don't know. I've been working here less than a year."

The stranger cast a glance around the inside of the barn. He had blue eyes, a clear complexion, and wavy brown hair. "How does he make a living?"

I thought the question was a bit personal, but I shrugged it off and said, "Like anyone else. Buys and sells cattle. Has cattle of his own but not a big range to graze 'em on. Buys and sells horses once in a while, as well."

"Does he have a fellow named Holbrook working for him?"

"Yes, he does. Ross Holbrook."

The stranger nodded. "And is there a woman named Evie Burns here?"

I looked at him straight and said, "I don't know how many of your questions I should answer."

He waved his hand. "That's all right."

I imagined he assumed that if Evie was not around, I would have said so. I narrowed my gaze on him and said, "What's your name, friend?"

"My name's Paul," he said. "Paul Pimentel."

"Good enough. Would you like me to tell Finn you were looking for him?"

"However you'd like. And your name?"

"Emerson Danforth," I said. "Everyone calls me Dan."

"That's good enough, too." He glanced around again and said, "I won't keep you from your work. Pleased to meet you."

"And the same here," I said.

THE STRANGER WASN'T GONE LONG when Evie showed up. She was wearing an everyday dress of dark blue and had put on a light-colored straw hat with a wide brim and a round crown. Her dark brown hair fell to her shoulders, and her eyes, which varied in color, showed green. She had a worried expression on her face, and her hands worked together as if she was buttoning a shirt or winding a watch.

"Who was that man who stopped in?" she asked.

"He said his name was Paul Pimentel. He was asking about Finn."

Evie drew her brows together. "Was he asking to see him?"

"Not outright. He asked whether this was Finn's place, what he did for a living, if he had Ross

Holbrook working here . . . and whether you were here."

Her face clouded. "I don't know why anyone would ask about me."

"Neither do I. And if it's any comfort, I didn't answer his question about you. That is, I told him I didn't know how many of his questions I should answer, but I think he would conclude that the reason I didn't answer was that you were here."

Her eyes met mine for a couple of seconds. "Thank you anyway." Her chest went up and down as she breathed, and with her eyes fixed at some point a few yards away, she said, "There was something familiar about that man, some sense I had, but I know I haven't seen him before."

"Well, he was a stranger to me. He seemed polite enough, even if he asked a lot of questions. Inquisitive, as my grandfather would say."

"Did he mention where he was from?"

"No. The only thing he said about himself was his name, and I had to ask for that. We might get a chance to know more about him, though. He didn't seem like he was going to leave right away."

She let out a short, weary breath. "I wouldn't expect anything good to come out of this."

"You never can tell," I said, but I knew I didn't have any wisdom to share. It was just something to say.

Finn came to the bunkhouse while Ross Holbrook and I were finishing breakfast the next morning. Holbrook and I were the only two living in the bunkhouse at the time, so Finn didn't mind much about what he said or how loud he said it.

"Some son of a bitch came by here yesterday afternoon." Finn bored his brown eyes at me. "You talked to him, didn't you?"

"Not much," I said.

"Not much. Tell me what he said, or what he asked and what you told him."

I took a couple of seconds to pull my thoughts together. "Well, he asked if this was your place, how long you had it, what you did for a living, if Ross was working here, and if Evie was here. I gave short answers to all of the questions except the last one."

Finn scowled. "And you gave him a long answer to that one?"

"I didn't answer it."

"Well, saddle up. Both of you. We're going to town to have a talk with this bird. What did you say his name was?"

"He said it was Paul Pimentel."

As we rode into town, Holbrook pulled up next to Finn and asked, "How do you know he's here?"

Finn made a sound like "Puh" and said, "I just know things." He squared his shoulders, snorted, cleared his throat, and spit off to the side. He was a well-built fellow, of average height, and he carried himself straight up if he was in the saddle or on foot. I had never seen him tangle with anyone, but I had noticed that men did not crowd him.

We rode on without speaking, and in less than an hour we covered the five miles to town. We dismounted and tied up in front of the barber shop and post office. The barber shop was not open yet. Finn sent Holbrook into the post office to ask about the newcomer.

Holbrook came out a minute later. He took the toothpick from his mouth and rubbed his nose. "They said to try the café."

"Well, go ahead," said Finn.

The café was three doors down on our right, so Holbrook turned and strolled along the board sidewalk. He had something of a rolling gait, with his head tipped back and his arms swinging. He was heavier-built than Finn, and he had an air about him that said that anyone who wanted to knock his hat off was welcome to give it a try.

Holbrook went into the café and came out a minute later. He stood on the sidewalk under the wooden awning and made a motion with his head. Finn and I walked in the street toward him.

As we drew up in front of the café, the door opened. The stranger I had seen the day before stepped out and came to a stop with his hands on his hips. Looking at Finn from the sidewalk, he said, "What is it?"

Finn drew himself up to his full height. "Is your name Paul Pimentel?"

The man glanced at me. "That's what I told your workman here."

"I heard you were looking for me."

"I didn't say that."

"I heard you came by my place and was askin' questions about me."

"If your name's Finn Cole, that's true."

"Well, I don't like people comin' by my place when I'm not there, and I don't like people askin' questions about me."

"Neither of those things is against the law."

Finn's face stiffened. "I don't know what your game is. You sound a little too smart to me. Why don't you step down here into the street and back up your smart words?"

"Take off your gunbelt, and I will."

By now, a few onlookers had gathered, and everyone could see that Pimentel was not wearing a gun.

Finn unbuckled his belt and handed it, along

with the holster and six-gun, to me. As if on second thought, he took off his hat and gave it to me as well.

Pimentel stepped forward, took hold of a post that held up the awning, and turned his back to us as he swung down into the street. As he did so, he slipped his right hand into his pants pocket. When he drew it out, I saw him close his fist around a pocketknife with a short, thick, brown handle. I did not know how many others, if any, saw the movement.

When he stood around square in the street, he took off his hat with his left hand, and with a bit of a flourish, he sailed it onto the sidewalk. He put up his fists with his forearms curved and his elbows forward, as I had seen boxers do. He gave a mocking smile and said, "Come on."

Finn moved forward with what I imagined was his own sure method. He settled on his left foot and swung with his left fist, trying to knock down his opponent's guard. Then he stepped forward with his right foot and swung a right punch.

Pimentel stepped back, bounced on his feet, and came in with a straight-arm left jab that shook Finn's head. Then he came across with a hard right punch that caught Finn on the jaw and cheek and dropped him to the ground. As Pimentel stood back, he slipped his right hand into his pocket and brought it out empty. With his palm upward, he said, "Is that good enough for the moment?"

Finn raised himself to one elbow and rubbed the side of his face. "I guess so. But this isn't the last of it."

Pimentel shrugged. "Either of us could decide that."

I WAS CLEANING the stall later that day when Evie came from the house. She was wearing a brown dress and hat, which helped give her eyes a light brown tone. She had a worried expression like the day before, and she was clutching one hand with the other. I waited as she drew within four feet of me and spoke in a low voice.

"You didn't tell Finn what I told you, did you? About my thinking there was something familiar about that stranger?"

I shook my head. "I didn't say anything about our conversation. He didn't ask me, and I didn't volunteer anything."

"He got it out of me that someone had come by, and so I had to tell him I talked to you. But I didn't tell him anything about that strange sense I had."

"Well, he's seen him for himself by now, anyway."

"That's what I heard. He's furious about it. He said the man caught him off guard and hit him with something. I'm sure he wants to get even."

I twisted my mouth and nodded my head. "Seemed that way to me."

FINN AND HOLBROOK returned from their afternoon ride as the sun was going down. I was slicing potatoes, as it was my turn to cook, and I saw them through the open door.

Holbrook came into the bunkhouse in a huff. He said, "Let's not take too long with supper. Finn wants to go into town, and he wants both of us to go with him."

We hurried through the meal, cleaned up, and grabbed our hats. Finn was waiting for us with a horse already saddled for himself. Holbrook and I made short work of catching and saddling horses for ourselves. The night was dark, but the horses knew the trail, and we made it to town almost as soon as we did in the daylight.

Finn and Holbrook led the way to the Buckeye Saloon. We tied up at the rail and walked into the lamplight of the saloon. It was not a large establishment, maybe twenty-five feet wide and thirty-five feet deep. Men stood along the bar, and a few sat at tables.

Halfway down the bar, Paul Pimentel stood with his left elbow on the bar and his right hand on his hip, in a posture that allowed him to watch the front door. As before, he was not wearing a gun.

Holbrook and Finn walked up to him, with me following. Pimentel's eyes roved over both of them.

"What do you need?" he said.

To my surprise, Holbrook answered. "You seemed pretty sure of yourself earlier in the day. How would you like to try your luck with me?"

Pimentel raised his eyebrows. "Take off your gunbelt, and I'll give you a gentleman's chance."

"Sure." Holbrook stepped back, and with a smirk on his face, he unbuckled the gunbelt and handed it to me.

The bartender came bustling from the far end of the bar. "See here," he said. "If you're going to fight, you need to take it outside."

Pimentel held up his left hand and said, "This won't take long." With a swirl of the hand, he took off his hat and set it on the bar. At the same time, he slipped his right hand into his trousers pocket and brought it out in a fist.

Men stepped back to give the two fighters room, and the men sitting at the tables scraped the chair legs as they stood up.

Pimentel raised his fists in front of him, tossed his head, and said, "Come on."

Holbrook, lighter on his feet than I expected, bounced in, tossed a punch that hit Pimentel's forearms, and bounced back. From out of nowhere, it seemed, he produced a shiny-bladed knife that he opened with a flick of the wrist and a click.

A gasp went around the small crowd.

Holbrook said, "You've got a knife in your hand. Use it."

Pimentel's face fell as a mutter went through the crowd.

Holbrook made a thrust forward, with his hand and elbow high. Pimentel jumped back, keeping an eye on the shiny blade. Holbrook lunged again, taking a swipe that cut the sleeve on Pimentel's shirt as he raised his arm in defense.

No one made a move to interfere. Holbrook leapt forward again, this time with his arm low and the cutting edge of the blade up.

Pimentel, moving back and to the side, kept an eye on the knife. "So this is the way it is," he said. "Like before." His chest went up and down. "I know who you are."

Pimentel brought his hands together to open his knife, and Holbrook rushed him. Holbrook pushed with his left arm against Pimentel's raised forearms, and with his right hand lower, he drove the knife blade into Pimentel's midsection.

Pimentel hunched and stood back, dropping his unopened knife and pressing his hand against his stomach. Blood leaked between his fingers. His eyes widened, and his face went pale as he raised his head. He said, "You low-down sons of bitches. Takes two of you. Just like you did with Pete." His eyes rolled up, and he brought them back. He blinked. Tears started in his eyes. He pressed his upper teeth against his lower lip, and he seemed to be trying to pull together the strength to say something more, but he lost everything and slumped to the floor.

"You all saw it," said Holbrook. "The man had a knife, so I took it to him on his terms."

I HAD dug out a broken corral post and was tamping in a new one, sweating on a hot and hazy afternoon, when Evie came my way at a determined pace from the house. Finn and Holbrook had gone off on an afternoon ride, as they often did, and I imagined she had been waiting for them to leave.

She was wearing a light blue dress and a cloth hat, and her eyes had a bluish-grey cast to them. Her face was clouded, and her voice quavered as she said, "What happened? I know something bad happened, but Finn won't tell me."

I took in a full breath to steady my own nervousness. "There was a fight," I said. "Holbrook goaded the other man into it. The stranger had a way of wrapping his fist around a short, thick, pocketknife, the way some men use a brass bar or a lead weight or something similar. That's how he knocked Finn down. But Ross was ready for him and shook out a knife with about a five-inch blade, what I've heard some people call a stiletto. He got the best of the stranger with it."

Evie seemed to sink as the breath went out of her. "I was afraid something like that would happen, that they would . . . take care of him. Did he say anything, this Paul Pimentel?"

"He did. Something strange to me, but I think it had meaning for Finn and Ross."

Evie's eyes were wide open. "What was it?"

I moistened my lips. I felt that I had to tell her. "He said he knew who Ross was, and it was like before. They were doing to him what they did to Pete."

Evie gasped. "He said that name?"

"Yes, he did. It was the last thing he said."

Tears were falling as Evie shook her head. "I knew it. I knew it. I knew there was something familiar about him."

I wanted her to tell me more, so I prompted her. "About Pimentel?"

"Yes, but I'm sure that wasn't his name. I think he was Pete's brother, come to get even."

All this time, I had been holding the shovel upside-down, as I had been tamping the post with the tip of the handle. I turned the shovel right-side-up and rested the blade on the ground. I said, "Who was Pete?"

She had fear in her eyes as she looked at me straight and said, "You can't tell anybody I told you."

"I won't." At the same time, I was uneasy about what I might hear at this point.

She sniffed as she took in a deep breath. She swallowed and exhaled. "Pete was the one I was with before...before Finn. They all worked together—Pete, Finn, and Ross—in some kind of a gang, I think. I didn't ask questions. But they made money, in some way. Then one day they had a fight among them–about money, of course, or at least that was what I was told. They said it was a fair fight and Ross came out on top. Pete didn't. Finn said we had to get out of there. Things were too hot. So we came here, and he bought this place, and they've been carrying on like normal citizens ever since."

"And so you just...ended up with Finn?"

Evie's eyes did not meet mine. "I'm ashamed to say it, but yes. I felt I needed the protection, and he has a way of making a woman feel as if she's under his power."

I had heard women say things like that before, and I didn't think I could do anything about her situation. I said, "Who was Paul Pimentel, then?"

"Pete's brother, I'm sure. That's why I thought I recognized something about him. But the name wasn't Pimentel. It was Hester. And Pete didn't ever mention a brother named Paul. He only spoke of one named Jim."

"So this fellow, Paul or Jim, came to get even for what they did to his brother."

"I think so. I believe he was in prison for a while, so it might have taken him this long to finish his sentence and then find out where Finn was."

I was feeling a little steadier now. I was beginning to form an understanding of the whole situation, and I felt as if I was on the outside of it all. I said, "Not that it matters much now, but where did this earlier part take place?"

"In the mining country in Colorado. Up around Leadville."

I had a general idea of where that was. I said, "Well, the ranch country in Wyoming is an unsuspecting place."

Her blue-grey eyes met me now. "You have to promise me you won't tell anyone I told you any of this."

"I already told you I wouldn't."

Her voice sounded calm as she said, "I'm done with him. I have to find a way to get away from him."

My pulse picked up. A few seconds earlier, I felt as if I was on the outside, and now I felt as if I was being pulled in. "Do you think you can?" I asked.

"I have to."

In that moment I did not see her as an outlaw's woman, though I did not know what one would be like. But I saw her as a desirable woman, and that did not do me any good. I knew I should be making a plan to get as far away as possible. But instead I said, "Do you think you can do it by yourself?"

Her eyes met mine again as she said, "If I need help, I'll tell you."

Finn showed up in a calm mood at the bunkhouse the next morning. Sometimes he smoked tailor-made cigarettes, and on this occasion he drew a small case out of his vest pocket and took out a cigarette with neat, packed ends. He rapped it on his thumbnail, put it in his mouth, and lit it.

"Dan," he said, "I need you to go to the place up north for a couple of days. Get a precise count on the cows and calves in that pasture, and patch any weak spots in the fence. I think some of them have been gettin' out, and I don't know if any of them have strayed."

"I'll do it," I said. "How much grub should I take?"

"Figure enough for one night and two days. You can be back here for supper tomorrow night."

I counted the meals. "All right."

"And clean up the kitchen here before you go. Ross and I have a long day ourselves."

"I will."

I finished my coffee and began picking up my own plate, the platter the bacon had been on, and the tin plate that had held the biscuits. I wondered if

Finn and Holbrook were up to something. They had been keeping close company for the last few days and had been leaving me to work on my own. Now Finn was sending me several miles north, where he leased two sections of fenced pasture. I knew the place well enough, including the shanty we used as a line shack.

I had finished the cleanup and was putting a few personal items in my warbag when I heard a knock at the back door. I took soft steps across the room and cracked the door open.

Evie whispered, "Quick. I've only got a minute."

I opened the door and saw her pale, worried face. "What is it?" I asked.

She spoke in a rush. "Finn's in the outhouse, and Ross is getting their horses ready. I can't let them catch me here. But I had to tell you. We're on our own now."

"What do you mean?"

"I told him I was thinking of leaving, and he knocked all the resistance out of me. He has his ways. He told me I was never going to leave. Then he got it out of me that you told me what happened in town the night before last. I'm sorry I told him, but I couldn't help it. I was on my back, in bed. He had his full weight on me, and he had his hands on my throat." She was wringing her hands, and fear showed in her eyes. "I'm sorry. I have to go. But I had to tell you."

I studied her lost expression. I didn't know what to say or do. I was trying to take it all in.

Still in a whisper, she said, "I couldn't do anything else. I have to run now. I'm sorry. And Dan–"

"Yes?"

"If we both get out of this, I'd like to see you again."

She was gone on a fast run, a grey dress retreating in the clear light of morning.

I shook my head as I tried to catch up with what I had just heard. Finn was onto us, both of us. He knew why Evie wanted to leave, and he knew that I knew. I remembered what Evie had said the first day the stranger came by. She didn't expect anything good to come of this. I was beginning to agree.

My first impulse was to tie my bag on the back of the saddle and ride like hell as fast and as far as I could go. But a few things worked together to make me go through the motions of doing what the boss told me. First, I did not have my own horse, so if I went anywhere out of line, I could be accused of stealing another man's horse. Second, no matter where I went, I could count on Ross Holbrook tracking me down. He wouldn't take the trouble to brace me in front of other men. A bullet in the back would be fine with him. A queasy feeling ran between my shoulder blades.

Then there was Evie. I had the flaw of not being

able to see where she was at fault. I found it plumb easy to see how Finn was crooked and corrupt, and I despised the idea that a man could take the woman of a man he had killed or had had killed. And Evie had gone with him. I couldn't get past that, but I couldn't focus on it strong enough to make me decide I should get out of this spot any way I could and run like hell. I wanted to get out, but I wanted to see if she would, too.

So I went on about packing my things, along with a bait of grub. I carried my bag and my bedroll out to the barn, where I left them in the hay while I picked out a horse.

I selected a dark horse that I often rode. He was brownish-black with a thick, black mane and tail, and he had black lower legs. Some people would call him a bay. I just called him a dark horse. I chose him because he could go all day and never get tired, and because he did not have any light markings that could be seen at night.

Finn and Holbrook were lolling around at the hitching rail in front of the house, smoking cigarettes. For as much as they had a long day ahead of them, they didn't seem to be in a hurry. I assumed they were waiting for me to leave first, and I would be a bigger fool than I already was if I doubled around and came back to talk to Evie. So I saddled the horse, tied on my gear, and waved to Finn and

Holbrook as I set out on my way to the place up north.

I HAD the cattle counted by noon of the first day. The pasture consisted of only two sections, rolling country with no side canyons or hidey-holes. I came up with twenty-three cows and twenty-three calves, the same number we had put into the pasture some six weeks earlier, and the same number we had counted more than once in the meanwhile. I thought that Finn's concern about stock getting loose was a fish story, but orders were orders. With my gear stowed in the shack, I found the fence pliers, staples, and hammer, and I spent the afternoon riding fence and fixing weak spots.

I put the dark horse in the small corral as the sun slipped in the west. I had noticed earlier that there was a small stack of firewood inside, by the cast-iron stove. I split a few of the larger pieces with the loose-handled ax that stood in the corner by the stove wood, and I built a fire to fry the salt pork I had brought along. I left the door of the shack open, to let the out heat and to make it easier for me to keep a lookout.

I did not think that Holbrook would come for me in daylight. I more or less assumed he would come, just as I assumed that Finn would stay at home and keep an eye on Evie.

The sun went down, and a red-orange moon between a quarter and a half hung in the sky to the south. I plumped up my blankets to make my bedding look as if someone might be sleeping there, and I took my place behind the door.

I had not waited very long when I began to wonder whether I would have the calmness of mind and the steadiness of hand to fire a straight shot in the dark. I thought of an option. I crept across the room, found the ax in the faint light that came in the window, and tipped it up to let the head slide off. With the handle in my hands, I took a seat behind the door again.

I waited about two hours, and nobody came. I began to doubt my own judgment. Then I told myself that if I let my guard down, someone would come. For all I knew, a man like Holbrook might know when a victim was most likely to be in his deepest sleep, or in more general terms, he might know when all sleeping things were at their lowest ebb. That would be the time to be on the prowl.

My uneasiness began to eat on me. I wondered if anyone was going to do anything. I wondered if anyone was doing anything out of the ordinary back at the ranch.

My worry and my curiosity got the best of me. I saddled the dark horse and made ready to go take a look. I left my belongings and the grub in the line shack, but I took the ax handle.

The horse and I made good time in the thin moonlight, and I slid off to walk the last half-mile into the ranch. I took off my spurs, put them in the saddlebag, and left my hat on the saddle horn. Light was showing through the cracks in the barn, which did not surprise me. I tied the dark horse to a corral post in back, and holding the ax handle at my side, I made my way to the door. Light spilled out where the door was ajar, so I edged up to get a peek.

My stomach thumped at the sight of Finn Cole and Ross Holbrook, smoking cigarettes in the lamplight. They stood by the hind ends of three horses, one of which was saddled. Only Holbrook was wearing a hat, but both of them wore gunbelts.

Finn's voice carried. "We can get up there and back in a little more than two hours. Take care of numskull, leave her off, and go into town in the morning."

I wondered if I heard him right. What he said didn't make sense until I realized how many horses were tied up. I shifted to get a better look inside, and what I saw sent my blood to my feet.

Evie's body lay in a heap on the straw. She was wearing the same grey dress she was wearing when I saw her alive for the last time.

I did not know whether Finn had planned to do her in or if he had done so in the height of an argument, but it was evident what he and Holbrook were planning to do from this point on. They were going to make it look as if Evie had gone to the line shack to see me, I had done violence to her, and they had caught me red-handed.

Finn's voice rose again. "I need to go to the house. Go ahead and saddle these other two, and I'll be back in a few minutes."

Holbrook nodded, then palmed his face as he took a drag off of his cigarette. He did not seem bothered by the work at hand.

I sank back into the shadows as Finn walked out and left the door half-open. His spurs clinked as he continued on his way to the house.

I crept to the door and took another look. Holbrook had his back to me as he laid the blanket on the back of a sorrel horse and swung the saddle up and onto the blanket. He bent down, reached under, and pulled the cinch to him. When he straightened up again, he had the cigarette sticking out of the side of his mouth as he ran the latigo through the cinch ring and then the D-ring on the saddle.

I told myself it was now or never. I took the quietest steps I could, came up behind him, and raised the ax handle to shoulder level with both hands. The sorrel horse nickered, Ross Holbrook turned around, and the last thing he saw was the ax handle coming full force at the side of his head.

His hat fell away, and he went down like a sack of potatoes. I took in a quick, deep breath. Finn would be back any time, and I did not know if I would be lucky enough to do the same thing twice.

I heard footsteps and the light jingle of spurs. I did not have time to move to the side of the door, and because it opened outward, I would not have had a good hiding place anyway. I moved to the third horse and stood crouched on the other side of its hip.

Finn came into the lamplight at a jaunty pace, wearing a hat and carrying something I did not recognize at first. He stopped short, transferred the object to his left hand, and laid his right hand on his gun. I saw then that the object he carried was a small set of saddlebags, the kind that a rider drapes over the swells in front.

"Ross," he said. "Is there something wrong with you?" He squinted his eyes, looked to both sides, and moved forward. He started to kneel, then stood up and looked around again.

I could tell he had not placed me yet. With my gun drawn, I stepped to the hind end of the horse, stood sideways to give him less of a target, and aimed.

He drew his gun quicker than I would have imagined, but he did not make a good enough shot. I felt my left arm jerk backward with the impact of a bullet as my right forefinger pulled the trigger.

Finn Cole spilled over backwards and to the left, dropping his pistol and falling on the little set of saddlebags. As he went down, I saw a dark spot staining his vest.

I walked over to the place where Evie's body lay slumped in the straw. My voice did not sound strange to me as I said, "I'm sorry you didn't get more of a chance, Evie."

Though I had plenty of contempt for Finn and Holbrook, I had nothing more for a speech. My left arm was stinging and throbbing, so I rolled up my sleeve. A gouge had been taken out of the flesh on my lower arm, but as far as I could tell, no bone was broken, and no blood vessel was cut. The wound was bleeding, but the blood was not welling out.

Everything was quiet and still as I tore strips from my sleeve and used my teeth to tighten a bandage around my wound. The horses had jumped and grunted and crowded when the shots were fired, but they were quieted down now.

I had a dizzy sensation, a strange sense that I had lived through some of this before or that it had to happen as it did. I shook my head to be sure I was not dreaming. There was no changing what had taken place.

I walked out of the barn and into the faint moonlight. My mouth was dry, but my mind was clearing. My thoughts ranged from small to large. I realized there were two things I would never know—what

Finn had in the little saddlebags, and whether I could have killed a man and ended up with his woman.

I shook my head again, slower this time. I wasn't even sure I could kill a man until I saw what happened to Evie. Then there was no question.

I stood near the barn for a moment, breathing the night air and focusing on what I had to do next. Taking the horse of a man who had planned to kill me did not bother me a bit. I made my way out back, pulled myself into the saddle with one hand, and rode the dark horse away, into the night.

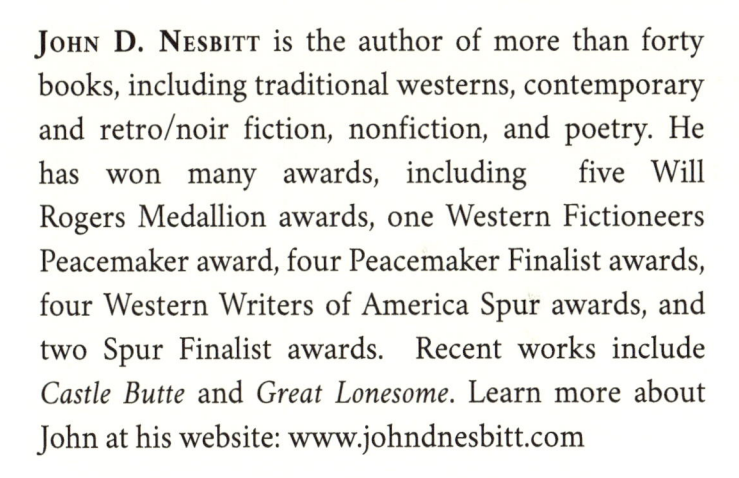

JOHN D. NESBITT is the author of more than forty books, including traditional westerns, contemporary and retro/noir fiction, nonfiction, and poetry. He has won many awards, including five Will Rogers Medallion awards, one Western Fictioneers Peacemaker award, four Peacemaker Finalist awards, four Western Writers of America Spur awards, and two Spur Finalist awards. Recent works include *Castle Butte* and *Great Lonesome*. Learn more about John at his website: www.johndnesbitt.com

A REQUIEM FOR LORD BYRON

RICHARD PROSCH

Bereft of my youthly idealism after the war betwixt the states and minus any accrued financial resources, I found myself behind a desk in the summer of 1875 mentally copulating with the ponderous sweet prose of young Algot Carlson.

Ah, precious Algot, a master baiter of reluctant words, he possessed the uncanny skill of coaxing a perspiration thin anecdote into a thick as honey narrative, leaving the reader's mind silent and still.

I reveled in his literary ability if not his penmanship.

With the golden glow of sunrise gracing my window, I made checkmarks on his paper next to the obvious cliches. For Algot, all was fair in love and war. He was, after all, *head over heels* in love, but rest assured—he assured us—*time would heal all wounds.*

The boy had a heart-shaped appreciation for all things trite and mundane.

And yet there was the quick wit of the Bard about him. The promise of a Keats, if only I could put my finger on it.

I let my attention be drawn by the birdsong outside my window, the final tremolo of the field sparrow, its call starting strong, receding like a penny drop. The Wyoming range marred only by a single structure, inspired vast contemplation--the delicate perfume of blooming wildflower and sage suggested the tenuous nature of life.

What hidden talents might any of us possess? Who knows when and where they might become manifest? A right turn, the wrong execution, who knows what position we'd achieve?

Young Algot had the makings of a Byron. Who except I would discover it?

Turning back to the composition, I studied Algot's structure, admired his sentences. His declarative phrases were bold, his confessions absolute. Here was not the usual obfuscation, soft and doughy, but instead a bold, resolute admission.

His prepositional phrases offered concrete relationships to objects and other characters.

His narrative pacing was dead on.

His descriptions were vivid, especially when it

came to coitus and killing, subject matter the young writer naturally shies away from.

Finished with the essay, I dropped back in my hardwood chair catching my breath, marveling at the talent of Algot Carlson, wondering how fate allowed me to discover such a gem.

Dare I say *a diamond in the rough*.

But perhaps such common indulgence of my own is the reason I never rose in the ranks at University, instead dropping away, settling for a job in the American West.

Removing my pocket watch, I took in the time.

Nodded to myself.

I put the watch back in my vest, beneath the tin star with its spear-like edges, its razor-sharp responsibilities.

Outside, the sun floated just above the far horizon, behind the wood scaffold where the hangman marched Algot Carlson to his death.

I carried the boy's last confession to the window, held it to my chest as the black hood was fitted, the lever tipped, the boy dropped.

Somewhere the field sparrow sang.

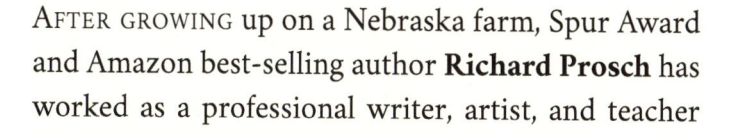

AFTER GROWING up on a Nebraska farm, Spur Award and Amazon best-selling author **Richard Prosch** has worked as a professional writer, artist, and teacher in Wyoming, South Carolina, and Missouri. His western crime fiction captures the fleeting history and lonely frontier stories of his youth where characters aren't always what they seem, and the wind-burned landscapes are filled with swift, deadly danger. Visit him online at RichardProsch.com.

HIRED GUNS: MULE'S GOLD

STEVE HOCKENSMITH

Diehl glanced off to the right, up the rocky incline that came to a jagged peak high against the blinding-bright afternoon sky. It was a brief look, no more than three seconds. But it was all Diehl needed.

When he looked away—focusing again on the narrow trail and the switchback just ahead that veered sharply up the mountain—he was gritting his teeth.

"Son of a bitch," he muttered. "You've done it to me again."

"What did you say?" Newburgh snapped.

Diehl stopped his dust-covered paint, forcing the men riding behind him—Newburgh on his big Morgan and Romo bringing up the rear with the swayback nag and the sluggish, balky pack mule—to rein up, as well.

"Have *I* done something wrong?" Romo asked.

"I wasn't talking to you either," said Diehl.

Newburgh tried to look back at Romo, but he was a hefty man perched precariously on his oversized horse, and he could only turn so far.

"He knows we stopped listening to him hours ago," he said. "Perhaps he's started talking to the mule."

"Well, I don't think it would do him any good," Romo said with a thin, wobbly smile. "I'm beginning to think she's deaf."

"So's the person I was talking to," said Diehl.

He swiveled to the left to gaze out at the vast yellow-gray vista of the desert. He lifted an arm and pointed at a distant mesa.

Newburgh and Romo peered at it.

"Umm...what are we looking at?" Romo asked.

"Nothing," said Diehl. He waved his hand as if making a point about the craggy bluffs stretched across the horizon. "I'm just pretending to admire the view."

"A lunatic," Newburgh said, shaking his head. "The man's a lunatic!"

For a moment, Diehl—tall, broad-shouldered, dark-haired, with a touch of gray at his temples and weariness in his brown eyes—said and did nothing. Then with one swift, smooth motion, he pulled his Winchester from its scabbard and dropped from his saddle. He walked to an outcropping of large rocks beside the trail, turned his back to the biggest, and started tugging at the top of his trousers with his free hand.

"Now what are you doing?" Newburgh asked.

"What does it look like I'm doing?" said Diehl.

He dropped to a crouch beside the boulder.

"It looks like you're about to...well...you know," said Newburgh. He cleared his throat. "Relieve yourself."

"Exactly," said Diehl. "And I'm hoping the men watching us from the bluffs aren't wondering why I took my rifle along."

Romo stiffened.

Newburgh harrumphed.

"Look the other way, will you?" Diehl said. "I'm supposed to be doing something disgusting down here."

"Oh, but you *are*," said Newburgh, averting his eyes. Unlike Diehl, who was wearing a battered Stetson and faded denims and a plain yellow shirt, he was dressed like Stanley setting off to find Dr. Livingston—puttees, jodhpurs, khaki jacket and pith helmet. He pulled out a handkerchief and patted his sweaty, fleshy face. "This is what I get for a partner. A gibbering ninny afraid of his own shadow. What do you think, Romo—does the Mexican sun bake some men's brains? He seemed sane back in Tucson."

Romo eyed the barren, craggy slopes above them and said nothing.

Diehl levered a round into the chamber of his Winchester. The hard, metallic sound of it seemed to stir some unhappy memory in him. He looked down at the rifle and frowned.

"I'm telling you someone's up there waiting for us to round the bend and come closer," he said. "At least four men. Probably more."

Newburgh snorted. "Oh, really. Just like somebody's been following us all day?"

"Somebody *has* been following us all day," Diehl said.

"So you keep insisting. Only tell me this." Newburgh jabbed a chubby finger up at the summit. "How did they get ahead of us without being seen? By anyone other than you, I mean."

"I didn't say the somebody following us and the somebody ahead of us were the same somebody."

Newburgh rolled his eyes. "Somebodies, somebodies everywhere...and all of them with bloody machetes, no doubt."

"Machetes would be nice. Better than rifles," said Diehl. "Just in case, you two ought to take cover, too. Whoever's up there is sure to have noticed all the *pointing*, Newburgh."

Moving quickly but calmly, Romo dismounted and pulled out his own rifle—a battered carbine that looked older than him. He hustled over to join Diehl by the rocks.

Newburgh just leaned back in his saddle, the leather creaking as he jutted out his round belly.

"Oh, that's just lovely," he said, flapping a hand at Romo. "Now he's got you doing it. You who should know better."

Romo squatted beside Diehl, then pivoted to squint up at Newburgh. His small frame and boyish, earnest face and simple, well-tailored clothes—black suit and white shirt—made him look like a college student confused by a teacher's disapproval.

"Why should I 'know better'?" he asked.

"Because you're Mexican, Alfonse. You're Mexican," Newburgh said.

"Alfonso," Romo corrected.

Newburgh went on as if he hadn't heard him.

"Just because we're in Sonora you're not going to see bandits lurking behind every cactus. Or so I would have hoped."

"But there *are* bandits in Sonora, Mr. Newburgh," Romo said.

"And have you seen any today?" Newburgh asked.

Romo's eyes darted toward Diehl. "Well...no."

"And these bandits you haven't seen," said Newburgh, "they'd be so stupid they'd waylay a party of prospectors that hasn't even begun prospecting yet? With nothing to steal but pickaxes and pans and slats for a sluice box?"

"And food," said Diehl. "And guns. And ammunition."

Newburgh pounded his saddle horn with a clenched fist. "But no gold yet. No *gold*! Think, man! They don't rob you going *up* the mountain. They rob you coming *down* the mountain…if they rob you at all. You shouldn't believe all the blood and thunder you read in the newspapers, Diehl."

"You just don't want to get down off that elephant you're riding," Diehl said, "because you can barely haul your big ass on."

Newburgh let out another harrumph. "You're trying to goad me. Well, I will overlook the offensive nature of that remark…while acknowledging that I do indeed have no desire to waste my time or energy on ups and downs and scurryings about based on the unfounded fears of a fainthearted shop clerk."

Diehl scowled and looked away.

"I've been more than a shop clerk," he mumbled.

"So…what are we going to do?" Romo asked.

"*You* are going to get back on your horse before it wanders off with our mule," Newburgh told him. "*I* am going to carry on and find that abandoned mine you were supposed to lead us to. And *Mr. Diehl*…he can just keep cowering here until he comes to his senses and regains his manhood."

Romo's eyes widened slightly. He made no move to get up and return to his horse. Without a word, he turned to look at Diehl.

Diehl nodded down at the young man's carbine.

"You any good with that old thing?" he asked.

Romo shrugged. "I can't say. I just bought it yesterday in Nogales."

Diehl's head dropped.

"I'm a fair shot, though," Romo went on. "At least I used to be. I bagged a lot of turkeys and quail when I was a boy."

"Turkeys and quail. When you were a boy," Diehl said, staring down at his boots. "Well, *Alfonso*, your targets are about to get a bit bigger."

He leaned to look up and down the trail winding along the mountainside. He pointed to his left, back the way they'd come.

"I'm going to head that way then work my way up higher for a better look," he said. "You cover me."

"Cover you?" Romo said.

"You know…if someone tries to shoot me, you shoot them? Preferably before they *do* shoot me?"

Romo nodded. "Oh. Right. I understand."

"Tommyrot!" Newburgh said. "I'm not going to sit here broiling for the next half hour while you go scampering about in the rocks looking for *banditos* who exist only in your imagination."

He looked up at the mountaintop and cupped a hand to his mouth.

"Hola! Amigos! We have-o mucho oro! Oro oro! Gold! Come-o and-o get it-o!"

"Newburgh, you damn fool!" Diehl spat.

Newburgh held his hand out toward the peaks and gave Diehl a haughty "told you so" look.

"See?" he said. "Nothing."

There was a *pop* from somewhere in the bluffs above them, followed by a thud and a puff of dust from the front of Newburgh's jacket.

The horses flinched and whinnied. The mule didn't.

"Dios mío!" Romo gasped.

"Oh," said Newburgh.

There was another *pop*, another thud, another puff of dust from Newburgh's chest.

The horses nickered nervously. Again, the mule didn't react at all.

Newburgh slowly, slowly, slowly slid sideways from his saddle.

When the big man's bulk came crashing to the ground, the horses trotted forward a few steps, shaking their heads. The mule, tethered to Romo's saddle, brayed as it was unwillingly dragged along.

Newburgh rolled onto his back and groaned.

"*Stay still*," Diehl hissed at him.

"It appears...I owe you an apology," Newburgh said weakly.

He began struggling to push himself up.

"Don't move, dammit," Diehl said.

Newburgh sat up.

Romo started toward him. Diehl thrust out an arm to hold the younger man back.

"I do believe...I have been shot," Newburgh said, staring down in shock at the two bloody holes in his jacket. He looked up at Diehl and Romo and smiled. "Is there a...doctor in the house?"

More shots rang out, louder than the first — from a bigger, closer gun.

Newburgh flopped back, arms splayed wide.

The horses bolted. The mule, tied loosely with a bowline hitch so it wouldn't drag Romo along if it went over a cliff, dug in its hooves and jerked its lead rope free. It came to a stop beside Diehl and Romo as the horses galloped along the curve in the trail and charged on up the mountain.

The sound of pounding hooves died away slowly, then there was silence. It was broken by a burst of fast, harsh Spanish. One man was shouting, then another, then yet another.

Diehl could only understand the curses.

"What are they saying?" he asked Romo, who was staring in horror at Newburgh's bloodied body on the other side of the mule.

The younger man blinked, then cocked his head and listened.

"They're yelling at whoever finished off Mr. Newburgh," he said. "They're mad at him for spooking the horses." Romo frowned. "He says it doesn't matter because there was bound to be more shooting anyway."

"Cállate! Cállate! Cállate!" one of the men bellowed.

Diehl didn't need a translation for that.

"Shut up! Shut up! Shut up!" he was saying.

The other men obeyed.

So there was a leader.

"Hola, Americanos!" the man called out. "Bienvenido a Mexico! Hablas Español?"

Romo looked over at Diehl.

"Don't answer," Diehl said.

"Sí? No?" the bandit yelled. "Huh?"

He paused, waiting for an answer, then went on in Spanish Diehl couldn't follow.

"He says he's sorry about our friend, but it shows that they're serious," Romo translated. "They'd rather not fight, though. They'll spare us if...."

Romo grimaced and shook his head.

"What?" Diehl said.

"They'll spare us...if we leave them the gold."

Diehl turned to glower at Newburgh. Not that Newburgh noticed. He was on his back, motionless, his round belly and wide, unblinking eyes pointed up at the sun.

A shaft of gold suddenly appeared between Diehl and the body.

The mule, oblivious to everything, was unleashing a stream of urine.

"Come-o and-o get it-o," Diehl sighed.

The bandit chief began shouting down to them again. Diehl caught the words "oro" and "amigos." And something more.

He heard the clatter of rocks and pebbles sliding down toward the trail off to the left. Then he heard it on the right.

The leader kept jabbering at them about *misericordia*— mercy—even as his men were creeping down the incline.

It was too late to outflank the bandits. They were doing the flanking first. The only question now was when the shooting would start again.

It didn't stay a question long. There was a blast from the right, and a bullet ricocheted off the top of the boulder, showering Diehl and Romo with a spray of gray chips.

Diehl and Romo instinctively shrank down further.

The mule just stopped pissing and stared off placidly at nothing.

Another shot from the same direction thudded into the ground near Diehl's boots.

"Well, damn," Diehl growled.

He took one quick, crouching step away from the rocks, pivoted toward where the shots had come from and started firing. He didn't even spot who he was shooting at until he pulled the trigger the third time and a man in a white shirt and a wide-brimmed hat arched his back, dropped his rifle and started rolling down the slope forty yards away.

There was a loud *crack* behind Diehl, and when he dived back behind the boulder he saw that Romo had popped up to fire in the opposite direction.

"Get down!" Diehl barked as the young man laboriously cocked the hammer and worked the lever in preparation for another shot.

There was a ragged volley of return fire, and bullets slammed into the rocks and dirt all around Romo. He yelped and ducked down beside Diehl.

The mule swished its tail as if shooing off a fly but otherwise took no notice of the battle going on around it. There could be no question now as to whether or not it was deaf.

"We won't get away with that again. There's too many of 'em," Diehl said. "Our only chance—and it's not a good one—is to stay hunkered down here and hope we can fight 'em off when they...what?"

Romo was gaping in dismay at the mule.

Diehl peered beneath the animal, thinking some of the bandits might be slipping over the ridge beyond it. He saw nothing but rocks and sky.

"What?" Diehl said again.

Romo lifted a trembling hand and pointed at the mule. Or at something strapped to it, to be more exact. The biggest box on its back.

The one marked DYNAMITE.

"Son of a *bitch*," Diehl said.

If just one stray shot hit that box, every stick of dynamite inside it would go off.

Diehl was about to be killed by an exploding mule.

He shook his head. Then he started to laugh. Then he stopped and shook his head again.

He picked up a rock the size of a teacup and threw it at the mule's haunch. It bounced off and clattered down onto the trail.

The mule kicked back with its right leg and craned its neck to throw a glare at Diehl.

And that was all. It didn't leave.

A bullet smashed into the boulder behind Diehl and Romo. Then another plowed into the ground between them and the mule.

Romo clasped his hands and closed his eyes and began murmuring softly.

He was praying.

"Don't give Him the satisfaction," Diehl said.

Romo opened one eye. "Qué?"

Diehl nodded down at the other man's carbine. "Your hands'll do more good on your gun."

Another shot spat up dust and pebbles not far from their feet. The bandits were getting a better angle now. It was only a matter of time. One way or another — caught in a crossfire or blown to bits by a bomb-mule — their time was almost up.

There was a soft, slow, steady crunching noise to the right. Then the same sound came from the left.

The bandits were close enough now to hear their footsteps.

"Get ready," Diehl whispered.

Romo nodded, both eyes open again, and clutched his carbine tightly.

Darkness fell over a big rock about thirty feet off. A shadow.

Diehl brought up his rifle.

The boom came before he squeezed the trigger. A distant blast that echoed longer than any previous shot.

There was a grunt, then a thud and a clatter. The shadow Diehl had been watching disappeared, and he heard quick, whispered questions all around it.

Qué? Quien? Dónde?

Who? What? Where?

Another shot rang out, and this time the grunt-thud-clatter that followed was accompanied by the sight of a limp body rolling down onto the trail.

"Vamonos! Vamonos!" a man cried, and there was nothing soft or slow about the sound of footsteps now. The bandits were fleeing.

"This is our chance!" Diehl said.

He popped up over the boulder and looked for a target. He saw one immediately—a man wearing bandoliers scrambling up the slope. Diehl drew a bead on the point where the bandoliers crossed—X marks the spot—and put a bullet in his back. Romo rose up beside him as he did the same to another man, then another.

Romo brought up his carbine...then lowered it again.

"They're running away," he said.

"Right," said Diehl, hunting for a fresh target. "And we don't want them coming back."

He trained his Winchester on a bandit as he rushed toward a crest forty yards up the incline.

There was another far-off bang, and the man threw out his arms, dropped his rifle and toppled backwards.

Three of his fellow bandits scrambled past him and disappeared over the ridge.

"Damn," said Diehl.

Three bandits—four if you counted the chief, who'd probably stayed safe at the top of the grade to begin with — was more than enough to ambush them again down the trail.

Diehl slowly moved his gunsight along the ridgeline, hoping to spot the rounded yellow dome of a sombrero rising up as one of the men dared a peek back at him. A surprising sound echoed down instead.

A short, piercing shriek. Followed by another scream that lasted longer but ended just as abruptly.

Two shots rang out from the ridge, but there were no bullet strikes around Diehl or Romo or the mule. Whoever was doing the shooting and whoever was getting shot — both were up the hill.

A man in a checked shirt and moccasin boots stepped out onto one of the jutting bluffs. His long, dark hair and breechcloth fluttered in the breeze. He lifted the rifle he was carrying over his head with one hand.

"*Ay de mi!*" Romo cried, bringing up his own rifle.

Diehl reached over and shoved the barrel down.

"Don't," he said.

"But don't you see?" Romo said. "An Apache!"

Diehl nodded. "Oh, I see."

He let go of Romo's rifle, then cupped his hand beside his mouth.

"*Hola*, Eskaminzim!" he called.

"Hello, you dumb bastard!" the Apache called back.

Diehl dropped his hand and sighed.

"You *know* him?" Romo asked, shocked.

"He called me a dumb bastard, didn't he?" Diehl said with a shrug. "We know each other."

He cupped his hand to his mouth again.

"Where's Hoop?" he shouted.

Eskaminzim pointed down at Diehl with his rifle. Even from fifty yards off the big grin on his face was easy to see.

"Where do you think, you blind pendejo?" the Apache laughed.

Diehl looked over his shoulder. Romo turned, too—and his jaw dropped.

A tall, brawny black man was climbing up onto the trail about thirty feet away. He was wearing a navy blue shirt, a tan hat with the brim pinned flat in front and trousers held up with gray suspenders. In his hands was a long, heavy-looking rifle.

Diehl gave the man a nod.

"Hoop," he said.

The man nodded back.

"Diehl," he said.

He had a Southern accent that stretched the name out till it broke in two. *Deee-ul.*

Diehl stepped out to glare around the mule at Newburgh's body. Flies were already finding the holes in it.

"Told you we were being followed," Diehl said to the corpse.

"Who are these men?" Romo asked.

"Old...colleagues," Diehl said. "Looking for me, I assume...?"

"That's right," the man called Hoop said. He gave Newburgh a brief, dismissive glance as he walked toward Diehl.

The mule noted that someone was joining them on the trail with nothing but a twitch of the ears and a swish of the tail.

"Got a message for you," Hoop said. He pulled a

folded piece of paper from a trouser pocket and held it out to Diehl. "From the old man."

Diehl took the letter but didn't open it.

"Job?" he asked.

Hoop nodded. "Job."

"Same old shit?" Diehl asked.

Hoop nodded again, this time with the slightest hint of a smile curling one corner of his mouth.

"Same ol' shit," he said.

"Well...," Diehl said, "lucky for him I just happen to find myself at liberty and ready to entertain offers."

Hoop's smile widened ever so slightly.

"Broke and hungry, in other words?" he said.

"That, too," said Diehl.

He looked down at the letter in his hand and took a deep breath. He'd thought he was done working for the old man—thought he was done killing—but what the hell. It was better than being shot or starving.

He'd squandered his chance to start over. Maybe he was getting another one.

Maybe God wasn't out to get him after all.

The mule finally noticed that Diehl was standing behind him.

It kicked him.

STEVE HOCKENSMITH'S FIRST NOVEL, the mystery/Western hybrid *Holmes on the Range*, was a finalist for the Edgar, Shamus, and Anthony awards. He's gone on to write five sequels (so far) as well as the New York Times bestseller *Pride and Prejudice and Zombies: Dawn of the Dreadfuls*, the tarot-themed mystery *The White Magic Five and Dime* and other books. He's also a widely published writer of short stories and mysteries for children. You can learn more about him at stevehockensmith.com.

HOLLY JOLLY COURTSHIP

JACQUIE ROGERS

Henderson Flats, Owyhee County, Idaho Territory—1885

Jack Wade, feeling a mite dapper in his new town clothes, whistled as he drove his shiny new courting buggy through Henderson Flats on his way to his new farm eight miles west of town. After he'd sold his first year's crops for a tidy sum, he'd gone on a buying spree—he had a purpose. Jack had worked his fingers to the bone all summer and fall, so during the winter he planned to achieve his goal and have a good time doing it.

Yep, he planned get hitched. It was time.

He didn't have much money left but he reckoned with nice clothes and a brand spankin' new buggy, he'd be sure to catch a smart and beautiful wife before Christmas. Maybe even without talking, which was a mite troublesome for him when it came to pretty gals. But he needed a helpmate, for he was getting mighty tired of his own cooking. A man could eat graveyard stew only so long. And it took two to make a family—there was no way around that.

An old man driving a carriage waved to him as they passed. Jack waved back, but then his buggy lurched and his team jerked. The buggy rolled and Jack ended up face down in the powdery alkali dirt.

The tall, thin-haired old man sat on his carriage and scowled through his spectacles at Jack. "You hurt, boy?"

Jack spat a clod out of his mouth and pushed himself to his knees. "Nope." Just his pride. And dang, after three years of fighting in the Indian Wars and a year toiling on his new farm, he sure didn't consider himself a boy.

He stood and glanced around at his buggy—the horses seemed all right, just a mite jumpy, but the overturned wadded up buggy was unrecognizable.

"My fault," the old man said. "I cut the corner too tight and my rear wheel caught your buggy's wheel and flipped it. He reached into his vest pocket and pulled out some money. "Here's a few dollars to tide you over. I'll arrange for the bank to pay the blacksmith for repairs out of my account. Tell him Moses Alden said so." He doffed his hat. "Good day." He flicked the reins and drove off.

Jack scooped up a handful of rocks and flung

them dirt as he watched the buggy kick up dust down the road. He was mighty het up, what with the old man not even offering to take him back to town and all. At least the old geezer had left a few bucks. Moses Alden. Jack would remember that name.

Getting his team unhitched proved to be quite a tussle what with the lines wound around the twisted singletree. Both horses snorted and stomped, unnerved about the unfortunate accident. After a considerable amount of cooing and patting, he managed to get them both calm enough so he could free them from the harness.

His new sack suit had rips down one britches leg and another in the jacket sleeve plus tatters everywhere else. Not fifteen minutes after he'd bought the first new suit he'd ever owned—his Christmas present to himself—the dang thing was ready for the rag bag. He mounted the calmest horse bareback, took the other by the lead rope, and rode directly to the livery.

The burly middle-aged smithy, Jonas Howard, was hammering away at some hot metal on his anvil into a shape that looked to be a hinge of some sort.

"You know that buggy you just sold me?" Jack asked.

"Yeah," the blacksmith said without missing a beat with his hammer.

"Some old man ran into me and busted it all up.

Said if you'd fix it, the bank will pay you out of his account."

Howard tossed his hammer in the bucket and wiped the sweat from his brow. "The hell you say."

"Yep. Goes by Moses Alden. You heard of him?"

"Nope. He ain't from these here parts."

"I was afraid of that. I'll go over to the bank and see if he's good for it."

Howard followed Jack out, grabbing his hat as he passed through the door. "I expect you want to me fetch the buggy and bring it here."

"Yep. Much obliged. If you can't fix it, you might as well keep it for scrap. I'll help you move it after I talk to the banker."

Once Jack got back from the banker, who assured him that Moses Alden had left plenty enough money to pay for repairs, Jack asked Howard what he thought about fixing the buggy.

"I went out and seen it." Howard shook his head and pursed his lips—Jack knew he was about to get some bad news. "Ain't hardly worth fixing, but I can get 'er done."

"Might as well go ahead—the buggy's brand new and my pockets are empty, so it's either that or no buggy at all." He sure didn't want to go courting in a hay wagon.

"It'll never look brand new again, but I'll give it my best shot."

Henderson Flats, Owyhee County, Idaho Territory —October, 1885

Greta loved dancing so Saturday nights at the Claytonia Dance Hall was the highlight of her week. She'd come with her much older sister and brother-in-law, Grace and Fred Ross, with whom Greta had lived since her mother had passed on when she was only three. Her father's job took him on the road most of the year, so he'd been unable to care for a small child. And now, she might as well stay until she graduated from school.

The Rosses' four boys, Greta's nephews, were the same age or older than she, so their friends were her friends. All four were a lot of fun, popular with the ladies, and she loved them dearly, especially her dance partner, Joe.

"Better have a drink while you have the chance." Joe handed her some lemonade. "A big crowd's here for the dance tonight—a lot of new folks." Joe waggled his eyebrows as a group of single ladies came in, giggling and pretty much keeping to themselves. "Looks like a full house. Full of dang fine women."

Greta elbowed her cousin. "You have some good pickins—they're very pretty. How many of them will fall under the spell of your nimble dancing by the end of the evening?"

He winked and said, "All of them."

She punched his shoulder and their other friends laughed. She and Joe had learned to dance together and they were good at it even though Joe was fourteen inches taller than her not-quite-five-feet.

Attendees had a habit of not wanting to be the first dancers on the floor, so the owner of the new dance hall had taken care of that by asking six of the regulars who could dance well to start off each dance. Greta and her cousin being two of them. In exchange, they received free admission and refreshments.

The chosen dancers stood just inside the front door greeting and assessing the crowd as people filtered in. Several couples came in, then three men in their mid-twenties.

"Oh, look at that bunch," her friend Vanette said.

"I am. I am." And Greta was—at one in particular.

The first was a stringbean type with big ears and a bigger smile. He wasn't very handsome but Greta bet he did all right with the ladies. The second, good-looking enough, turned and bowed at the prettiest lady in the room, which was her friend Mary. They wouldn't have any trouble getting him on the floor.

The third was the one who caught her attention. He had a jaunty stride, broad shoulders, and a confident smile, but he went straight to the refreshment table without greeting a single other person. Ah, a shy one. Dark-haired, heavy-browed, strong. Greta had to take a second look. And a third. Silently, she laid claim.

The third dancer, Mary, nudged her. "Look at those shoulders—wouldn't you like to rest your head on them? Think we can get him to dance?"

"You shouldn't waste your time on him," Joe said. "Looks like he came with his friends and doesn't have any intention of dancing with the ladies."

Greta agreed that he didn't look eager to dance, but she sure didn't consider him a waste of time by any means, and she'd never back down from a challenge.

Mary, who had striking blond hair rather than dark like Greta's own, or brown like Vanette's, clasped her hands to her breast and bobbed about with excitement. "I'll get him to dance—just you wait and see!"

Not to be outdone, Vanette said, "Sure, after I get him warmed up for you."

Mary stuck her chin out. "I'll bet you two bits I can get him to dance."

Greta couldn't believe that Mary would bet money on such a thing, but neither was she about to be left out. Besides, he was hers—they just didn't know it yet. "You both will owe me two bits before the night's over. Mark my words."

The owner came over and clapped his hands at the six dancers. "Are you ready? I'll give the band the nod in less than five minutes, so each couple take a side so you don't all come out from the same place."

Joe steered Greta to the side opposite the handsome man in question, who stood next to the Christmas tree.

"You're not making this easy for me, Joe. Just see if I help you out."

"I don't need any help."

There was some truth to that. The ladies stumbled all over themselves to dance with him.

"Even so, once we split up, you'll not be able to get in my way."

It wasn't just the competition between girls. The shy man, without a doubt, was the most interesting man in the room and she couldn't help but sneak peeks at him more often than she'd ought. His powerful shoulders and roguish grin attracted the attention of every woman in the hall, although he seemed utterly unaware of it.

Joe elbowed her. "You're staring."

Greta was saved by the music, for the band struck up a lively polka. She grabbed Joe and off they went. She loved to polka, and with Joe's height, sometimes she felt as if she were flying.

Joe spun her around the room. She glanced at the fine fellow as she and Joe danced by the refreshment table and she smiled when he caught her looking at him.

"Yes, Greta, he's watching. He marked you the minute he walked into this room."

"You're joshing me. Any man would be interested in Mary or Vanette before they'd give me a second look."

"I don't agree at all. You're cute as a button—short and sweet. And you surely have to know you've never had to sit out a dance. There's a reason for that."

When the owner gave the sign to split, Joe twirled Greta and she backed away, laughing. When she turned around to ask a man to dance, she ran right square into the man in question. He didn't budge—was more like a brick wall. A brick wall with muscular arms that steadied her.

She gazed into his eyes. Dark green eyes—full of kindness and mischief all at the same time. Her words wouldn't come out when she tried to ask him to dance. She stared at him and he gazed right back. Finally, she gathered her wits and asked, "Would you finish this dance with me?"

"No, miss. I can't polka."

"Can you two-step?"

"Well, my brother showed me how. He ain't much of a dancer and he ain't pretty at all—not like you." He looked away.

Greta vowed that he'd not only dance with her—she'd get him to ask to court her.

Jack had the best woman in the place right here in his arms, and he didn't even know how to dance. Now if that wasn't a heckuva note. First dance, too. Maybe she'd go out to the porch and sit with him on the swing. Then again, if he danced with her, he wouldn't have to think of anything to say.

"We have to dance or people will talk, what with you holding me."

He noticed she hadn't seemed to mind, though. "A two-step is all right?"

She tugged him onto the dance floor. "Yes, it's just fine."

He wasn't quite sure where to put his hands. She was a foot shorter than his brother. But when his left hand settled on her waist, she took his right.

"You lead," she said. "Just step to the beat of the music and you'll be fine."

Music? It was as if they were the only two in the room, and he'd honed in on her lilting voice—and didn't hear a single note the band played. But he paid attention so as not to make more of a fool of himself than he already had. She'd never sit on the porch with him if he acted like a big ox.

The first two steps went all right. The third, he stepped on her foot.

"I'm sorry."

"It's fine. Just keep dancing and I'll watch for both of us."

It had to be the longest song in the world—or the shortest, because he didn't want to let her go. He concentrated on counting his steps and not walking all over the prettiest girl in the room. His friends Larry and Jim both danced up a storm, and they'd come for her next—Jack didn't want that.

"Would you dance the next song with me?" he asked.

She leaned into him, which made him hopeful.

"No, I can't. I'm supposed to dance with different men to keep everyone on the floor."

"Oh." Now he did feel like a fool. "That's why you came to me, then."

"No, I came to you because I wanted to dance with you first. Ask me for the third dance—I'll say yes. And after that, I might need some refreshments."

The music stopped and she spun away to the tall man he'd seen her with before. Jack had to wonder why her partner hadn't been more attentive.

Both his buddies had already found women for the second dance. Jack had no interest in any of the women except the short black-haired girl, and he didn't even know her name. He went back to the Christmas tree and stood as close to the dance floor as he could get without someone tromping on him.

He kept a close watch on his lady—she'd danced with two other fellows. Her bright smile made him feel good all over and he could hardly wait until the third song started, even if he did have to dance to get her in his arms. No obstacle was too steep. He caught her gaze a time or two and she beamed a smile at him, which he caught in his heart.

THE MINUTE the second dance ended, Greta turned around and the very man she was looking for stood right there.

"May I have this dance?" His baritone voice gave her the lightest, happiest feeling.

"Yes, you may—as soon as the music starts." Although she already felt as if she were dancing, just being near him.

"I have a better idea. We could go sit on the porch swing. It'd be easier on your toes."

She'd like nothing better. "Sorry, but I have to stay in here, at least until one dance after the intermission."

"I don't want you to dance with all them other fellers. Stay with me."

She looked for Joe—she was his partner and she didn't want to leave him in the lurch, but she did want to know this man better.

"Do you have a name?"

"Me? I'm Jack Wade. You?"

The music started up and Jack's friend—the tall

one with big ears—swung Vanette by them. She leaned out and said, "Her name's Greta."

Greta put her hand on his shoulder and her other in his palm. "Let's dance before the owner hollers at me."

He pulled her close—much closer than he should've, but she didn't care.

"Mmm," he murmured in her ear, "we wouldn't want that."

The fourth dance was a slow one, which suited Greta just fine because her toes were getting a mite tender from Jack stepping on them. And she sorely regretted her commitment to stay the entire three hours and dance with different men. Still, she'd given her word.

"I have a buggy," he mumbled in her ear as they swayed to the music. "I can take you home."

"I won't be leaving until closing time, and I came with my sister—she's old enough to be my mother and doesn't let me out of her sight. But maybe you could drive me and the rest of the family could follow. I'll see if Joe can talk her into it."

"Who's Joe?"

"My dancing partner." She pointed to Joe, who was flirting with one of Greta's school friends. "And my nephew. He's a year older than I am—and a sweet talker. My sister can rarely deny him."

"You're staying at your sister's place for the weekend?" Jack asked. "Where do you live?"

"Yes, and every weekend. I live with my sister and her family on the other side of the river."

"I live the opposite direction—over by Graveyard Point, so likely I'll just take you to the ferry and go home. Elsewise, it'll be too hard on the horses."

Greta was flattered he'd even take her to the ferry considering Graveyard Point was eight miles the other direction. "I'd like that. Thank you."

Jack's friends wanted to leave and go to Wilson's Saloon, but Jack told them to go ahead—he was staying at the dance.

"Found yourself a cute little calico, I see," Larry teased.

Normally, that wouldn't have set Jack off, but he had to hold himself back to keep from punching his friend in the kisser. "She's a nice girl," was all he said.

After two hours of watching his gal dance with every dang man in the room, he was all too happy when the owner announced closing time. Jack headed straight for Greta. She grabbed his hand and led him to an older couple.

"Jack, this is my sister Grace. Grace, this is Jack—he offered to take me home."

"How do you do, Jack." Grace offered her hand and he kissed the back of it.

"Over my dead body," the man standing next to

her said, but he smiled. He offered to shake and Jack did. "My name's Fred Ross. And no insult to you, son, but she looks to be five years younger than you. I think you better go find yourself another woman—one a little older."

"But Fred!" Greta protested, her eyes sparking.

And that was the end of the night. Jack went home, looking forward to the next Saturday night dance, which wouldn't happen for more than a month. Most particularly, he looked forward to seeing Greta again—he could do without the dance. But if dancing was what it took to woo her, then he'd do it.

GRETA HAD FLOATED on air since Jack had attended the next dance the second week in December. The third Saturday would be the annual Henderson Flats Christmas Social and later, a dance at Claytonia. She looked forward to the event—always fun—but she really and truly looked forward to seeing Jack again.

She and Vanette checked the mail on the way home from school. "I got a letter from Jack!"

"Looks like you've got yourself an admirer." Vanette grabbed the letter from Greta's hands and Greta snatched it right back.

"I'm opening it now. We're meeting at the Christmas social on Saturday, and then going to the dance after." She carefully opened it, for she planned to keep it in her hope chest.

Dear Greta,

I can't come Saturday because of farm chores and a sick cow.

Your friend,

Jack

Tears welled in her eyes with her bitter disappointment. She read it again, just because. And again.

"What's it say?" Vanette asked.

"He's not coming to the Christmas social or the dance, either." She folded the letter and put it back in the envelope. "So it looks like I'm going by myself. Joe already asked Mary to the social, and they're planning to dance together, too, so that leaves me alone."

"Oh, pooh. But there are plenty of men who'll gladly dance with you, and you know it. You don't need a beau at the social—we'll all be there having a good time. You won't even miss him."

Yes, she would. Sorely. She missed him every minute.

A FEW DAYS LATER, she received another letter.

Dear Greta,

May I pick you up Sunday for dinner with my family?

Your friend,

Jack

Her spirits lifted considerably and she scribbled out an acceptance right there in the post office and mailed it. The clerk told her that he should receive it Friday, "If he picks up his mail."

Vanette wanted to go shopping but Greta couldn't get into the Christmas spirit.

"What do you want for Christmas?" Vanette asked.

"Jack." And it was true. She couldn't think of anything she wanted more.

"Let's get some red and green hair ribbons for the Christmas social, and I bet Jack won't be able to resist them next time he sees you."

Greta bought two red ribbons, and a white one just because she thought it contrasted nicely with her dark hair. The green ones looked quite splendid in Vanette's hair and she bought two. Then Greta saw a pair of sheepskin earmuffs. It took every penny she had but she bought them for Jack's Christmas present, for his ears had been red with cold when he'd arrived at the last dance at Claytonia.

"I'll be to your house an hour early and we can get ready for the social together," Vanette said.

"I'm more concerned about Sunday. If my sister will let me go, I'll meet Jack's family at his dinner."

"Oooh, his family. He must be a serious beau. I

bet you'll have a ring on your finger before Christmas."

"Not if we don't see each other more."

"Is he picking you up after church?"

"I don't know." Greta hadn't seen him in church —Henderson Flats folks had church in the schoolhouse. "I think he's new to the area, and he's been farming all summer, so I doubt if he's been. Besides, it's eight miles from his farm, so it would be hard for him to get to morning services after his chores."

"I wonder what his house looks like."

Greta wondered, too. "I'll find out Sunday." He'd told her the house only had two rooms—a kitchen and a bedroom—but he'd planned to build two more rooms next year after the crops were planted.

On Saturday, Greta had fun but she kept hoping Jack would show up. He didn't, but his friend Larry came to the dance.

"Jack sent a message that he'll see you in church tomorrow."

So that settled it. He'd meet her at church and they'd leave from there. She'd already cleared it with her sister and Fred, although they were reluctant to give their assent, and only agreed when Vanette offered to chaperone.

GRETA'S HEART nearly burst when she saw Jack drive up in his buggy. The buggy's wheels didn't align quite right, and the seats were torn up, but she reckoned it would be more comfortable than Fred's freight wagon.

"He's here," Vanette said, as if Greta's gaze hadn't already locked onto him.

"I hope the sermon's short." Greta tried to make her voice sound a lot steadier than she actually felt. "I really want to see his place."

"I don't expect that you're anxious to sit close to him for eight miles, either." Vanette giggled and elbowed her.

"That, too. Although I'm a mite nervous about meeting his family. Fingernail-chewing nervous. What if they don't like me?"

"They'd be crazy not to. And anyway, if he didn't think they'd like you, he wouldn't want you to meet them yet."

Sunday services went by quickly, for Jack sat beside her. He didn't hold her hand, but reached over several times, then pulled back. Finally, church ended. Everyone there knew that Greta was meeting Jack's family and the two of them took a lot of ribbing.

The ride out, he didn't hold her hand, either, because he was holding the reins. She sat beside him in the middle of the seat, and Vanette sat on her other side, chattering most of the way. Greta didn't pay attention to most of it because Jack's leg pressing on hers held every bit of her attention, and also heated her up—a blessing on a cold December day.

Finally, after more than an hour's ride, he pulled up to a little gray shingle house with a red tile roof. "Here we are." He hopped out.

A big yellow dog bounded across the farmyard to meet them and sniffed Greta as Jack lifted her from the buggy. "That's Pinkie," he said when he helped Vanette down. He reached down and gave Pinkie a couple pats on her side, then took Greta by the waist and escorted her into the house, with Vanette following.

Inside, the warm house bulged with family—he introduced her to his father, step-mother, younger brother, and two little sisters.

"Nice to meet you." She smiled and resisted the urge to wring her hands. They eyed her up and down and she wondered if they approved. "Could I help with something?"

"Not much to do but make gravy," Myrtle said as she took a roast out of the oven. "We lived in this house until last year, when Neil bought our new place and built a house there. He sold this farm to Jack. So I know my way around the kitchen."

"I can make the gravy—I like doing it."

"You're our guest. You should be visiting."

"I'll set the table, then."

"On the other hand, maybe Jack should taste your gravy. After all, gravy is his favorite food, and he's never brought a girl home before."

One thing Greta was good at was making gravy—smooth, dark, and just the right thickness. She was a little nervous but whipped up a gallon of it in no time, just like she did at home.

Jack loved it by the way he dumped a healthy ladleful on his second helping of potatoes. He winked at her as he saluted her with his fork heaped with potatoes and gravy.

"Never had better," he said, then enthusiastically cleaned his plate.

After the dishes were washed, Greta and Vanette bundled up to go home, but before they got to his buggy, Greta gave him his Christmas present. "Merry Christmas—open it."

He did, and grinned wide when he saw the earmuffs. "Thanks, they look nice and warm. I'll put those on right now." He glanced at Vanette and whispered, "Do you think you could get her to go back inside for just a minute?"

"Sure." Greta turned around, pointed at her friend, then pointed to the house. Vanette nodded, tossed back a mischievous grin, and hurried back inside.

Jack pulled a small package out of his vest pocket. "I have a Christmas present for you, if you'll take it." He handed it to her.

She unwrapped it quickly and opened it. A wedding ring! "Um, is this a proposal?"

"It is. You're the only girl for me. And you make dang good gravy."

Greta was nervous as she'd ever been—not because of her impending Christmas engagement party, but because her father would be there. He'd never met Jack before and she hoped with all her heart that the two men would cotton to one another. Fred had finally come around, which helped, but he was a farmer like Jack. Her father owned a bank. Not only that, he could be more than a little stern on occasion.

The clock struck twelve. Jack would arrive anytime. He said he'd come shortly after noon, depending on the ferry. Her father had shown up mid-morning, as had Vanette and all four Ross brothers. Greta bustled around the house making sure everything was perfect—the Christmas decorations arranged just right and the food would all be ready at the same time.

Jack's father and his wife showed up. Neil had agreed to play carols on his fiddle after dinner. Greta introduced everyone. They all seemed to get on well, and for that, Greta was grateful. She only hoped Jack wouldn't be late.

She stood at the window and waited. Ten minutes later, he drove up in his crooked buggy.

"You stay right there," Grace said, pointing to the couch. "I'll answer the door when he knocks."

Greta could hardly wait to see him, but she agreed to sit. He knocked. Grace opened the door. "Welcome, Mr. Wade. We're expecting you." She stood back.

He walked in carrying a rather sorry-looking bouquet, which Grace took. "Thank you, ma'am," he said to Grace, but his gaze was on Greta.

She stood and ran to him. "I'm so happy you're here. You can meet my papa." Jack held her hand for a mite longer than necessary. He had big hands. Strong.

Dinner was ready so she didn't want to delay introductions. She dragged him to her father, who stood.

"Papa, meet Jack Wade, my fiancé."

Her father chuckled and held out his hand. Jack stared at him a minute. "Moses Alden?"

"In the flesh."

Greta was confused. "You know my father?"

"Uh, we ran into each other before."

"Oh? Where?"

"Graveyard Point Road."

Greta was still confused. To her father, she said, "Why were you out there?"

"Hunting. I ran into him and wrecked his buggy."

Greta giggled. Now it all made sense. "So that's why your buggy is crooked."

Jack nodded, and wrapped his arm around her waist. "That's why."

Jack decided Moses Alden wasn't so bad after all, considering he produced the prettiest girl in Idaho Territory. "I'm pleased to meet you again on better terms, sir."

Moses pursed his lips, then said, "Seems to me that you have something to ask me today. We might as well get that out of the way before the food gets cold."

"Yes, sir. I'm asking for your daughter's hand in marriage."

"Granted, if she'll have you. Take good care of her." He headed for the table. "Let's eat." He sat and put a napkin on his lap with a flourish. "Looks like you'll need a new buggy. Stop by the bank in Boise and I'll have my secretary fix you up."

After dinner, Jack finally got Greta alone on the porch. He squeezed her hand. "I hope you like milk cows."

She smiled back. "Never had any before. I hope you like cats." She stepped closer to him. "It's cold out here."

He put his arms around her. "That better?"

She nuzzled his chest. "Mmmm. And cats?"

"I get a kick out of them. Have you heard of Deputy Duke? He's Sheriff Sidney Adler's deputy—big orange cat that claims Deputy Kade McKinnon as his human. Duke looks dreadful ragged but Adler won't go anywhere without him."

"Yes, and I adore Duke but he'll never win any beauty contests, that's for sure."

"But you could."

Jack chose Larry as his best man and he married Greta in a ceremony the next spring. It was a nice wedding if you didn't count Larry's knees knocking together from nervousness. Greta laughed about that. In fact, she laughed about nearly everything and maybe that's what Jack loved the best about her.

Yep, he'd found a better woman than he'd ever dreamed of, and she was his wife.

"Let's go home."

She put her hand on his cheek. "Looks like this fellow could use a big stack of spuds and gravy."

"He sure could." He swooped her up in his arms and carried her to his—their—new buggy. "I hope your father stays off the road until we get home."

AWARD-WINNING AUTHOR **JACQUIE ROGERS** has been writing since 1997 and currently has two series available: *Hearts of Owyhee* and *Honey Beaulieu – Man Hunter*. Both series have won several awards and the latter won four Will Rogers Gold Medallions as well as the Laramie Grand Prize. She lives in Idaho about two miles from where Greta lived with her sister and brother-in-law, and about ten miles from Jack's farm, where she grew up.

In fact, this short story is mostly true—the story is of Jacquie's parents' first meet, and of course Jack's first encounter with his future father-in-law. This tale has been repeated at many a family affair. In this retelling, the last names have been changed to protect the guilty.

Jacquie is the past president of her local Romance Writers of America chapter and current vice president of Western Fictioneers. She's the author of seventeen novels and at least two dozen short stories and novellas.

Visit her website and sign up for the Pickle Barrel Gazette! http://www.jacquierogers.com

MERRICK

⚛

BEN BOULDEN

Sweat beaded on Merrick's brow.

Slow moving horses beat a tepid rhythm on the road above. A wagon squeaked, its wheels rumbling across dry clay and shale.

A man laughed.

Another clicked his tongue at the laboring beasts before saying, "You should have seen it, me and Janie Frain as naked as God made us…"

Merrick drew a breath and held it. His heart was thumping in his chest. The Remington was cool in his right hand.

"…and in comes Janie's—"

A crash and a thud bounced on the road above as the armored wagon slammed into the four-foot rectangular trench that was dug for the purpose. The double tree hitch busted with an ear-shattering crack.

Merrick moved up the incline. His boots were slippery on the shoulder's pale rocks and paler dirt. He stepped onto the road's flat surface. The Remington was steady on the wagon's tailgate.

Dust clouded and shimmered in the desert light.

The draft horses panicked and pulled the broken hitch several yards down the road before stopping. They snorted and stomped, then stared at the ground.

"Holy shi—"

"Shut up!" Clarence Tilley said as he moved across the road. An ancient Army Colt white-knuckled in his left hand, a carpet bag in the other. "How's the driver?"

Before the little man named Spider could answer, the company's shotgun rider moved away from the wagon. A Holland & Holland side-by-side scatter in his hands. He clicked the hammers back and pulled the gun to his shoulder.

Spider Robison stepped forward. A shiny new Winchester at his shoulder, its large bore aimed directly at the security man's chest.

"It ain't worth dying for."

Tilley moved in a hurry from the road's opposite side, at the shotgunner's back. He said, "No reason for you to get hurt today, but the money's important to us and we'll kill you, if you insist on it."

The security man looked from Tilley to Spider. A dim stupidity clouded his eyes.

Merrick thumbed the Remington's hammer. "I'm sure you'd like to see your wife and daughter when we're done here, Mr. Baylor. Maybe read that pretty Allison a story before she goes to bed tonight. Make love to your wife and kiss her goodbye in the morning."

The shotgunner's confusion and fear at hearing his daughter's name was plain on his face.

Clarence had done his homework for the job.

The shotgunner said, "How?"

"The how doesn't matter, Marty." Merrick motioned for the big man to drop his gun. "It's more about the why, and why is always about money."

Baylor, pale and sick looking, disengaged the scatter's hammers. After a moment's hesitation, he dropped the heavy gun to the road. "You ain't going to hurt my family, are you?"

Merrick gave the devil's smile. "Not today, Marty."

Spider scurried from his position at the front of the wagon and retrieved Baylor's H&H. A mean look settled on his face a moment before he kicked Baylor in the groin. The big security man dropped to his knees, both hands covering his privates. He rolled onto his side and curled into the fetal position. His eyes closed with pain. A whimper escaped his throat.

Spider's eyes flashed with glee. He giggled and spat coffee-colored snot on the security man.

Merrick slapped the little man on the back of his

head. Spider jerked away, his face reddening. A vein throbbed at his temple. He raised the Winchester—

"Stop it!" Tilley shouted.

Spider froze with the Winchester midway to his shoulder. Its ugly black bore pointed several feet to Merrick's right. His eyes bounced with rage and what Merrick thought was fear.

Merrick brought his Remington up. His mouth was a grim line, eyes unreadable and hard. "If I kill him, do I get his share, Clarence?"

Tilley sighed. "You stop it, too, Merrick."

Spider's left hand palsied on the forestock, and the Winchester quivered dangerously in his hands.

Merrick said, "Take your finger off the trigger."

"Goddamn it, Spider," Tilley said in a harsh whisper. "Put the rifle down."

Spider looked at Tilley. A twitch bobbed above his left eye.

"Spider," Tilley said, "Merrick will burn a hole in you and we'll let you rot on this shit road till the birds find your eyes. I'm asking you to lower your rifle so we can finish the job."

Spider gulped. His Adam's apple bounced. A whimper escaped his mouth and defeat smoldered in his eyes. The little man lowered the Winchester with shaking hands. He said, "Why'd he go and hit me like that?"

Merrick lowered the Remington. His eyes never moved from Spider.

Clarence glared at Spider. "I reckon because you're a dumb shit that can't control himself. Now help Baylor to his feet and if you lay another unnecessary hand on him it won't be Merrick who kills you." Clarence rubbed a palm across his chest and in a milder voice said, "You take care of the driver, Spider?"

The little man took a deep, ragged breath. An ugly smile spread across his thin lips. "That sucker bounced on his face. Didn't even twitch."

Tilley grimaced. "He dead?"

Spider shook his head. "Don't know."

"Check him."

Spider bent over Baylor, placed a hand on the man's shoulder. "You need help standing?"

Baylor grunted something Merrick couldn't hear, but whatever the words were, they prompted Spider to step away. Baylor rolled onto his knees and found his feet. His legs wobbled, but he stood.

When Baylor was standing and the tension had drained away, Clarence hollered, "Porter!"

Porter was all arms and legs as he ran from around the road's curve ahead of the wagon. He shambled to a stop a few feet from the still swaying Baylor. The six-gun was ugly in Porter's long-fingered hands.

"Where's the money?"

Baylor didn't hesitate. "It's in the box."

The wagon had been fitted with a large strong

box in the bed. It was four feet wide by four feet high, and six feet deep. All burnished steel and iron. Its weight alone made it the safest way to transport cash money from bank to business and back.

Porter said, "Keys?"

Baylor shrugged.

Porter slapped his face with an open hand. The flat sound echoed hard across the road.

The shotgun rider stepped back from the blow—

And stopped, his hands raised over his head, when Merrick's Remington found his skull.

Merrick said, "Open the box."

Baylor's neck stretched as he looked over his shoulder at Merrick. His head was shaking. "The keys were sent ahead with another rider."

Merrick looked to Clarence. "What now?"

Spider spat oily brown tobacco juice that splattered with a thud on the dirt road. He said, "Do we believe this piece of shit?"

Clarence didn't bother answering, but instead he walked to the back of the wagon. An iron bar held the door tight. An iron padlock was attached at each end. Tilley tugged both locks and when he was satisfied they were locked he called Porter over.

Porter, a smile on his emaciated face, eagerly pulled a leather pouch from his shirt pocket. Guncotton appeared in his hand. He dropped to a knee and stuffed the nitro concoction into the locking mechanism behind a padlock's keyhole. He did the same to the other.

Merrick moved back. He had known more than one explosives man that had lost a hand, an arm. A few that had lost their lives. He didn't like explosives, but they were a valuable tool in his trade.

When Porter was satisfied with the guncotton's position, he looked back at Tilley. "We ready?"

Tilley moved across the road and stepped a few feet down the embankment. The other men followed, including Baylor who looked pale as death.

Tilley said, "We're ready."

Porter placed rigged fuses in each lock, studied his work for a moment and then looked to where the men were hiding. An eager smile shimmered on his face. "Here goes!"

He struck a Lucifer on his denims and placed its flame on the fuse cord, held it steady until the fuse sparked orange-blue with life. He lit the other. Their sizzle seeped across the road as the fuses burned.

Porter moved away from the wagon on bent knees. His head down. The fuses were timed to burn for two minutes, but it wasn't uncommon for fuse cord to jump and ignite the explosives seconds or even minutes ahead of expectation. The cheaper and older the cord, the more likely it would jump, which is exactly what happened.

A fuse flamed bright and then flashed. The spark

jumped an inch and ignited the guncotton inside the lock with a pop.

The lock shattered.

Iron shrapnel exploded outward. Porter dropped to his belly and squealed when hot iron shimmied across an ear. He covered his wound and mumbled about his mother.

His blood painted the road's hardpan red.

The lock's remnants were scattered in a wide circle around the wagon. The iron security bar bent in an ungodly shape.

The other fuse was still burning. Its padlock flapped and bounced from the explosion.

Porter started to stand. His eyes were wide with pain.

"Stay down!" Merrick said as he watched the fuse burn.

Porter shook his head. His jaw worked open and closed as he tried to regain his senses.

The second lock exploded. Its force knocked Porter to his belly. He screamed and lay still.

Merrick, the explosions still sharp in his ears, moved onto the road and kneeled next to the explosives man. He rolled Porter onto his back, expecting to find him unconscious, but instead the man grinned. Blood dripped from his wounded ear.

Porter said, "Holy shit! Did you see that?"

Tilley, with disgust in his voice, said, "I told you to buy new fuse cord."

"Damn your mouth, Clarey." Porter got to a knee. He looked at the blood on his hand. "That should have been perfect. I've used Hercules cord for years, never had a problem."

"Till now," Merrick said. "Let's see what's in the back before somebody comes along."

Spider rabbit-hopped across the road, yanked the wagon's door open. The interior was dark and black smoke billowed from inside. The little man waved his arms to clear the smoke and stuck his head inside the safe.

"Get back to Baylor!" Merrick growled.

Spider ignored Merrick and pulled a thick canvas bag from the strong box. He giggled when he opened the bag's leather top. Neatly bundled greenbacks were stacked inside. Spider's job was keeping the wagon's crew busy and Merrick knew that when one man lost concentration, the whole team was in jeopardy. And Spider had already proven himself a liability.

Merrick raised an eyebrow at Tilley, willing him to take control.

Tilley grabbed the money from Spider's hands. He pointed to the front of the wagon. "Get your ass back in position."

The little man jumped. His tobacco fell from his mouth and bounced on the road. A black liquid slithered down his chin. He retrieved his lost plug, dusted it with his hand, and popped it back in his cheek.

"Now!"

"Okay! Damn. It's not like Baylor's doing any—"

A shotgun blast thundered, charged the atmosphere. Merrick dropped low and moved down the hill for cover. He looked up in time to see Baylor disappear around the wagon's front corner. He heard the metallic snap of the shotgun opening and then closing with fresh loads in its chamber.

Merrick measured the scene. Porter was down. His left arm was twitching; crimson bubbled at a spot between his shoulder blades and dripped onto the dry roadbed.

Tilley crouched behind the wagon, the money on the ground and a Colt in his left hand. Spider, the little sonofabitch, was nowhere to be seen.

"How's Porter?"

"Bad," Tilley said. "You see Baylor?"

"He's at the front with a fresh load in the scatter and god knows what else."

Spider's assignment was to secure the driver, shotgun rider and any weapons. The shotgun in Baylor's hands was a bad sign there were other guns, too.

"Baylor?" Clarence said in an even, cool voice. "It doesn't have to go like this."

When there was no answer he continued, "This money's insured. It costs no one nothing. It's not worth your little girl being orphaned. No sense at all. I know you're a good man with a sense of duty, but you need to think about what you're doing here. You can't win, son."

Merrick used Tilley as distraction and eased close to the wagon. He moved on his toes towards the front. The big Remington .44 locked in his hand. He paused, listened for movement, trying to block Tilley's non-stop chatter from his mind.

"...that little girl of yours. What's her name? Allison, right? She's the prettiest little girl I've seen..."

Merrick moved to the wagon's front edge. The driver's seat was a few inches above his head. He removed his broad-brimmed campaign hat with his left hand and peeked around the wagon.

Merrick flinched back as the shotgun's barrels tightened on him.

Wood splintered from the wagon; smoke belched. The ear-splitting blast shocked Merrick. He fell backwards onto his butt. His hat bounced to the ground.

Baylor stormed around the wagon's edge. The shotgun aimed at Merrick.

Merrick reacted without thought. The Remington boomed. He thumbed the hammer and pulled the trigger again.

Baylor jerked to the side. He changed direction, but kept walking. The shotgun was loose in his hands. After a few steps, he fell to his knees and collapsed. His face hit the dirt with a bounce. A pool of blood spread from beneath his chest.

Merrick jumped to his feet. He grabbed Baylor's shotgun and trotted around the wagon. The driver on the ground was still unconscious. A Colt fastened to his hip. Merrick grabbed the Colt and lobbed it over the embankment.

"Spider! You lazy sonofabitch."

A gun's blast pounded across the road.

Merrick flinched, dropped to a knee. He tossed Baylor's shotgun as far as he could and grasped the Remington in his right hand. He moved quickly to the back of the wagon. As he stormed around the corner, flat pain crunched his skull, vibrated down his spine.

His vision faded; stars danced across a black sky.

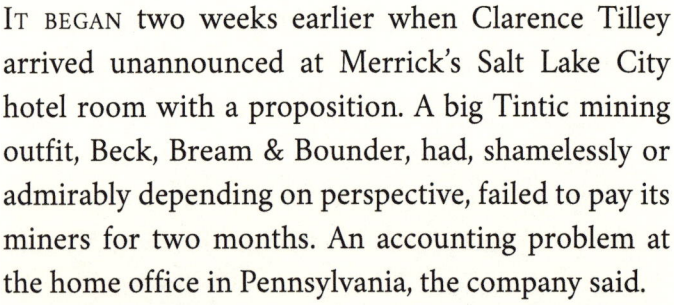

It began two weeks earlier when Clarence Tilley arrived unannounced at Merrick's Salt Lake City hotel room with a proposition. A big Tintic mining outfit, Beck, Bream & Bounder, had, shamelessly or admirably depending on perspective, failed to pay its miners for two months. An accounting problem at the home office in Pennsylvania, the company said.

When the miners started grousing, BB&B paid labor agents to crack skulls. But when the strong arm failed to stop a looming strike, the company agreed to replace its accounting department and pay the miners.

A little bird told Tilley the miners would be made whole with a single payroll on a certain day. Clarence, Clarey to his friends but always Clarence to Merrick, had a payroll heist planned to the last detail. But he had a hitch.

A gang member ran off with the teenage wife of a wealthy Mormon polygamist, leaving Tilley with three men on a four-man job.

Or as Tilley said, a self-conscious frown on his livered lips, "A tiny hiccup. Nothing at all, really."

"And you thought of me?" Merrick said.

Clarence, his dopey half-smile in place hiding a cleverness most men found disturbing, nodded. "You being in town and all."

"You're in a pinch?"

"Not a pinch, really. There are others I could bring in, but since we go back…" Clarence shrugged his shoulders to show Merrick how little he cared.

"What's my share?"

"Ten percent of net." In a past life Clarence had been an accountant. He enjoyed using fancy words like *net*. If BB&B were smart it would hire him as its accountant and the miners would keep working for free.

"Four guys and all I get is a *tenth*? Of net. What the hell's *net*?"

Clarence waved his big hand at Merrick like it was nothing at all. "After expenses."

"So, I'd get less than a half share of *profits*? And a full share of what you've paid for whores, hotels and whiskey since you came to town?"

Clarence shook his head and scowled.

Merrick shook his head, too. "What's the expected take?"

Clarence beamed. "Fifteen thousand. That number reflects the gross amount, of course."

"And after expenses?"

Clarence looked at something above Merrick's head. His lips moved like a cash machine. "Say thirteen thousand, five hundred. If it's less I'll guarantee your end at thirteen-fifty."

An amount that would keep Merrick flush for a year. "I'm in, but I need fifteen hundred guaranteed."

Clarence bent over at the waist like he'd been sucker punched.

Merrick said, "Five hundred payable now."

Clarence straightened and a smile twitched at the edges of his mouth. He pulled a fat wad of greenbacks from a shirt pocket and counted out ten bills.

After the money had been exchanged, Merrick said, "How much did I leave on the table?"

"Plenty." And Tilley left it at that.

Merrick cursed and closed the door behind Tilley's waddling backside.

Merrick came to a slow awareness. A steady ache cracked his skull. He opened his eyes to a flash of blinding white and wrenched them closed again.

He inhaled, held it a moment, then exhaled and counted to ten.

Merrick opened his eyes to an azure sky. A hawk foiled high on rising currents. The left side of his scalp was sticky with blood. He eased into a sitting position, but lay flat as the world swirled around him. When the ground stopped moving, he propped himself up on an elbow and studied his surroundings.

His thinking was muddied with an unsettling confusion. He had been on the road when the world disappeared. But now he was on juniper and rock covered ground that sloped down to a copse of trees and a trickling creek.

The embankment below the road, Merrick thought.

Above, voices encroached.

"An easy deal, you said. Nothing to it, you said."

"It's done, ain't it?"

"And what about Baylor? What am I going to tell his wife?"

"Quit crying. We got fifteen grand in this bag and we split half."

Merrick recognized the voice as Spider's.

"I can't. This can't—"

A shotgun blast dropped like a hammer.

Merrick went to his belly and reached for the Remington, but found an empty holster instead. He held his breath, afraid to move or even look up the embankment.

Boots scraped across the road.

And then nothing.

Merrick listened and waited. After what seemed like hours, he rose to his feet and scurried up the embankment. The road was empty of life. Tilley was dead, lying on his back, eyes staring at hell. Porter prostrate, the wagon driver at the road's edge, cut nearly in two from the shotgun blast.

Merrick knew in an instant that the other voice he had heard belonged to the driver. Spider's betrayal was an inside job. It must have gone sideways when the driver was knocked cold. But Spider made it work.

He searched the road for his Remington, but found nothing but Tilley's ancient Colt under the wagon. He placed it in his holster. He picked his hat up from where it had fallen earlier, knocked the dust from it and covered his head. Merrick moved to the front of the wagon and stepped over Baylor's motionless body and swiftly went up the road to catch Spider Robison.

The horses were gone and nothing more than dust

marked the little outlaw's trail. With no chance to catch Spider on foot, Merrick walked back to the wagon and eyed the draft horses. He grimaced at the thought of riding one of the large animals, but quickly went to work. He freed the smaller horse, eighteen hands high if an inch, and positioned it next to the wagon. He climbed on. His legs spread wide across the animal's back. His feet barely scraped its belly.

Merrick clicked his tongue and brushed a spur across the horse's flank. It responded with a snort.

"Giddy-up."

The horse tried to look back at its passenger, but the blinders covering its peripheral vision blocked the view.

"Go, dammit!" Merrick's patience thin, he dug his spurs into the animal's belly.

The horse snorted with belligerence, but moved forward with a slow and measured gait.

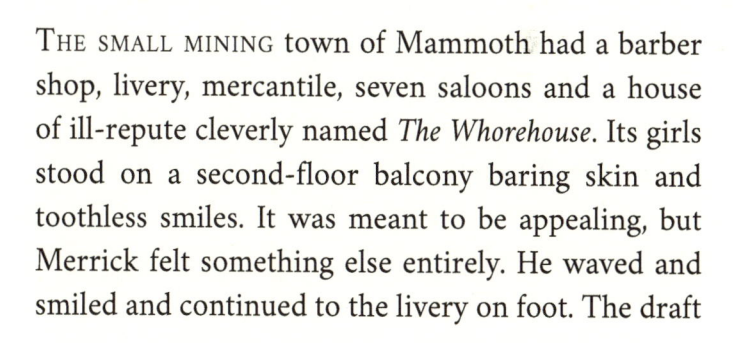

The small mining town of Mammoth had a barber shop, livery, mercantile, seven saloons and a house of ill-repute cleverly named *The Whorehouse*. Its girls stood on a second-floor balcony baring skin and toothless smiles. It was meant to be appealing, but Merrick felt something else entirely. He waved and smiled and continued to the livery on foot. The draft horse abandoned outside town in case the robbery had been discovered.

An old scarecrow waved as Merrick entered the livery barn. "Help you?"

Merrick said, "I need a horse."

"Rent, buy or trade?"

The old man, bald except for a small island of greasy white hair high on his crown, smelled worse than the barn.

"Buy."

With a bent finger, the man pointed to the corral behind the barn where four sway-back mongrels chewed moldy hay. "Your lucky day since we got plenty of fine stock."

Merrick wasn't a horseman, but none of the animals looked like much.

"Any better than the others?"

The old man paused and brought a finger to his ruddy face. "You need to understand, they're all fine horse flesh, but if it were me, I'd take the mare."

"How much?"

The old man poked the air like he was working an abacus, said, "Let's see, five to rent and thirty to buy."

Merrick flinched.

The old man squinted, hunched his shoulders. "Twenty-five?"

Merrick took a wallet from his front pocket, still surprised Spider hadn't thought to take it, and pulled out two bills. He showed the money to the old man. "Twenty for the horse and a saddle."

The liveryman grinned and snatched the money from Merrick's fingers.

THE HORSE RODE better than Merrick had a right to expect. It took him across fifty hard miles of white stained alkaline desert, skirted the southern edge of misplaced sand dunes and then west to Delta. A Mormon agricultural town as different from Mammoth as one could imagine, but it had the same appeal as Mammoth's whores.

For Merrick, none.

The livery was larger than Mammoth's and its proprietor still had teeth and hair. A great thatch of angry red was on his head and a pale blond beard on his face. When Merrick led his nag into the barn the liveryman, hands on hips and a frown on his face, said, "I'm guessing that glue bag came from Jensen?"

Merrick shrugged.

"That old bird in Mammoth?"

Merrick said, "She's a better horse than I figured her for."

The big man shook his head. "You looking to trade?"

"I'm looking for something better."

"That should be easy. I have a handful of dead

animals in the back. We'll have to do some digging, but any one of them is better than that thing." He pointed at the mare and laughed heartily at his own joke; saliva splattering his beard.

Merrick kept his tongue.

The liveryman stuck his hand out. "I'm John Ivins. They call me Red John, but you can call me R.J. Everything in the yard's for sale. The prices vary, but they run between twenty and fifty. I'll give you two dollars for the mare."

"I'd hoped you'd give me five."

"Hope's been dead for years." The man's wide smile contradicted his words.

Merrick said, "I'm a friend of Clarence Tilley."

R.J. straightened and looked at the open barn door for visitors, then back to Merrick. "You alone?"

"I am."

Red John held a finger to his lips. The barn's interior darkened as the door closed on squeaky hinges.

When he returned, he spoke in a whisper, "That runt said the job went bad and everybody died."

"That's true, except me."

"And the runt."

Merrick looked around the barn's shadowy interior. The sides were lined with horse stalls and about a third of them were occupied. He turned back to Red John. "How long since Spider, the little guy, left?"

"*Spider*? That's a perfect name for the little

bastard. He traded four horses for two, straight across, and I'm pretty sure every damn one is stole."

"How long since he left?"

Red John's eyes narrowed. "Why?"

Merrick dropped his hand to Tilley's old Colt. "He killed Tilley and another man."

Red John stared at Merrick's hand on the Colt for a moment before he raised his hands, palms out. "Don't get offended. I was just asking."

"How long?"

"Four hours, I guess."

"What direction?"

"He told me he was headed east for Gunnison, but he rode west."

Merrick removed his hand from the holstered Colt. He knew where the traitorous bastard was going. He grimly chastised the little prick for his lack of imagination.

"Now," Merrick said, "How about that horse?"

Red John studied his visitor for a beat, smiled. "You headed into the Snakes?" When Merrick frowned, the liveryman continued hastily, "I'm asking because I've got a little paint that was raised in that country. Knows it so well all you'll need to do is hold the saddle horn."

Merrick nodded. "That'll work."

The landscape changed with the rising elevation. The lowlands were barren and ugly. White alkaline spotted with pickle weed and greasewood. The foothills nurtured pinyon and juniper, the soil darkened to acorn brown and then a rich black. As Merrick moved higher into the Snake Range Mountains, patches of quaking aspen, fir, and lodge pole pine cluttered the slopes. The temperature cooled, a lavender and pine fragrance mingled with the clatter of fast-moving water.

The small paint moved sure-footed up the steep slopes, following Spider's trail unless another route made more sense, but she always reclaimed the tracks. The minutes turned to hours and Merrick allowed the horse its head. He watched the horizon for trouble, hoping for a glimpse of his prey.

The sun blistered in the western sky.

It took some time, but Merrick found the slim passage. It was a water and wind eroded slash in the granite. The paint stopped a few feet from the entrance, snorted and looked at Merrick with a nervous eye. Merrick patted the horse's neck before he pivoted from the saddle and dropped the reins to the ground.

The hard man moved soundlessly through the aspen grove that was clustered against the granite cliff. The Colt's tattered grip more comfortable than it should have been in his hand. The tunnel's interior was shadowy and calm. The track four feet wide at the entrance, rising as high as Merrick could see.

He knew this place well, had been a guest more than once. A sanctuary for liars, killers and thieves nestled in the valley hidden on the other side.

A placed called Vigilance.

THE PASSAGE LED into a pristine alpine meadow isolated from the outside world by steep granite walls soaring a thousand feet on three sides. The fourth, a conifer covered slope that rose to a rocky and perpetually snow-covered peak. The long grasses, quaking aspen and ponderosa pine made for a sun-licked haven against the craggy and wild background. Yellow and blue wildflowers grew in bunches. A crystal alpine lake shimmered in the afternoon sun. Along its edge six tiny rough-hewn cabins; farther back against granite cliffs, a corral.

A rangy man dressed in a black suit, a flat-brimmed black hat on his thick head, sat on a stump outside the nearest cabin and whittled a crooked stick into a smaller crooked stick. He hummed a tune familiar to Merrick, but one he couldn't place.

Merrick stepped into the meadow. The paint was straggling behind on its own accord. The whittling man looked up. When he saw Merrick, a grin spread across his ugly face.

"Brother Telfair." Merrick used the man's preferred Mormon affectation.

The Mormon stood from the stump. He hobbled on a wooden leg, pocketed the knife and tossed the stick onto a pile of other sticks.

Merrick offered his hand, Telfair accepted. "You're still making toothpicks, I see."

"What brings you to my home, Merrick?" The man's voice was a growl and a sober smile crept onto his face.

"Work, I'm afraid."

"I thought maybe so. Anything to do with a little man named Spider?"

"He's here?"

Telfair pointed at the third cabin down the line.

"With blessing?" Merrick knew the hideout was owned by the Elders. A Mormon gang controlling damn near everything criminal in the Utah Territory. Its membership went high in the Church. Its protection did, too.

Telfair said, "He's paid his tithe."

"I'm looking for something that belongs to me."

The old man shook his head and splattered tobacco juice in the long grass.

"Are you going to stop me collecting?"

"Brother Robison know he has something of yours?"

"He thinks I'm dead."

Telfair's eyes went hard. His hand dropped to the well-used Colt on his hip. "You on that payroll job?"

Merrick knew Telfair had been a fair gun hand in his day, but times change. Men grow old, and so do their reflexes. Some men, like Telfair, lose a leg and get sent to pasture in a place like this. "I'm not here for you, Telfair. All I want is my money."

"That job had no sanction from the Elders. There was no tithe offered or received." Telfair's mouth barely moved. His eyes darted back and forth between Merrick and the gun strapped to his leg.

"I'm sorry your outfit didn't get paid, Telfair. I was hired help. I'm not responsible for fees, but I'll pay your tax on my share. I'm owed a thousand for my end. I figure another two hundred for my trouble collecting. That makes an even one-twenty to the Elders."

Telfair said, "Not a tax. A tithe."

Merrick glanced at the corral. Five horses. If two belonged to Spider, it meant the camp was sparsely populated. The place was probably empty except for the old gun hand and Robison. "His mount corralled?"

Telfair's fingers wrapped tight on the revolver's handgrip.

"You alone? You and Spider?"

The tall man stopped breathing. His head went still as night.

"No need you dying for a rat like Spider. You and

me know each other, Telfair. We've always been friendly. But I'll drop you where you stand without any thought or feeling, leave you here for the buzzards and never think about you again."

The man drew sharp breath. "They'll kill you, Merrick."

"Yeah. But you and Spider will be long dead when it happens. And that money will buy me more than a few years between now and then."

Merrick dropped his hand to Tilley's Colt.

The crippled man's eyes followed the movement.

"It's your move, old man. Your life for Spider's."

Merrick watched the other man's eyes, saw the flint drain away, the tremors start. Telfair took his hand from the gun and lowered his gaze to the ground.

"Goddamn you to hell, Merrick."

Merrick knew he should kill the old outlaw. That he had made Telfair an enemy by shaming him, but killing was wasteful and he and Telfair always got along well enough. And their past should count for something.

"Anybody else here?"

The old man dropped down on the stump. He looked across the small valley and shook his head.

"I need to take your gun?"

Telfair squinted up at Merrick. "You already took everything I had."

Merrick studied Telfair. "It was time that broke

you, not me." He paused, then said, "Spider in his cabin?"

Telfair glared at Merrick with hateful eyes.

"Well?"

The old gunman nodded once. "You going to kill him?"

Merrick looked at the cabin a few hundred yards away. Its walls aged silver. He wondered if Spider had heard the exchange. "If he makes me."

"The Elders won't let me stay here after this. It took more than talk to get the job in the first place, but after this… I'll need money." The man looked spent. He was pale and sweaty.

Merrick turned back to Telfair. A weak breeze rustled the grass. The lake's smell was in its grasp. "Spider's share is yours, but you'll have to earn it."

Telfair rubbed his forehead with a palm. "How?"

Merrick lowered a hand and helped the old man up.

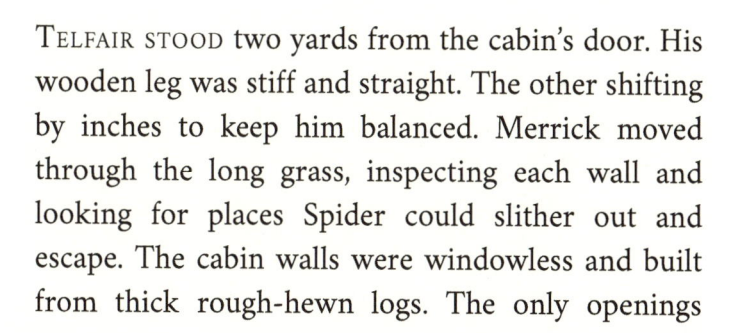

Telfair stood two yards from the cabin's door. His wooden leg was stiff and straight. The other shifting by inches to keep him balanced. Merrick moved through the long grass, inspecting each wall and looking for places Spider could slither out and escape. The cabin walls were windowless and built from thick rough-hewn logs. The only openings were three thin vertical slits near the roofline; maybe one inch by ten and used to ventilate the cabin's interior.

Merrick moved to the cabin's front corner and palmed the old Colt in his right hand. He motioned for Telfair to knock. The old man limped to the door and rapped on it with his knuckles.

He stepped back. "Brother Robison?"

From inside the cabin, Merrick heard a metallic snick, boot heels clacking on plank flooring and a faint scratching, like cotton on a rough surface.

"Yeah?"

Telfair glanced at Merrick with eyes wide.

Merrick gestured for him to answer.

Telfair coughed. "I'm fixing to make my dinner and wondered if you'd care to join?"

The door opened inward. A dark line ran across the edge closest to Merrick. The little man was hidden in shadow.

"A little early, ain't it?"

Telfair shrugged. "Not for me. I'm an old man and my belly starts rumbling about three o'clock. It gets real cranky by four and demands I collapse at five. I'm hoping to avoid all that this afternoon and have my dinner ready to eat at four." He studied his watch theatrically for a few seconds. "Which gives me thirty minutes."

When Spider didn't answer immediately, Merrick worried the old man's longwinded speech had caused suspicion. When he was ready to make his move at the darkened door Spider opened it a little wider.

Merrick held his ground.

Spider said, "What's it going to be?"

Telfair scratched his head. "Venison stew. The venison's fresh. I got canned carrots and potatoes both. You're welcome to join if you care to."

A reflection hit Merrick's eyes. A blued barrel appeared from the cabin's darkness.

Telfair looked at the object like it was an angry snake crawling from his boot after a long night. His eyes darkened with fear. He put his hands up, palms out, and stepped back. His wooden leg caught an edge and he fell hard to the ground. Air whooshed from his lungs.

The gun flashed in the dark doorway; blood sprayed from Telfair's shoulder. The gun's sharp crack blossomed across the valley.

Spider pulled the trigger again.

Telfair's body jerked. The old man's pupils flittered from side to side. He jerked his hand to the sucking wound in his abdomen where the second bullet burrowed. His head lolled toward Merrick. His mouth opened without words.

His eyes stared into a darkness Merrick could only imagine.

Spider, just visible in the doorway, yelled, "Merrick coming to dinner, too, old man?"

Merrick moved in a hurry. He raised the old Colt to shoulder height and pulled the trigger. Wood splintered from the doorjamb an inch from Robison's head with a crack. The little man bent backwards, away from the bullet's impact and disappeared into the cabin.

The door crashed closed.

Merrick stopped a few feet from the door. Its vertical plank construction was the cabin's most vulnerable spot. He searched the ground, found a grapefruit sized rock and hefted it in his left hand. The Colt was in his right hand.

"All I want is my share, Spider. I'm owed a thousand. Another two hundred to cover your leaving me for dead. You give it to me and no one else will get hurt."

The scraping sound again, cloth against wood, came from inside the cabin.

Merrick was certain it was Spider leaning against the door, listening. He tossed the rock underhand. It landed with a thud, bounced once and clattered against the door.

The door bounced against its hinges, rattled, as two shots from inside tore through its weathered plank boards. Dirt geysers sprang from where the bullets smashed into the ground. Merrick held steady.

Minutes passed.

The valley was silent.

Then, "You out there, Merrick?"

More silence, followed by clattering boot heels on pine boards.

"Well? Come on, Merrick! You still out there?"

Merrick didn't respond.

A hinge squeaked as the door hesitantly opened. The narrow shadow reappeared at the door's edge. Merrick's muscles tensed and then relaxed as he prepared for the impending violence.

The door opened an inch more.

"Merrick?"

Merrick waited, silent. He knew the little man couldn't see him without showing himself. And he knew Spider's fear and desire for escape had overcome his common sense.

The door opened a few more inches. Spider's bald head appeared in the doorframe. His eyes popped wide and he shrank back into the cabin when he saw Merrick charging.

But Spider was too late and Merrick brought the Colt's barrel down on his head with a sickening thud. The little man's knees buckled. His eyes spun back into his head. He dropped motionless to the ground. His upper body lying outside the cabin door and the rest of him was hidden in the cabin's dark interior.

Merrick holstered the Colt, yanked Spider from the cabin and retrieved the little man's gun. A familiar Remington Model 1890. He pulled Tilley's old Colt from his holster and tossed it into the grass. He slammed the Remington into the holster where it belonged.

Merrick entered the cabin and paused. When his eyes were adjusted to the dark interior he found and lit an oil lamp hanging on the wall. Its orange flame revealed a straw mattress at the back. An unsteady table stood in the right corner and a tiny rocking chair in the left. A heavy money bag sat on the table. Its leather top latched closed.

Merrick opened the bag. He stared blankly inside.

Grimness overtook him. He upended the satchel and dumped its contents on the floor. The rocks clattered out and dust lifted into the air.

"Sonofabitch."

Merrick searched the small room, but found nothing. He did the same for each cabin along the lake's edge. When he finished, Merrick went back to where he'd left Spider. The little man's eyes open, his mouth wide. For a moment Merrick thought the man had awakened, but his blue lips and pasty pallor made death obvious.

He rifled the Spider's pockets and found ten waded up bills.

$500.

With Tilley's down payment from a few days earlier, Merrick was still five hundred short for the job. He smoothed out the greenbacks, folded and tucked them into his wallet.

Merrick looked at his paint munching the valley's virgin grass, then at the two dead men sprawled under blue sky. He didn't dare stay on at the camp much longer. The less The Elders knew about the killings, the better. They would kill him for his perceived trespass on their territory. Make his death painful if they decided he'd pulled the trigger on Telfair.

Then he thought about Red John back in Delta, wondered about his relations with The Elders. Whether the big man would let it slip he had seen Merrick chasing Spider Robison into the Snakes. He could go back and kill the liveryman, but the more time he spent on the trail in the Utah Territory, the more likely he would run into The Elders. A meeting that would end badly for everyone.

Merrick sighed and wondered about going to San Francisco. Maybe Scottsdale. Then he trampled into the long grass and found Tilley's old Colt and threw it into the alpine lake.

The outlaw retrieved the paint and worked his way out of the valley.

When he found the trail, he turned west, towards California and the coast.

A thousand dollars would take a man like Merrick a long way.

BEN BOULDEN WRITES THE *SHORT & Sweet: Short Stories Considered* column for *Mystery Scene Magazine*. He has published more than two hundred articles and reviews about books. His short fiction has appeared in *Down & Out: The Magazine*, *Bullets and Other Hurting Things*, edited by Rick Ollerman, and Paul Bishop's *Murder and Mayhem* series of anthologies: *Pattern of Behavior*, *Criminal Tendencies*, and *Bandit Territory*.

SHOT FOR A DOG

CHERYL PIERSON

It had been an accident—a trick of the relentless, shimmering heat that had made Luke pull the trigger. At least, that had been the story he told, and the tale he stuck to in his own mind, until he had almost come to believe the fabrication himself.

He and his younger brother, Jeremiah, had been finishing up hoeing the corn. The late afternoon sun had begun to relent, and though this July day would never cool off enough to be comfortable, at least it was becoming tolerable.

"I'm hungry," Jeremiah declared.

"We gotta finish," Luke answered flatly. At sixteen, he was responsible for Jeremiah, who was only half his age—and with no more brains than a turtle.

After a moment, Jeremiah stopped hoeing. "I'm goin' back to the house," he stated, straightening to stretch his back muscles.

"You ain't goin' back 'til I say we're done, *brother*," Luke said mildly, but when his blue gaze met Jeremiah's dark eyes, the animosity couldn't be hidden, nor did he bother to try.

Luke had hated his half-brother from the day he'd been born, with his coal black eyes and hair the color of a raven's wing. Jeremiah was not like the rest of the Marshall clan, all fair and blue-eyed, with light hair. More than once, Luke had noticed the disapproval in the eyes of his aunts and uncles when they came to visit his mother. When he got older, he realized it was two-fold. The fact that she had slept with an Indian was almost worse than her having a child out of wedlock. A bastard half-breed baby was what Jeremiah Marshall was—and he was only a "Marshall" because Ma had been before Pa died.

"It's dinner time, and I'm goin' back." Jeremiah picked up the Mason jar containing a half-inch of now-tepid water, and started through the corn rows carrying his hoe and the jar.

"Hey! Hey, come back here, you little—" Luke broke off as Jeremiah kept walking. His anger swept over him, making him almost sick with the impotent feeling. His fingertips itched in murderous rage.

Even worse was the unhurried way his little

brother moved, as if Luke's authority meant nothing to him. *By God, I'm older, I'm in charge, and I'm whiter than you.* He thought it, but he didn't say it—not then.

"Dammit! I said come back here, you little bastard!"

The rustling stopped, and Luke knew Jeremiah was thinking about running back the way he'd come from and barreling into him, his fists flailing. The last time he'd tried that, Luke had given him a shiner for his efforts—claiming it to be an accident, of course.

Luke stood listening, hopefully. But there was no noise, except for the evening breeze whispering through the cornstalks. He ignored the cooling spell it tried to weave around him, too angry to think of anything but teaching Jeremiah a lesson he wouldn't forget.

"Jeremiah! Get your ass back here!"

There was no response, and the wind mocked him, as if it tried to cool his anger, as well as his body. He wouldn't let it happen.

Luke jerked up his hoe and the old rifle that had been his father's, according to his mother. Leaving his own Mason jar at the end of the corn row, he started through the same row of corn where Jeremiah had disappeared moments earlier.

The corn was above his head, and in his fury, he shouldered his way through until he came out, breathing hard, at the far end. He'd have to wait to show Jeremiah who was boss. Anger tasted almost like blood, he thought. It would be hard to pretend nothing was wrong when they sat down to eat dinner. But he could wait.

From the corner of this eye, there was a flash of movement in the falling shadows. Reflexively, Luke dropped the hoe and raised his rifle, sighting down the barrel.

Soulful brown eyes stared back at him, under hair as black as night. The screen door of the little cabin was thrown open. Jeremiah stood for only an instant looking into Luke's twisted soul with the eyes of age; age that Luke couldn't fathom, and an understanding that speared him deep in his gut.

Elizabeth Marshall followed her younger boy out onto the porch, her own gaze questioning, until she saw Jeremiah running across the yard toward his beloved dog, Shadow.

"No! Jeremiah!"

Luke still aimed at the big dog, refusing to let go of the terrible idea that had seized him. His finger pulled back on the trigger, and there was a moment of conscious decision at the next level, that urged him forward in this course of action

Just as the trigger came back fully to send the bullet forward, Jeremiah entered his sights. By that moment, Luke couldn't have stopped if he'd wanted to.

With the reverberating shot echoing in the evening stillness, he understood that what he'd done had been a ruthless act that would change his life forever. But, no matter—that damn boy should have listened to him!

A cry of mingled despair and victory escaped him, and he lowered the rifle as his younger brother's body was flung, like a puppet, to the ground along with the dog. They both lay still, then Jeremiah's shaking fingers moved to stroke the dog's velvet-soft ear.

The dog was not quite gone yet, his loyal dark eyes looking up into Jeremiah's as the boy reverently touched his fur and whispered to him.

Elizabeth screamed, then rushed toward where Jeremiah lay, his face on Shadow's bleeding chest. She laid a hand on his head, but he didn't seem to notice. He whispered brokenly in the soft ear beside him, his words for no one but the only friend he'd ever known.

She turned to look up at Luke. "What in the world? Go get Doc Myers! Now!"

"It was a mistake," he said tightly. "I—I thought it was maybe that big cat that's been stealing our chickens—"

"You thought *maybe*?" Elizabeth's eyes glinted with anger and fear in the twilight. She turned her attention back to Jeremiah, trying to see how bad he had been hit.

"Ma, I said I didn't mean to! I made a mistake—"

"Luke…" She spared him a glance, shaking her head. "Surely, you could see that it was Shadow, not a bobcat—and your brother—Go! What are you waiting for?"

"Ma! I didn't mean to!"

"I ain't so sure of that," she murmured in a low voice, humming with fury.

Luke's anger overcame his indignation. "That little blanket baby been lyin' on me to you?"

Rising quickly, Elizabeth took a step toward him. The slap across his left cheek echoed, and fixed him rooted to the spot. Elizabeth still stood with her hand upraised, her breathing rapid and heavy, staring at the red imprint of her hand on her son's pale skin.

"I can't stay here," Luke muttered finally.

Elizabeth's mouth was drawn and set. "No, you can't. But you go get the doctor! Your brother's hurt bad."

Luke's chest clenched. He hadn't expected that. He'd thought his mama would forbid him to leave. He'd expected her to protest, to tell him things would look better in the morning…but maybe this was something that would *never* look better. Maybe this was something that could never be forgiven.

He couldn't help looking over at Jeremiah. His little brother lay in a pool of Shadow's blood, mingling with his own. The dog's dark eyes held a faint spark of life, accusatory as they met Luke's, but also with an understanding that wrapped around Luke's heart like choking vine, making him take a step backward. The dog had always belonged to Jeremiah, since Old Man Jackson had brought him to their little cabin four years earlier. But Shadow had never shown aggression toward Luke; neither had he shown any particular affection.

Now, as he lay dying, Luke was filled with a sudden, unreasoning fear at what he saw in the big dog's eyes. It was as if Shadow could see deep down into him, and Luke let go a relieved sigh as the light in Shadow's eyes finally guttered out.

Jeremiah must have felt the final breath rush out of his companion's body. He put his face up to the big dog's soft snout, his own body shaking.

"Just look what you've done," Elizabeth muttered vehemently, kneeling again to see to Jeremiah. "You are pure evil, Lucas. *Pure evil.*"

"Ma, I didn't do it on purpose!"

"I don't believe you! Go fetch the doctor! No more arguing!"

Though desperation warred with this fearsome side of his mother he'd never seen, Luke tamped down the urge to beg for forgiveness. He swallowed hard. It was time for him to get out in the world on his own anyhow.

"I'll get my things."

"Later!" Elizabeth said tersely. "Saddle up Bessie and get to town."

Jeremiah lifted his head finally turning to look at Luke. His black eyes were filled with pure hatred. His face was streaked with Shadow's blood, making him look like a young Indian warrior painted for battle. *For death.*

The grim set of his mouth showed no sign of forgiveness, just as there was none apparent in his expression or the tense lines of his body. His dark hair glistened wet in places with the dog's blood, where he'd laid close to comfort him in his last moments.

As long as he was going, Luke decided he might as well have some satisfaction from this. *He wasn't some little child to be slapped like a rented mule!* For just a moment, he thought of hugging his mother, throwing himself at her mercy, and asking to stay. Where would he go? What would he do, now? But one look at her told him things had gone far beyond that. She looked at him as if he were a stranger, and one she didn't ever want to see darkening her doorstep again. Worry knit her brow, all for that little red heathen, and none for him.

Luke turned away stiffly and walked toward the cabin. Light spilled out from the door and windows, casting a melted buttery glow into the falling darkness. He refused to allow any feeling to enter his heart other than relief that this was all finally over.

"Lucas! Ride for the doctor! Go now!" Elizabeth's frantic calls could be easily heard in the surrounding stillness. He'd do what he damn well pleased. *Let that Injun heathen bleed. What did he care? He was leaving, anyway—cast out by his own mother.*

Luke came up the front steps and pushed the door completely open. The light was hard to get used to—he'd been in the falling darkness, and Ma had already lit all the lamps. He made his way to the stairs that went up to the loft room he'd shared with Jeremiah. And he took his time about it.

He climbed slowly. Reaching the last rung in the ladder, he looked around their bedroom for what was to be the last time. He hoisted himself up into the room and walked slowly to the chest where his spare clothes were.

He fingered the splintered wood at the corner of the top drawer before he pulled it open, his eyes unseeing as he finally gave it a gentle tug. He didn't have many clothes; they'd all fit in a pillowcase.

His lips thinned as he pressed them together tightly. In one moment, he wanted to open the window and yell out to his mother to forgive him—and, in the next, he thought of burning this damn house down before he left it.

All because of Jeremiah. He shook his pillow out of the case.

As he loaded his clothing into the empty pillow case, he thought of what else he might take with him. There wasn't much; they didn't have much to begin with. Jealousy of his younger brother made him want to destroy the things he couldn't carry. Instead of thinking of his own needs for his journey, his mind turned to what he might keep Jeremiah from having—if he survived.

The damned dog was first on the list. That hadn't been as hard as it might have been, had he given any thought to his actions. But he *had* given thought to them. And he'd done just what he had tried to do— punish Jeremiah for not obeying him. Jeremiah had been a fool to get himself shot for a dog.

Still, all that had happened wasn't enough. Not when he was being forced out of the home that was rightfully his! Luke's gaze fell on the small book that Jeremiah used for his drawings. He walked to the bed and picked it up, thumbing through it quickly, a sneer on his face in the gloom.

All of the pictures were of Shadow. *That damn dog. Didn't Jeremiah think of anything else?* Well, he would now, Luke gloated. Shadow was dead. Savagely, he ripped the pages from the book and stuffed them in the pillowcase on top of his clothing. For all he knew, Jeremiah was dead, too. He wouldn't be needing these anymore.

There was one last thing near and dear to Jeremiah's heart, he thought. A silly flute he'd made and taught himself to play like some damn savage—which was just what he was.

Luke knew where it was—under Jeremiah's pillow. He shoved his hand under the softness and groped until his fingers closed around it. He pulled it out, looking at the crude drawings his brother had made to decorate it—turtles and snakes, mostly.

He raised a knee, and brought the flute down sharply across it, snapping it in two. But that wasn't good enough. He wanted to feel his brother's utter destruction, and what better way than to break the flute completely so it could never be mended? Besides, he might not be using it again anyhow.

The wood wasn't that strong after all, he thought, as he broke one of the pieces in two again, then the other. Carefully, he scattered the wood pieces under Jeremiah's pillow.

Feeling better about everything, he shouldered the sack with his belongings and started down the ladder. Maybe he'd send Doc Myers out this way if he passed through town.

No need to ask any kind of forgiveness now, he thought. He didn't want it or need it. He had something better—the satisfaction of revenge.

Lucas didn't bother to say a proper goodbye—not to his mother and certainly not to Jeremiah, the sorry little savage who had run him out of his own home. Let him lay out in the yard by that damn dog all night, if he lived.

He glanced at the barn, thinking of taking the only horse they owned. He had his rifle and some bullets. He'd leave the damned horse. He struck off down the road on foot, his belongings slung across his back, rifle in hand. He ignored his mother's cries as they turned from the pleas for him to go to for the doctor to the angry cursing him for a devil for leaving them, leaving his brother, to die on the ground.

When he'd walked far enough that the cries faded, and he'd almost lost sight of the little cabin when he turned, he couldn't help but noticed the cheery yellow glow in a field of darkness. Just for an instant, the thought of going back seized him so violently it clamped his chest like a vise, but it didn't linger. "I'm just hungry—that's all," he muttered to himself.

He hadn't taken any food. The thought of the warm golden cornbread on the kitchen table tempted him, and made him curse himself for a fool. He should have taken some of it.

No. He turned away, putting his back to his home determinedly, thinking how sorry that little savage would be when he had to hoe the corn all alone—when he was well enough. And how angry he'd be when he discovered the pieces of his flute under his pillow.

A grim smile touched Luke's lips. The first bit of gladness of the day filled him. It was a good thing he'd done—killing that dog. He could feel the joy rise up inside him again as he remembered the way the rifle had kicked when he'd pulled the trigger. The dog had fallen without a sound, but his brother had been yelling Shadow's name as he ran toward him in those final moments. *But the way Shadow had looked at him...and then, the way Jeremiah had...*

A shiver ran up his spine. Would he ever be able to forget that steady accusatory gaze from the beast? And suddenly, the pure hatred for him that he'd seen in Jeremiah's fading, pain-filled gaze rose up to haunt him as well.

Luke shrugged it off. "Shoulda kept out of the way," he muttered.

SLEEP WAS a while in coming to Luke that night. He'd found a place in Old Man Jackson's barn to bed down. The old coot didn't have but one horse, so Luke figured that would be as good a place as any. The horse shouldn't mind sharing, especially since

Luke was sleeping in an empty stall near the back of the barn.

He'd slung his pack down on a bed of straw that hadn't been changed in a while. It wasn't fresh, but it was welcome, as Luke stretched out slowly in the darkness and rested his head against his pack.

Just as sleep began to steal over him, a noise floated to him on the midnight breeze. It was a soft, melodic sound that was somehow…familiar. Luke opened his eyes and sat up, hearing only the sighing breeze outside and the rhythmic breathing of the horse two stalls down.

Only a dream. He settled back down into the straw, closing his eyes again. Weariness seeped through his bones. He let himself relax once more.

Somehow, sleep eluded him. Something crinkled in the pack, and he remembered the pages he'd ripped from Jeremiah's book.

He sat up again, opening the pack, feeling for the papers. He drew them out slowly and rose, walking back toward the barn door. The night wind had picked up, and Luke could hear the low rumble of thunder in the distance. From far off, lightning flashed. Clouds scudded across the moon, but there was enough light for him to see his younger brother's drawings.

He'd never truly looked at them before. They weren't important. Nothing about Jeremiah was important. But… these drawings were much better than he had anticipated. Though Jeremiah was only eight, the drawings showed the hand of a much more mature artist. Luke was surprised.

But as he looked at the pictures Jeremiah had sketched, he could see something even deeper.

The first few sketches were of Shadow. There were eight pages. Paper was such a rare commodity that most every page of Jeremiah's drawings was filled from top to bottom on both sides.

The common subject of many of the drawings was the familiar figure of Shadow, crude and childish, in the beginning. But with each new drawing, there was improvement in the skill and deftness of touch, culminating in the last picture...

Luke stood staring at that one. It was a rendition of Shadow lying in the yard, feet outstretched. The dog's eyes were open, barely—and they were looking straight at him. They gleamed at him, as if they were alive.

The wind gusted, and he was tempted to let it carry the handful of papers with it, scattering those drawings to the four corners of the earth. But he held on tightly to them, for some reason, and forced himself to look at that last picture again.

No matter how he turned the picture, those eyes followed him, holding his own stare. Finally, he wrenched his gaze away, folding the pictures. It had been a trick of the dappled moonlight, he told himself.

"Little bastard," he muttered, turning back toward the depths of the barn and making his way to this straw bed. He shoved the wad of papers back into his pack, wondering why he didn't bury them under the straw.

Sleep finally stole over him, but it was restless and shallow, with dreams of dying dog eyes, the clear melody of the broken flute, and Jeremiah's face streaked with blood, hungry for vengeance of his own.

The pointed end of Old Man Jackson's shotgun awoke him abruptly. Luke turned, easing himself over to look up into the weathered face.

"You git up and git out," the crusty old man said.

Luke couldn't understand the animosity that was evident in the narrowing of his eyes, the hard set of the eighty-year-old jaw. The last time they'd passed on the road, there had been a pleasant exchange of a few neighborly words. Now, the old man had hate in his eyes and lead in his hands—a bad combination for someone lying on a bed of straw too far from his own rifle for it to do him one damn bit of good.

"Mr. Jackson? It's—It's me—Luke Marshall. Your neighbor." Maybe he just hadn't recognized him.

"I know who you are, you murderin' little bastard. Anybody who'd kill like you done ought to be shot for a mad ravin' dog! But that's too good for the likes of you, Lucas Marshall, *isn't it*? You're nothin' but a cold-blooded murderer. A rabid dog can't help that he's got the hydrophobe and has to be put out of his misery. You got all your sense about you, boy. You're just dang stinkin' pure evil. Ought to shoot you right now, myself."

Luke started to sit up, but the old man took a step back and cocked the rifle, aiming it dead-center at Luke's chest.

"I may be old, but I still got my eyesight and the use of my hands. I don't mind pluggin' you, either."

"Mr. Jackson—"

"Save it," Jackson bit out. "Your brother was here last night. He told me all about what you done. You're a sorry excuse for a human being. I don't want you on my property."

Anger shot through Luke like a fire that flamed to life in his gut and fanned outward, setting his limbs tingling. *That little bastard! Why would he have come...but he couldn't have, could he?* Because when Luke had left, Jeremiah had been lying in a pool of blood—his and Shadow's.

"I needed a place to sleep—"

Jackson nodded once, a grim smile on his leathery lips. "You might say I'm mucking out my stables, and this is the first stall I'm cleaning the shit out of. Git your gear, and git out!"

Seething, Luke rose slowly, picking up his pack and the rifle that rested on it.

"So that's the gun you murdered that poor animal with," Jackson stated.

"I thought he was a wildcat," Luke replied sullenly.

The old man cackled. "That's your tale—I sit on mine!" Abruptly, the smile left his face. "Git the hell off my land."

Luke took a step toward the door and Jackson moved to stand behind him, prodding him in the back with the gun barrel again.

"Mr. Jackson—what did Jeremiah tell you?"

"He told me what happened. An' you're lucky I didn't shoot you on sight, you damn vermin!"

"But, what did he say?"

"Boy, I'd like to plant my boot up your ass right now, but it would slow you down, and I want you gone. You know what you done."

"But what did Jeremiah—"

"I give that pup to your ma for y'all to have a good guard dog, once Jeremiah come along. Yer ma was alone there with two young'uns. She needed protection. Looks like she shoulda been guardin' from *within her own family*," he snarled.

"It was a mistake!" Luke turned to face Jackson.

Jackson shook his head. "Nah. Wasn't no 'mistake' to it. Jeremiah, he told all about how it happened. You got mad, let your jealousy boil over—

all 'cause little Jeremiah didn't do what you said. You seen Shadow come into the yard, took aim, and shot him dead to get back at Jeremiah—but that wasn't *all* you done, was it, boy?"

Luke's mind whirled. When he'd last seen Jeremiah, he had been in no shape to walk the distance to Old Man Jackson's place. He hadn't looked like he'd be able to make it into the house...yet, the old man knew...*he knew*!

"When was he here—my brother?" He turned around again and kept walking as Old Man Jackson nodded for him to move.

"During the night..." His voice trailed away and Luke sensed he was confused about something.

"What time?"

"It don't matter none! All you need to know is it was after suppertime –after you did your killin'."

It was a good four-mile walk from Old Man Jackson's back to the Marshalls' cabin. Luke knew his ma would never have allowed Jeremiah to come, even if he'd been able. A chill swept through him. *How could the old man know what had happened?*

"Where was my ma at, Mr. Jackson?"

They had reached the edge of Jackson's property line, and the rutted road lay beckoning a few feet away.

Jackson stopped, but Luke knew the rifle was still pointed at his back. He didn't turn around until he reached the road.

Old Man Jackson gave him a contemptuous look.

Luke couldn't stop himself from asking, "Did she say she wanted me to come back home?"

For a moment, Luke thought he saw a flash of pity in Old Man Jackson's aged blue eyes.

"No. It'd be damn hard for a mother, even, to forgive what you done, boy."

"I—I killed a damn dog!" Luke would not admit, even to himself, that he had done it in cold blood… and that even when Jeremiah had run forward toward Shadow, there was still that split second he might have held up on the trigger and saved them both.

Jackson shook his grizzled bald head. "No, you done a lot more'n that. In the killin' of the animal, you broke that boy's heart. You done somethin' to him he couldn't never get over; you betrayed his trust and killed his best friend. And you…" He broke off and scratched his head, as if he wanted to say something about Jeremiah's killing. But if he did, Luke realized he'd have to admit that Jeremiah couldn't have come to him in the night.

But he knew. And how could he have known if someone hadn't told him?

"You forced yer ma to see the ugly part of you she didn't never want to look at. She wouldn't let a stranger do what you done without blastin' back at him. But you're her boy. She couldn't shoot you. So, though it broke her heart, she sent you on your way.

An' I know you never even thought of goin' for Doc Myers. Not even when she begged you."

He cocked his head. "Don't envy you a'tall. You ain't gonna be welcome anywhere you go…startin' right here. Now, git."

Luke had a lot of time to think about Old Man Jackson's words. The old coot had spewed them out like he was some damned prophet or something, Luke thought angrily.

He stopped around lunchtime as he neared a place in the nearby creek where he knew the water ran clear. He was thirsty, but more so, hunger gripped his empty stomach like a clamp.

He stumbled off the road, down toward the creek bank, and flopped down close to the water to get a cool drink.

But as he reached to make a cup of his hands, he noticed something—a movement behind him in his reflection in the water. He whirled quickly, but saw nothing. It must've been his tired eyes… He leaned forward again.

In the water, reflected beside his own face, there was another. *Jeremiah!*

He turned again, but Jeremiah was not there. It had been his imagination. He shook his head, and reached for a handful of water to splash across his face. *That had not been real. Couldn't have been.* How would Jeremiah have come this far on foot—especially after Luke had winged him with that bullet. And *why* would he be here?

Luke looked behind him again. Only the wind in the trees and the sounds of wildlife came to him. Nothing seemed out of place. He leaned up to get a drink again, closing his eyes this time.

A soft laugh sounded next to him, just as the water touched his dry lips. He jumped and rolled to his back, reaching for the rifle—and coming up empty.

Jeremiah stood over him. "Hello, brother."

Luke's breath caught in his throat. This was not the Jeremiah he knew. He was taller, older, stronger. His face was ageless; streaked, still, with Shadow's blood. The dark eyes that pinioned him to the ground were filled with soul-burning hate.

"J-Jeremiah?" Luke's voice came out breathy. "What are you doing here?"

Jeremiah's sardonic chuckle chilled Luke, in spite of the hot summer sun.

"Why, I'm here to keep you company on your journey, *brother*." He stepped forward and dropped one knee to the ground, kneeling beside Luke. "I'm here to let everyone know what you did."

Luke couldn't stop himself from reaching out to touch the apparition; for that was all it could be, he decided—his brother's ghost. His fingers passed through Jeremiah's leg. Luke closed his eyes and shuddered.

"You're d-dead, then," he stated, when he could draw a deep breath once again.

Jeremiah didn't answer until Luke opened his eyes. He stood, looking down at Luke with a mixture of disgust and pity. "You have no idea what you did, Lucas."

Luke moistened his lips. "Are you—going to kill me?"

Jeremiah grinned slowly. "Always concerned about *yourself*, aren't you? Don't you even wonder what happened after you left last night?"

Before Luke could answer, Jeremiah continued. "I'm going to tell you, and you're going to hear me."

Luke bristled at Jeremiah's tone. Ghost or not, Jeremiah was Indian scum that would never best Luke, in this world or the next. "Watch your words, Jeremiah." Luke rolled to a sitting position and slowly came to his feet.

"You're hardly in a position to give orders anymore."

Luke looked into Jeremiah's eyes. They were close to the same height, with Jeremiah being slightly taller—not the eight-year-old that Luke had always been able to physically dominate. But…he'd never controlled him in any other way. Maybe that's where his resentment stemmed from. Jeremiah had been as wild as a forest animal; feral and more independent than Luke had ever been.

Old habits were hard to break. Luke took a step toward Jeremiah, but his movements were slow and unnatural. He reached for Jeremiah's shirt front, but Jeremiah knocked his hand back easily, in plenty of time.

"Things are different now, Lucas. *Very* different." He pinned Luke with a blazing look of disgust.

Luke swallowed hard and shook his head. "This is a dream—nothing more." But his voice was quiet, as if he were trying to talk himself into believing it.

Jeremiah shook his head slowly. "No dream. You will reap what you've sown."

"I'm going home to see to Mama," Luke said. "She'll need me now. Now that you're gone."

Jeremiah's lips spread slowly, a laugh rumbling from deep inside him. It rose up and spilled out, ringing across the woods in a wild cacophony that set the birds to flight.

"Gone? *Gone?*" Jeremiah wiped his eyes as sis smile faded. "What a kind word to replace 'murdered', Lucas. *You murdered me.* I'm not *'gone'*—and I never will be. I'm going to be right here with you… as long as you draw breath."

Luke tried to ignore Jeremiah, but there was no way to do it. His words had struck more fear into Luke's heart than the mere fact that Jeremiah was here, standing beside him, in an ageless, adult form.

As Luke bent to pick up his gear, Jeremiah said, "Did you forget about your thirst?"

"No," Luke answered. "Just don't care for the company here. I'm gonna move downstream a little ways." He walked away without looking back at his brother. As he walked, he made no move to see if Jeremiah was trailing him.

He didn't really have to look. He had an odd sensation that someone was with him, though he couldn't see Jeremiah, or hear his footsteps.

He walked until his thirst would allow him to go no further. He had to have a drink. There was a place ahead of him where the creek ran clear. A rock outcropping allowed for a person to be able to lie flat, close to the cold water, and drink.

Luke scrambled toward the flat, warm rock, thirst burning in his throat as the sound of the running stream became clearer. He could barely wait to dip his hands into the water.

Just as he lay down, he felt a strong-muscled arm close to his. He turned his head to see Jeremiah beside him. Their eyes met briefly before Luke turned away and plunged his hands into the refreshing coolness.

He cupped his hands and closed his eyes, anticipating the way the water was sure to taste. But there was an odor to it that wasn't as it should be.

"Open your eyes, Lucas," Jeremiah murmured. "You need to see what you're drinking."

Despite his urge to defy Jeremiah, Luke let his eyes crack open, just as he brought the liquid up to his lips.

It wasn't water in his hands. *It was blood*. The entire creek ran red with it, thick and redolent with the odor of old copper, or iron.

Lucas scrambled back away from the bank, revulsion twisting at his insides as he tried to wipe the sticky residue from his hands onto the sparse grass.

When he looked back toward the creek, he could see nothing had changed; it still ran swift with a current of crimson.

He gasped, finally forcing himself to look up at Jeremiah, who gracefully came to his feet and walked to where Luke sat on the grass. He stood over Luke, a sneer twisting his mouth.

"H-How did you do that?" Luke demanded. Anger overrode his fear at what had just happened. How dare this—this *ghost*, or whatever he was—try to intimidate him?

Jeremiah chuckled mirthlessly. "You have no idea what I'm capable of, Lucas."

Luke jumped to his feet, squaring off against his brother. "Turn it back into water, damn you!"

"Don't you want to see what else I can do?" Jeremiah taunted.

Luke didn't. He didn't want to see anything but cold water in the creek bed. His gaze was drawn to where blood had just flowed freely in place of the water. The creek bed was now bone dry, as if it hadn't seen a drop of water for years. In the next instant, it was full of water, so plentiful with fish that they leapt out of the water onto the banks.

"My God..." Luke took a step toward the creek, the fish making splashing noises as they surfaced. But with the next step he took, the water became blood once more. He turned savagely to Jeremiah. *"What the hell are you doing to me?"*

"You will never drink again."

Luke's heart clenched, but he wouldn't let Jeremiah know it. He'd never felt fear so deep and cutting, as if he couldn't draw breath without forcing himself to think of it consciously. He was exhausted, and all he could think of was a long, cool drink.

"Look, I-I tried to go for the doc, but I turned my ankle. I couldn't make it on into town—"

"Liar. You didn't go for Doc Myers. You let me bleed to death with Shadow, there on the ground."

"No! Honest—"

"But you are *not* honest. And we both know it." Jeremiah's tone was matter-of-fact. They stood looking at one another for a few seconds, hatred and fear rippling through Luke. But Jeremiah wore a look of expectation of the inevitable, and Luke's fear turned to bone-melting terror.

In a desperate effort to regain the upper hand, Luke bent to gather his scattered belongings, making a show of organizing them in order to collect his thoughts.

"Mama—" Luke said after a moment. "What's become of her?"

Jeremiah studied him coldly. "After Shadow died, I passed, too. Shadow was waiting for me. But as we journeyed in the spirit world, a cry came to me on the wind…such a cry as you've never heard." He glanced toward the river of blood, watching it for a few seconds.

"It was…our mother. She couldn't live, after what you had done. You killed an innocent animal, who'd done nothing but be loyal and faithful his whole life. You killed me, your younger brother, who wanted nothing more than your love and approval." He turned to meet Luke's wide eyes.

"But the worst thing was, you killed our mother as surely as if you'd shot her, too. Her heart died, to see you as you truly were. Jealous, vindictive, and vicious."

Luke stood speechless, looking at Jeremiah, knowing he spoke the truth. "What happened?" he croaked, his throat parched by this time.

"Oh, Lucas…" Jeremiah shook his head with the

barest hint of regret. "Why do you think the river runs red?"

"I DIDN'T DO IT!" Luke said, starting back toward the road. *Was Jeremiah still there?* There was no answer to his bold declaration. Resolutely, he put one foot in front of the other, heading for Salvation, two miles away.

Thoughts of seeing Shadow in his gun sights, recognizing him, pulling the trigger anyway—then Jeremiah running— *That had surely been an accident.* Even in Shadow's death, Luke felt not much more than a trace of responsibility. Hadn't Jeremiah—and, yes, even their mother—driven him to do what he'd done? His place in the family as the rule-maker for Jeremiah had been threatened. If Jeremiah had been a better brother, none of this would have happened, he told himself. *None of it.*

"That's always been your problem," Jeremiah said placidly.

Luke whirled to face him, but he wasn't there. It was only then Luke realized his brother's voice had come from inside his own head.

"You damn coward!" he shouted to the empty woods. "Where are you?"

In the next instant, Jeremiah stood beside him, so close Luke could have felt his breath on his cheek, if a ghost had breath in his body. Jeremiah's eyes were blazing with an unholy light that made Luke take an involuntary step backward.

That brought a slow, taunting smile to Jeremiah's lips.

"Remind me again, brother, who shot a gentle animal for no reason but a spiteful spirit? Remind me, how, when our mother begged you to go for the doctor as I lay dying, you gathered your possessions and took time to destroy mine. You never intended to go for help. It was then that she realized what kind of man she had raised; then, that her heart began to die.

"When she knew that I had gone to the Other Side—and no, there wouldn't have been time to fetch the doctor, even had you tried—she realized she'd lost everything. That's when she held me close to her for the last time.

"Her heart was pounding so hard, Luke. Like a bird in a cage trying to beat its way to freedom from the pain and sorrow." Jeremiah stopped and looked away as the memories washed over him.

Luke didn't want to hear any more. Jeremiah raised his head to meet Luke's eyes again. The chill that seized Luke was not just a figment of his mind; it was physical, as well. He shivered in the sunlight, his thirst forgotten for the briefest moment in the wake of his fear.

"But why *tell* you about it?" Jeremiah asked, his

voice silky and thoughtful. "Why not let you see it for yourself, since you ran away and missed it."

Quickly, he stretched his arm out and touched Luke's forehead with two fingers. Lightning seemed to shoot through Luke's body, searing him from the inside. He screamed as he fell to the ground in a boneless heap. Jeremiah's soft chuckle enveloped him.

"Now, you can see it all."

At first, Luke didn't understand what his brother was talking about. He could do nothing but lie on the ground, feeling sick at his stomach, a blinding headache overcoming him to the point that he felt he'd not be able to ever again open his eyes to the light of day.

But keeping his eyes shut was not the answer. When Jeremiah had touched him, he'd done something that Luke couldn't understand fully, but he was beginning to realize that a terrible change had occurred within him in the blink of an eye.

He noticed an image in the red-black shelter of his shuttered eyelids. As it came clear, he realized he was looking at a familiar scene…Jeremiah's crumpled body atop that of his beloved dog, their mother on her knees beside her fallen son and his dearest best friend.

As Luke watched, he saw himself walking away, then the look of utter despair come into his mother's eyes. She leaned over to kiss Jeremiah's forehead, her fingers lingering tenderly in his hair, just as his still lay upon Shadow's in death. Finally, she rose and began to walk toward the rushing river behind their house. She moved as if she were sleepwalking in the night; as if she didn't know what she was about to do...

But, Luke could see, she *did* know. She walked right into the water with all of her clothes on, scrubbing her son's blood from her hands with meticulous purpose as she began to sink into the water. She made no attempt to swim or save herself.

Luke tried to stop watching, but found he could not open his eyes. And even as his mother disappeared into the water completely, he still concocted excuses and justifications for what he had brought down upon his family.

When he'd seen everything, he opened his eyes very slowly. Jeremiah was gone. The sun beat down mercilessly on him, and he felt sick. He glanced toward the creek, tempted to try again to get a drink before he set off for town.

He got to his feet very carefully and managed to walk to the creek bank. But just as he dropped to his knees, close to the water, a feeling of trepidation spread over him. He looked around, half-expecting to see Jeremiah, but he was alone. He plunged his hands into the water, fighting back the wave of nausea. With trembling palms cupped, he brought the water to his lips, but the bile rose swiftly, and he turned his head to retch into the grass beside him.

He crawled back away from the creek, suddenly awash in a sheen of sweat. Gathering his pack and his rifle, he started toward the little town of Salvation again, but after only a few stumbling steps, he couldn't carry the things he'd brought. Up ahead, a large elm tree offered shelter under its branches for him to lay his pack and rifle until he could come back for them.

As he set them down, he felt an odd sense of leaving the place for the last time. Foreboding closed in. "I'll be back," he muttered, but he couldn't stop himself from opening the pack and taking out the sheaf of drawings Jeremiah had done.

He studied them, one by one, until he came to the one of Shadow with the eyes that seemed to accuse him, no matter how he turned the paper. The dog looked larger than it had the last time he'd looked at the drawing…and, if possible…even more realistic.

He folded it hastily and started to cram it back in the pack. Something stopped him, and instead, he shoved the paper into his pants pocket.

He'd be fine once he got to town among people. He'd go to Doc Myers's first thing…*But, he couldn't.* The old doc would look at him with accusing eyes of his own, like Shadow's, and ask why he was only just now coming into town?

Old Man Jackson's words echoed in his head as

he took several unsteady steps toward the road. *How had he known what had happened?* Jeremiah, damn his soul, must have been spreading lies about him to everyone. But Jeremiah was dead.

"I'm not dead, brother." Jeremiah's voice came from the trees, the dirt, the sky, echoing around him, then throbbing with the pounding of Luke's head.

"Yes, you are!" Luke tried to run, but his legs wouldn't cooperate. He fell in a tangled heap in the road, covering his head.

"I'll be with you forever, Luke. Forever. *Forever...*"

If he could just get to town. He managed to push himself up, his feet sluggish, and doggedly started for town again. It couldn't be much further—no more than a mile...

"You *are* a demon," he muttered, casting a quick glance over his shoulder. He hadn't expected to see Jeremiah, but there he was, following only a few paces behind.

"Go away!" Luke whirled, then bent to pick up a few good-sized rocks, throwing one at Jeremiah's head. He knew it was childish, and he wished he hadn't left the rifle behind. If he had it, he'd shoot Jeremiah a second time, ghost or no.

The rock he'd thrown fell to the ground in front of Jeremiah, who only smiled at Luke's frustrated anger.

"Getting thirstier, aren't you, Luke?"

Luke shook his fist. "I'll get a drink in town! Stay away from me!"

"Don't be afraid. I have no intention of laying a finger on you, dear brother."

"Son of a bitch!" Luke screamed. "Leave me alone!"

But Jeremiah shook his dark head. "No, I'm afraid we are going to be together for a very, very long time."

Luke whirled around, turning his back to Jeremiah and walking, resolutely putting one foot in front of the other. He had to get to town. He suddenly wondered if anyone else would be able to see Jeremiah.

"Not unless I wish for them to," Jeremiah said quietly from beside him.

Luke jumped, startled. He hadn't felt Jeremiah there so close to him.

Jeremiah gave him a slow grin. "Maybe you're losing your mind," he suggested.

Luke shook his head, wiping the sweat from his face. "No. No, I ain't goin' crazy."

Jeremiah lifted a dark brow. "Could be anything. There's...lots of ways—"

"I ain't crazy! Do you hear me, you little bastard?"

Jeremiah chuckled. "I hear you. And anybody in the next mile around can hear you, too." His eyes narrowed in warning. "I believe you *are* crazy. And just plain cruel. There'll be no help for you in Salvation." His voice was flat, certain; and that added to

Luke's worry... But he didn't reply. How could he argue with a ghost? What sense did it make? He wiped the sweat out of his eyes and forced himself to start moving. He tried to ignore the silent movements of his half-brother, walking so close to him down this dirt road.

"Why are you here?" Luke's voice sounded desperate and pleading to his own ears. He glanced at Jeremiah, who walked on in silence for a moment before he answered.

"To serve as a reminder to you, Luke. Until the day you die." His face was set grimly. "And, afterward."

"Leave me be! Do you hear?" Luke's mouth was dry, and nausea flooded through him, thick and violent so that he almost fell to his knees. But instead, he turned away to be sick and stayed on his feet, barely.

"You're still so filled with hatred there's no room for remorse or sorrow," Jeremiah stated.

"For *you*?" Luke spat. "I'm not the least bit sorry you're gone. I-I regret Mama—"

"*Regret?*" Jeremiah shot at him.

"I can't argue any more, Jeremiah. I'm—so thirsty."

But when Luke turned to face Jeremiah, he was gone. Luke stood alone in the middle of the road, the town of Salvation barely visible in the distance. He wiped his blurry eyes again and started forward.

"Here comes that Marshall boy, Ellis." Lucinda Moore laid aside the bolt of cloth she'd been matching thread for in the mercantile she and Ellis owned.

Through the front window, she could see Luke coming down the street with the unsteady gait of a man who'd had too much to drink the night before. He stumbled, managing to grab a hitching rail in front of Abe's Saloon and hold on tightly.

Ellis Moore came to stand beside his wife, looking out at Luke Marshall as well. Ellis narrowed his eyes, then they widened as Luke looked around the town, as if it were unfamiliar to him.

"Lucy, turn the sign. We're closed. At least, for the time being."

"But—"

"Just do it. Don't let that boy in, no matter what." Ellis shut the door and locked it tight, making his way around the store, checking all the doors and windows to be sure they were secure.

"Ellis, what's going on, dear?"

Ellis came back to Lucinda's side and they watched as Luke finally let go of the itching rail and slowly started forward again.

"That boy," Ellis said grimly, "has the look of a mad dog—like he's got…the hydrophobe. We don't want to take any chances. Not until we know what's wrong with him."

"You best go warn the sheriff."

Ellis nodded, making for the back door. "Come lock the door, and stay out of sight."

Luke's world turned and tilted, swaying as he did. He couldn't stand on his own. What the hell was wrong with him?

"Damn you, Jeremiah...Damn you...You did this to me, you damn half-breed bastard. You did this!" Nearly as strong as his desperation, anger washed over him. *"Look what you've stolen from me!"*

Jeremiah chuckled mirthlessly from beside him. But when Luke whirled to look at him, he was gone.

"Show yourself!" he yelled down the empty street.

The last of the townspeople who were on the boardwalks hurried into nearby doorways as he staggered forward, holding to hitching rails as he went.

"You damned...half-breed..." Luke's voice was thinner now. He would have sold his soul for a drink of cold water, yet, at the same time, the memory of the blood he'd dipped from the creek rose up in his mind, making him want to retch again.

"Show yourself, you damned Indian bastard!"

But through Jeremiah's laughter echoed in Luke's ears he remained invisible, leaving Luke to scream his utter frustration down the now-vacant streets of Salvation.

"HE'S HEADED THIS WAY, SHERIFF," Ellis Moore said hurriedly. "That Marshall boy. Comin' down the street just as crazy as a bedbug. Yellin' out all kinds of wild things—can't hardly stand up—"

Sheriff Ben Wolf pushed his chair back from his desk and stood up. "Well, Ellis, you go on back to the store and Lucinda and I'll see to it. I need to question him about his brother's death; we just brought back his mother's body, too, from downstream where Paddy Michaels found her."

"No!" Shock pinched Ellis's face, the blood draining.

"Oh, I'm sorry. I thought you'd heard." The sheriff reached calmly for his Henry and checked the chamber matter-of-factly. "Mrs. Marshall drowned." His fingers tightened momentarily on the gun, then relaxed again. "Her son, Jeremiah, was found shot, along with his dog. Looked like he tried to save the dog—same bullet got both of them. As for Elizabeth —uh, Mrs. Marshall—we don't know if it was accidental or if this—animal—killed his mother." He started for the door.

"You believe *Luke Marshall* killed his family..." Ellis could scarce believe it.

Before the sheriff could answer, the door banged open. Doc Myers quickly closed it behind him.

"Ben, you know what's going on out there?"

"Ellis came to tell me."

The doctor shook his head. "He's got it bad."

"What's that, Doc?"

"Either he's got hydrophobia or he's a stark raving mad lunatic."

Ben shot him a sharp look. "Hydrophobia? You're sure?"

"Can't be anything else. Way he's walking, raving like he's –talking to your—uh, to Jeremiah..." There was a moment's hesitation in is voice. He cleared his throat. "It's like he thinks Jeremiah's with him. Doesn't realize he's –uh...*gone.*"

Ben Wolf gave the doctor a long look. "I didn't do right by Elizabeth or Jeremiah. I can't do it over—it's too late. I know he's *'gone,'* Doc. You can say *'dead.'* Now, I've got a job to do—if you'll get out of my way."

The doctor stepped aside slowly, then touched Ben's shoulder as he opened the door. "Be right in your heart, Ben. Don't do this for revenge."

Ben didn't reply for a moment. He looked out into the empty street. "Animals with the hydrophobe gotta be put down. You want to try to cure him?"

Doc Myers shook his head reluctantly. "There's nothing I can do for him. You know that."

"I thought not. I'll go put him out of his misery, same as I'd do for a mad dog with rabies. You two stay put."

Luke hung draped across one of the hitching posts. The world looked upside down. In fact, it was moving all around him, but he knew he was holding still. There was no way he could move—the damn hitching rail was cutting him in two.

But if he tried to unwrap himself, everything would come undone, and he'd probably end up face down in the dusty street.

"Lucas Marshall!"

Sheriff Ben Wolf's voice cut through Luke's befuddled thoughts.

Ben Wolf. Sheriff. Half-breed. Jeremiah. Indian. Ben Wolf.

Luke decided he better unroll himself from the wood rail. He managed to slide down to where his butt hit the ground and he sat, leaning against the pole that held the hitching rail in place.

The sun assaulted him. When had it gotten so damn hot? He needed a drink. But when he thought of water, he remembered his bloody hands down by the creek bank. His stomach churned, and nausea washed over him.

"Lucas Marshall!" the voice called again.

Luke tried to croak a response, but nothing came out. He opened his swollen dry lips again, and a rusty sound, like metal sliding on stone emerged.

Sheriff Wolf approached, rifle in hand, until he stood only a few feet from Luke.

"Sher...Wolf..." Luke tried to moisten his lips with a tongue as thick as an oak limb.

"Ask for water," Jeremiah's voice prodded from nearby.

Luke turned quickly, and the street spun crazily. "Shut...Jerem...Shut your mouth."

Wolf looked around the deserted street. "Who you talkin' to, boy?"

Luke looked up at him with unguarded defiance. "My...little half-breed...brother...Don't'cha see him, Sheriff?"

Jeremiah's laughter roared through Luke's mind like bells that wouldn't stop ringing. He put his hands up over his ears. "Stop it! Stop...you..."

"Luke...were you bitten by an animal that might've had rabies?"

That brought a smile to Luke's parched mouth. "No. Little...red...bastard did this to me. I—shot... his dog."

"That ain't all you shot," Wolf said tightly. "You murdered Jeremiah and Eliz—your mother." Wolf watched Luke for a moment, then said, "Ain't that right, boy? You drowned your mother—"

"No! I didn't...she killed herself."

Wolf cocked his head. "How'd you know that, if it's true?"

"Jeremi...Jer...told me."

Wolf's eyes turned deadly. "Ain't nothin' to joke about. 'Specially not after you killin' him like you done. And there ain't no question about that."

"Aren't you thirsty, Luke?" Jeremiah taunted from where he sat beside Luke.

Luke made a grab for him, but it was wasted. As soon as his fingers should be closing around Jeremiah's neck, the specter had vanished, leaving Luke to clutch empty air. Jeremiah's soft chuckle lingered in his head.

"Get out. Get out of my...mind."

"Water...water...water..." Jeremiah's voice changed like an echo.

"He turned the river...bloody. Then dried it up." Luke tried to swallow and wet his throat as he turned back to the Sheriff.

"Who'll believe that story?" Jeremiah whispered.

"Stop talking to me!" Luke shouted. He crawled up the hitching post, using every ounce of the last of his strength.

"I have questions. I gotta find out—" Wolf began.

"No, not you. Not...Jeremiah—he keeps talking to me..."

"Guilty conscience, Lucas?" Wolf asked caustically.

"He's here."

"He can't see me, Luke," Jeremiah whispered. "Not unless I wish him to. Only you can see me, hear me. And after all this, you still feel no regret for what you've done."

"I'm glad I did it!" Luke shouted to the empty street. "I'm glad I killed you and that damn dog of yours, Jeremiah!"

The melodic sound of the flute drifted through the dusty street on the hot wind.

Wolf shifted the Henry up into better position. He wasn't taking any chances.

Jeremiah suddenly appeared bedside the Sheriff, arms folded across his chest. "Come for me, Lucas. No, I won't disappear this time."

There was a look of hot anger in Jeremiah's features that Luke relished.

Oh yes. If he would stay put, they could end this once and for all, Luke thought. He took an unsteady step forward.

"Stay back, Lucas," Wolf ordered, bringing the rifle purposefully aimed at Luke's chest.

"Didn't you hear him? I'm going to kill him!" he raged.

"You already done that! You said it."

"Not good enough." He took another step, and Wolf warned him again, but it didn't stop him.

"I'm here, Lucas. Yours for the taking," Jeremiah said with a smile. He unfolded his muscular arms and loosened them, crouching. "Come on, *brother*."

With a wild cry, Luke hurtled himself toward where Jeremiah stood beside Wolf.

Cursing, Wolf pulled the trigger. The roar was deafening in the deserted street. Blood sprayed from the close proximity that Wolf had had to take the shot to stop Luke from attacking him as he'd rushed forward. Now, the boy sprawled face down in the dust, unmoving.

Slowly, Wolf started toward him, and from all around, doors opened, and people emerged. Doc Myers came to stand beside him, then knelt beside the body.

Harley and Jonas Unrue, the undertaker's sons, arrived and turned Luke's body over, careful not to come into contact with his blood-spattered skin.

"What's this?" Doc reached for a folded piece of paper that lay beneath Luke. Slowly, he stood, unfolding it, then walked back to the sheriff.

"Guess this tells the story," he said thoughtfully.

Wolf reached for it.

Shadow lay on the grass in front of the Marshall cabin. Young Jeremiah sprawled across him, his fingers lovingly laid upon the dog's big head. Shadow's loyal gaze was fixed on Jeremiah, dying, both of them.

A lifelike rendering of Elizabeth Marshall, too

real to be anything but the actual portrait of her in that awful moment, took Ben Wolf's breath away. He fingered the edge of the paper, alone in the midst of the crowd. Her eyes were wide with shock and fear. Her blonde hair streamed behind her, undone from its neat bun with the wind…the rifle barrel was even drawn, as if the artist was creating the picture from the perfect vantage point to capture every nuance of the killing.

Who? Who could have drawn this? Ben glanced at Luke's body as the mortician's sons loaded it into their wagon, with Doc Myers's help, to drive the short distance to their father's funeral parlor.

Luke laid slack jawed, eyes open, staring vacantly. The bullet had caught him square in the chest, where most people had a heart, Ben thought. Anger at his own losses swept over him. No, Lucas Marshall hadn't the talent to draw something such as this; perfection, detail, and realism rolled into such a rendering would have been beyond him.

The wind whipped up, fierce and wild with the sudden hot gusts of a summer storm. Ben held tightly to the drawing and blamed the blowing dirt for making his eyes sting and water.

Just then, the drawing was yanked from Ben's fingers and swirled upward. He made a grab for it instinctively, angry at the feeling of it being ripped from his grip.

The tug on the drawing had been angry, too; as if

Ben was being blamed for something—maybe, he thought, an act of omission in not doing right by Elizabeth Marshall and their boy. If he had taken responsibility, this whole mess might never have happened. Who knew? Perhaps *he* was the one who had lost his mind...a mad dog—or worse. For he'd had the power to change it all—and had done nothing. He could have married Elizabeth. Could have been a father...a husband...

He glanced around at the townspeople. They stood by, doing nothing...nothing but watching; watching him, watching the paper as it danced higher in the wind in a frantic escape. Down the street, the Unrue brothers unloaded Luke's corpse from the wagon, closing the door of their father's business behind them.

The melody of a flute sounded clear and haunting through the wind...a dirge for the death of innocence; for love never sought nor claimed; for simple kindness never extended, or returned.

As Ben watched, the paper disintegrated into pieces of shimmering dust high above where he and Doc Myers stood. And the rain began to fall, along with the sharp glitter of dreams, and jealousy, and anger, on the just and the unjust who stood in the streets of Salvation.

CHERYL PIERSON IS a native Oklahoman with many novels to her credit as well as numerous short stories and novellas. Founding Prairie Rose Publications with long-time friend Livia Reasoner is a dream-come-true for her—there's something new every day. Helping other authors is at the top of her list, and she enjoys every minute of it. Cheryl is a past president of the Western Fictioneers professional writing organization. She has two grown children and lives with her husband in Oklahoma City. http://prairierosepublications.com/

HEADWATERS

VONN MCKEE

Lex Tucker knelt on the high mountain slope beside three fallen rocks wedged together into a pyramid. He'd found it, at last. A rivulet gurgled from beneath the stones, straight from the mountain's heart. Lex stuck his hand in the icy flow and immediately jerked it back from the shock. Cupping both hands, he quickly scooped up the clear water for a drink. His horse stepped into the shallows where they widened to an arm's breadth, eased his thirst and splashed across the stream to feast on a patch of sedge.

Riding over Stony Pass earlier in the day, Lex caught silvery glimpses of the Rio Grande—only a humble stream here in the San Juans. It threaded through alpine meadows to conjoin with other meandering trickles before dropping into the valley. Downriver, it would broaden and tumble and flatten and snake itself to south Texas, where the great Gulf of Mexico would receive its muddy waters.

Lex had left the trail to trace the stream to its beginning farther up the mountain. He had no reason for the detour, except perhaps to put off reaching his destination. Although, according to his father's letter that somehow found him in Silverton, time was not something he ought to waste.

Everything begins somewhere, he thought, and usually not without a fight. Pure, cold water, clear as a diamond, pushed up from a dark unknown source and squeezed through hidden cracks in the mountain until it gushed past these last three rocks in its path. Now, it was no longer an underground spring but a river, albeit it a young one with no notion of the journey ahead.

Young and wild, bound for adventure. Lex smiled, remembering how he'd once felt the same.

Rubbing chilled hands on his pant legs, he went to fetch his horse, crossing the Rio Grande in one step.

"When are you going to stop crossing rivers and mountains to see what's on the other side, Lex?"

Sarah stood barefoot, with arms crossed. She was almost as tall as he, and he met her dark sapphire stare, noting the cocked eyebrow. In the blue silk dressing gown he bought her in San Francisco, she looked like the lady her mother had raised her to be. But Sarah only acted like a lady when she chose to, and Lex happened to admire that about her.

"You haven't answered me," Sarah said. They stood at the front door.

Lex reached for his hat and gunbelt hanging on the hall tree. Before he put the pinch-crown Stetson on, he stepped forward and kissed Sarah soundly. "I'll stop when I run out of rivers and mountains to cross, I reckon."

Sarah frowned, and he caressed the crease between her eyebrows with his thumb. "If it means anything...I take you with me...always," he said.

"It means something." She closed her eyes. "It could mean you would rather hold on to a memory than the genuine article. Memories don't ask for much, do they, Lex?"

He kissed her again and walked out. The closing door rang with a finality that echoed in Lex's thoughts all the way out of town.

Jimmy Bowes had handed Lex the wrinkled, stained envelope with his good arm. A tumble down a mine shaft in the bowels of King Solomon Mountain had crippled his shoulder and, being no longer of value to the Las Animas Mining District, Jimmy found work in Silverton at the mercantile and post office.

He was apt to lost this job as soon as a New Yorker named Thomson finished building a massive brick and granite hotel on the corner of Greene Street, which would also house the new post office, a store, bank and city offices.

"Why, I never knew your name was Lexington," said Jimmy. "Mister Lexington J. Tucker. Sounds right dignified."

Lex grimaced. His pa had stuck the name of his west Tennessee birthplace on his firstborn son. That meant Lex could never completely escape his father's reach, in memory, in scars—visible and otherwise—and even when he signed his name.

With a quick nod to Jimmy, Lex left the store with a folded blue flannel shirt tucked under his arm and a new plug of tobacco in his back pocket. He'd open the letter when he got to his matchbox of a rented room.

So the old man was in La Veta. Lots of freighters and treasure seekers traversed the high pass between Silverton and Del Norte, and La Veta lay a hundred miles beyond there. Someone must have seen Lex, had a drink with him, maybe bested him at cards, which was unlikely. Lex had learned to let others grub for money or for gold and silver nuggets. It was easy enough to win them off the poor fools, slow and easy, with whiskey and a decent cigar at hand. Somehow, word traveled over the mountains to Pop.

If the unsteady scrawl was to be believed, the old man didn't expect to be around for long. Wanted to have a word with his sons. Lex tried to remember the last time the three of them had been in one room. Guess it would've been that shack up north by the Rabbit Ears, close to where a couple of creeks formed the North Platte. It seemed the Tuckers were drawn to places where rivers begin.

Lex put the letter out of his mind for a day. But then, after washing his face in the dry sink wedged beside his bed, he looked up at the small mirror, cloudy with age, that hung askew on a rusty nail. His brown curly hair, past his shoulders, was shot with gray, though he was six months shy of thirty years old. Dark eyes, near black, were among the few reminders he had of his New Orleans-born mother, who died two days after his younger brother was born. But the thin face with its square, clefted chin, the fierce eyebrows—one split by a scar from an encounter with a fire poker —the full lips set in a line. Lex Tucker took a step back from the mirror's truth—his mother's eyes, in his father's face.

It may have been curiosity, or a remaining shred of conscience, or a firstborn's inescapable bent toward responsibility that made Lex pack saddlebags and mount up for the road out of Silverton and toward Stony Pass, and La Veta. He questioned the decision with every mile.

Lex heaved the axe up to split one last piece of firewood for the day. His arms burned with fatigue, even though he was strong...for a ten-year-old. He could hear Deke Tucker inside, swearing at no one in particular and throwing a pan, a tin cup, turning over something. A chair? Lex locked eyes with Silas, younger by three years, who had emerged from the chicken coop, cradling four eggs in his small, dirty hands. They would wait until Pop quieted down to go inside, not that it guaranteed he wouldn't break loose again.

The boys slipped into the one-room cabin. Lex stacked wood against the back wall behind the small stove. Silas fetched the skillet from underneath the table where it had been flung, to begin cooking the eggs and a slab of salt pork on top of the stove. Pop lay on the bed, eyes closed but not sleeping. When the cooking smells filled the cabin, he roused, sat up, and reached for the nearly empty bottle on the floor. He took a noisy swig. Lex set the table, dreading the notion of sharing it with his father. Silas divided the eggs and meat onto the plates.

Pop walked past the stack of wood and paused. He stooped to pick up a piece and, with a poker, opened the door to the stove, then shoved the wood inside. He slammed the door hard and it bounced open from the force. Pop drew back the poker and swung hard at it, clipping the door's edge. It did indeed stay shut, but the iron poker slipped from his hand and flew across the room.

Lex turned his head at the sound of the slamming door, just in time to catch the end of the poker above his left eye. His head snapped backward from the blow. Blood soon streamed down his face and down the front of his shirt. He stood frozen, staring at Pop with the eye not blurred by blood. Pop looked stricken for several seconds, then the familiar dark cloud settled over his face.

"Well, hell, boy. Don't stand there and bleed on our supper. Get outside and wash in the trough."

LEX EXPECTED his second crossing of the Rio Grande, where it hooked south at Del Norte, to be uneventful. It was August, and the fury of early summer snowmelt had died down. Still, the Rio was wide and temperamental, even on its good days. He gently urged his horse into the current, angling for a shallow bank.

He never knew why the horse went under. Perhaps a leg caught a tree snag, or the river bottom fell away quickly. The sudden dip was enough to throw Lex forward and out of his saddle. He could see nothing, and deep burbling water noises filled his ears. As he scrambled to turn upright, the horse's thrashing front legs pushed him farther under and

Lex was trapped beneath the desperate animal as it tried to swim. His head thumped against the sandy bottom, stunning him for a few seconds.

With no sense of up or down, Lex stopped flailing and relaxed. He gave himself over to the river, moving with the current, underwater. Surely, only seconds passed, although they seemed like minutes. He felt carried along, as if in unseen arms. Then, he surfaced, face up, never so grateful to see a blue sky above.

He wasn't sure how he escaped the current, but he was aware of the sound of waves breaking nearby. The Rio washed him up on the opposite shore, a few hundred feet downriver from his intended landing spot. When he was able to sit up, he spied his horse safely on the bank, shaking himself.

Lex took off his clothes and squeezed out the muddy water, then unsaddled his mount. They rested for an hour, drying in the sun. When they picked up the trail west toward La Veta, he heard Sarah's voice, sounding for all the world like she was right behind him.

"When are you going to stop crossing rivers and mountains to see what's on the other side, Lex?"

HE COUNTED a half dozen saloons as he rode through La Veta, but there were also a number of saddle shops, mercantiles, law offices and other businesses among the storefronts. The tracks of the Denver Rio Grande ran right up Main Street. He thought of stopping at one of the saloons for a drink but changed his mind. In order to face Pop after all these years, he needed all his wits about him.

It didn't take long to find the plain, two-story boarding house tucked behind a gunsmith's shop, that Pop mentioned in his letter. He tied the reins to the gate post, proceeded to the door and knocked. While waiting, he looked around at the neatly kept porch and yard. A wooden plaque, with burned letters spelling HAAS, hung over the door.

A slight old man, who looked as though he were made of wax, answered. Lex scrutinized the man's face, but could see no resemblance to his father.

"Good afternoon. You must be Lexington Tucker," he said, a faint Germanic accent coarsening his words. He held the door open for Lex to enter.

"Yes, sir."

"Ah, it is good that you have come. I am Leo Haas. My wife, Mila, is…here…in back, I believe. Please, sit. I will tell Mister Tucker you are here." The man disappeared down a dark hall, leaving Lex in the stuffy parlor. He chose a wood bench by the open window and sat.

Lex heard mumbling and shuffling, then Haas emerged from the hallway with his hand supporting Pop's elbow—a frail and stooped incarnation of Pop.

Lex wondered which man looked the most likely to collapse.

As Pop settled into a chair, he fixed a milky-eyed gaze on Lex.

"Could you move me closer, my friend?" Leo helped Pop to a half-standing position and walked him forward a few feet, then scooted the chair under him.

"There. Better." Pop resumed his stare. A toothless smile eased the corners of his mouth upward. Lex could not remember seeing Pop smile before. Sneer, perhaps, but smile, no.

"How are you, son?" he said.

Lex squirmed, cleared his throat. "Getting by."

Pop nodded. "Getting by. Can mean things are good. Or … can mean things could be a lot better." He dropped his eyes to the braided rug.

"I…I thank you for making the ride. You sure as hell didn't owe it to me."

Lex did not care to discuss ancient history. "Silas been here?"

Pop shook his head slowly. "Your brother…won't be coming…"

Lex worried that something bad had happened to Silas, but he had no desire to ask Pop any questions.

"So I hear," Pop finished.

There was a half a minute of silence. Lex was ready to get the meeting over with, now that he had seen with his eyes that Pop was alive, for now. If he was soon to die, there was nothing anyone could do about it.

"Listen, Lex. I sit here…what's left of me…the sorriest excuse for a father that ever sucked a breath." At that, he stopped to inhale. Breathing and talking seemed to come hard for him. "Can't blame no one but me, but it was liquor that made me more of a devil than I already was. It was…it was the same with my Pop. In the blood, I reckon."

Lex heard kitchen noises, and heard Leo Haas talking—in German—and his wife answering.

"Yeah, well…can't change the past. We all live with our choices," said Lex. He thought of Sarah's front door, closing behind him.

"I won't ask you to forgive me—"

"Good!" Lex interrupted. "That sure ain't what I came for. Hell, I don't know why I came."

Pop sighed, and continued as if he hadn't heard. "I won't ask you to forgive me, but…I hope someday you will at least try to…give some thought to understanding why I—"

"Why you beat the life outa two boys, no matter how hard we tried to be quiet? Why you dragged us across Colorado, from one shit town to another? Left us with, with…whoever would agree to feed us for a few days while you…well, we didn't even know what you were doing or where."

Pop was silent. Lex grabbed his hat and rose to

leave. He couldn't think of anything more to say, so he just said, "Damn it. All of it."

As he walked to the door, Pop said, "Reckon I won't be seeing you again, Lex, but I want you to know…you and Silas were the only good things I ever had anything to do with, and that was mighty little." His breathing was louder and there was a wheeze with each exhale. "You boys…you will always be my sons, no matter what you say or where you go. You will always be … the only treasure Deke Turner ever found. And lost."

Lex pulled the door close hard, stomped outside and untied his horse.

When are you going to stop crossing rivers and mountains… slamming doors…?

He stood there, breathing raggedly, heart pounding, not thinking. Then, something seemed to burble up from a dark, unknown source … finding hidden cracks in rocky layers of indifference and detachment. The feeling moved from his gut to his chest to his throat, and finally broke from his mouth in sobs. Lex leaned his head against the saddle and cried, shoulders heaving from the release.

He felt like a little boy, and an old man all at the same time.

When the sobs let up, he kept his head bowed, feeling old weights lift from him, ounce by ounce, then by the pound. Lex wiped his face with his handkerchief and stood up straight. He retied the reins and walked back to the front door.

He didn't have to knock. It was Pop who opened the door, and Lex led him back to his chair and took his seat back on the bench. Both men looked at each other.

"Pop. Look, I...well, I stand by what I said. We all make our choices. You made some awfully bad ones. But...so have I." Lex twisted his handkerchief, untwisted it.

"In spite of...how it started...y'know, I've not had a bad life. Been to Mexico. Been to Frisco. Rode some good horses. Won a sight more hands than I've lost, Pop. You'll be glad to know that. Known some handsome women." He paused.

"Known one...that I..."

Pop's smile was back. "One you can't ride far enough to forget?"

Lex nodded. "Yeah, that's about right."

"Well, I reckon you better turn that horse around and get to riding back the way you came, Lexington."

It was Lex's turn to smile. "Maybe. If it ain't too late. But, Pop...I couldn't have done all those things if...well, you put me here, I guess. What little you had to do with it. I'm... lucky to be alive. Never occurred to me until just now."

"Leo, my friend!" Pop rasped, louder than Lex thought him capable of. Leo rushed into the parlor. "Get me that envelope laid out on my bed." Leo disappeared once more down the hallway, and returned in half a minute.

Pop slapped the sealed envelope on his palm, then held it out to Lex.

"You remember that place up in North Park? By the Rabbit Ears Range?"

"Sure." The memories weren't good, except for the ones of roaming the high meadows with Silas, pretending they were knights on horses.

"Well, by some luck, or by the gods, I hung onto the land all these years. Put the deed in a bank box when I was passing through Leadville, and there it's been, until I had 'em mail it to me once I started wasting away."

Lex reddened with shame. He had not asked about his father's health.

"Are you…"

Pop raised an eyebrow. "Well, who's to say how long. Time to pay the band, I reckon. I made my peace, Lex. With everyone but you. Anyhow, I got no use for a section of nice grazing land with a view of the mountains, but you might. You, maybe and…that woman you know."

"What about Silas?"

Pop blinked hard. He said, softly, "Your brother is dead. I didn't want to have to tell you. No fault of his own. Drowned, I heard, down in Texas. On the Rio Grande."

Lex felt the blood leave his face, remembering

the strangely peaceful experience of being swept underwater.

He slid the envelope into his pocket and stood up. He walked over to Pop, who braced himself on the chair arms to rise.

"I'll be all right, Lex. Leo and Mila are well paid to see after me. If you find yourself in La Veta again, stop on by. Your son-of-a-bitch father might still be kicking."

Lex held out his hand to shake, but Pop grasped his waist. Lex put an arm around the old man and patted him on the back.

"Goodbye, Pop." He could say no more. The burble from within threatened to rise again.

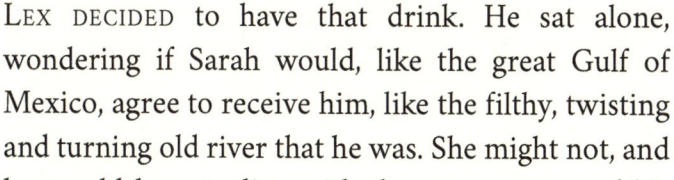

Lex decided to have that drink. He sat alone, wondering if Sarah would, like the great Gulf of Mexico, agree to receive him, like the filthy, twisting and turning old river that he was. She might not, and he would have to live with the consequence of his past choices.

After one whiskey, he asked for directions to the telegraph office. He caught the operator just as he was about to close up for the day. The man slid a pencil and blank form across the counter.

"Ten cents a word," he said.

Lex scratched his head with the pencil, then put it to the paper.

Miss Sarah Blackwell
Durango
Five rivers, six mountains, ten days until all crossings done.
I pray to place a firm hold on the genuine article for good.
Lex

Vonn McKee spent summers visiting her father's family, who raised cattle and broke horses in North Dakota and, later, northwestern Minnesota. Inspired by seeing her grandfather stretched out on a sofa reading Zane Grey novels (some of which were passed down to her), she owned a complete ZG set herself by age eighteen. After years of working at everything from riverboat waitress to country singer to construction project manager, Vonn is incorporating her experiences-and some of the interesting characters she's met- into stories of the old West.

ACKNOWLEDGMENTS

Thanks to sponsors, Mike Bray and Wolfpack Publishing, author Chris Enss, and the Western Writers of America. Thanks also to *Saddlebag Dispatches* and *Roundup Magazine* for their support in promoting our podcast.

Until we meet again be kind to each other, be kind to yourself, and treat your horses well.

We're outta here…let's ride.

Made in the USA
Columbia, SC
21 September 2021